skin
&
bones

Also by Renée Watson

Young Adult and Middle Grade Fiction

Ryan Hart Story Series

Picture and Early Chapter Books

Anthologies

skin
&
bones

A Novel

Renée Watson

LITTLE, BROWN AND COMPANY
New York | Boston | London

Copyright © 2024 by Renée Watson

Hachette Book Group supports the right to free expression and
the value of copyright. The purpose of copyright is to encourage
writers and artists to produce the creative works
that enrich our culture.

The scanning, uploading, and distribution of this book without
permission is a theft of the author's intellectual property. If you
would like permission to use material from the book (other than
for review purposes), please contact permissions@hbgusa.com.
Thank you for your support of the author's rights.

Little, Brown and Company
Hachette Book Group
1290 Avenue of the Americas, New York, NY 10104
littlebrown.com

First Edition: May 2024

Little, Brown and Company is a division of Hachette Book
Group, Inc. The Little, Brown name and logo are trademarks of
Hachette Book Group, Inc.

The publisher is not responsible for websites (or their content)
that are not owned by the publisher.

The Hachette Speakers Bureau provides a wide range
of authors for speaking events. To find out more, go to
hachettespeakersbureau.com or call (866) 376-6591.

Print book interior design by Taylor Navis

ISBN 9780316570886
LCCN 2023949277

Printing 1, 2024

LSC-C

Printed in the United States of America

In Loving Memory of Char Hutson
1971–2024

skin
&
bones

Our lives are more than the days in them,
our lives are our line and we go on.

—Lucille Clifton

the weight i carry

I don't want to die fat.

There would no doubt be whispers at the repast:

It's too bad she didn't take better care of herself.

They will speculate, assume.

Diabetes?

Heart attack?

If I die fat, I hope I die in a car accident or go missing and turn up bloated and bloodied in a river. No one will mention my weight then. I will die without conversation about the obesity epidemic and my family and friends can grieve without the added guilt from flashbacks of every time they wanted to say something about the pounds I was putting on and on but didn't.

Because here's the thing, I am not thick or big-boned or voluptuous.

I am fat.

Obese.

Morbidly obese.

That's what the nurse just typed into my chart. She is a wafer of a woman. The kind of woman who looks like she'll fall over should a big wind blow. This is the woman typing in the word *morbid* to describe this body.

Everything about me is big and Black. Big and majestic like the ocean. Every bit of me hard to contain. My belly spills over and so do my tears and so does my joy and every family recipe and every heartache and every weekend spent at Seaside Beach. It's all here with me. Heavy. It's all here sitting on this table, a layer of the thinnest tissue paper under me, holding all this Blackness, holding all this bigness. I feel the tissue paper rip under me. Wonder why they don't make it more sturdy.

I pull the too-small gown together as best I can. It is tight around my flabby arms and doesn't cover my breast or my stretch-marked stomach. I might as well be sitting here naked. You would think doctor's offices would have large robes for their patients. Don't patients come in all sizes?

The nurse doesn't realize that I can see what she's typed. She enters the words so matter-of-fact, and in the space for more notes, she types: *Morbidly obese but seems happy. Dressed well, good hygiene.*

I stare at the word *but*. Morbidly obese *but*...

She types again but I look away.

Can I take the urine sample now? I really have to go. I've been holding it.

We'll get to that. Give me just a moment. First I need to take your blood pressure and temperature. She wheels the mobile stand toward me and takes my temperature, then attempts to get the blood pressure cuff on my arm. *Hmm,* she says. Let me try this way instead. She switches positions, tries to get one side of the thick nylon material to connect to the other side. The Velcro won't connect. *You need a bigger one,* she says. *I'll be right back.* The nurse walks out of the room and returns with a larger cuff.

I want to ask her why both sizes aren't just available in each room. Wouldn't that be more efficient for the nurses and less embarrassing for the patients? But I don't say anything. She checks my pressure. My arm tightens to the point it feels like it's going to explode and then when she lets the air out, my arm relaxes. *Wow. Pretty great numbers,* she says. Like she is surprised, like she expected there to be an issue. *Okay, I'm going to get the doctor. Give her just a moment.*

While I wait, I fidget with the platinum miracle on my left hand. Two more weeks and I'll be Mrs. Lena Wilson, wife of Malcolm Wilson. *God, please let this bladder infection pass quickly.* I've got a honeymoon to Hawaii to be ready for. I twist the ring, trace the diamond with the tip of my finger. That skinny nurse didn't have a ring on. I hate that I just had this thought. I do not want to wear this engagement ring like an Olympic medal hard fought for, hard won. But it does feel like an accomplishment. I did work for this, for us. After everything I went through with Bryan, the on-again, off-again, so much heartbreak, heart-healing. Finally, I am here. Malcolm is my prize and I am his.

I look down at my dangling feet, thinking about the words the nurse used to describe me.

Morbidly obese but seems happy. Dressed well, good hygiene.

Glad I got that pedicure yesterday. My toes are painted a bright cantaloupe color, my heels smooth and silky.

I always leave the house casket-ready.

I got that from Mom, who everyone calls Honey. Whenever I'd leave the house, she'd ask, *You got on clean clothes?* and I knew she was not talking about my shirt or jeans or socks. She was asking about my bra and panties.

If you get in a car accident, you don't want to be unlady-like when the paramedics come.

Always a lesson from Honey and Grandma about taking care of myself, but never for myself. The house needed to be clean—not because that was a good discipline to learn for my own cleanliness, but just in case guests stopped by unexpectedly. Grandma always commented on my weight, occasionally mentioning my health, but mostly encouraging me to lose weight in order to become (even more) attractive, said I needed to lose this *baby fat* so a man would want me. And here I am, baby fat and then some—fourteen days from forty—and (finally) getting married. If Grandma was here, she'd be overjoyed, she'd be relieved that I found Malcolm, a man who loves me, loves all these pounds, loves my seven-year-old daughter, Aaliyah.

Don't marry the man you can't live without. Marry the man you can live with. Honey and Grandma said it all the time, that marriage is not about love only. *Love is a choice,* Honey always tells me. She never liked me with Bryan. This choice—me choosing Malcolm—she approves.

Just when I decide to find a cup and go to the bathroom, the doctor knocks, comes in. *And what brings you in today, Lena?* she asks, not looking at me. She scrolls through my file, reading while I talk.

I think I have a bladder infection. I get them often—since I was a child—so I kind of know the symptoms.

And your symptoms are?

Peeing every five minutes. And it hurts every time. Like it does when people have bladder infections.

Okay. I'd like to check your blood sugar too. Have you ever been tested for diabetes?

No, I haven't. But today...today I'm here for...I think I have a bladder infection. And, I, I came ready to do the urine sample, so if we can get that going, that would be...I uh, I have to go.

Yes, we will get to that. But I need to check a few other things first. A woman your size—we should, it could be something else. She says she needs to review my family history.

Diabetes. High blood pressure. Stroke. Hypertension. Heart disease.

It all runs in my family.

Great-grands and grands. Uncles and aunties, cousins—firsts, seconds, thirds. The passing down of big-boned genes, the passing down of cooking and feeding the ones you love to celebrate, mourn, rage. Food as medicine.

But also, there's been the passing down of family sing-alongs, gathering around Grandma's raggedy (but better than nothing) piano. What's been passed down is preachers and teachers, generations and generations of artists, a singer here, a poet there.

I want to tell her what's not on that chart. She wants medical history. Physical ailments. But I think she should know it all.

The almost dead, the died-too-soons, the divorces and sage loves, the births, rebirths, stillbirths, the car accidents, graduations, holiday dinners, the first days of school, last days of childhood, every birthday, every happy hour, Fourth of July picnics at Blue Lake Park, baptisms, breakdowns, excruciating laughter, Electric Slides at up-all-night house parties.

What's been passed down is Aunt Aretha's recipe for lemon pound cake that must be made for every arrival and departure of breath.

She asked for my family history. I could tell her, but I know better.

A knock at the door, and then a new person enters. She is not a thin wafer, she is not *morbid*. The woman draws blood. A quick sting from a needle. I look away, not wanting to see myself leaving myself. She is finished with pricking and sticking me and now we wait.

Am I going to give a urine sample? I think I have a bladder infection.

What are your symptoms?

I repeat myself: *Peeing every five minutes. And it*

hurts every time. Like it does when people have bladder infections.

The nonwafer, nonmorbid woman leaves, comes back with a plastic cup. Finally, the urine sample.

Then waiting and waiting, another knock and the words *bladder infection...antibiotics...*

And the blood sugar? I ask.

Normal...but you need to be careful carrying all that weight. I recommend trying to lose at least five to ten percent of your body weight. And then we can reassess and put you on a weight loss plan.

My doctor wants to put me on a weight loss plan even though my test results are normal.

Before she leaves the room, she offers an affirmation. *You know,* she starts, *you are a beautiful woman. I hope you know that. Your skin, your hair. Just gorgeous.*

I smile, kind of, I think. Yes, this is a smile, a thank-you. I open my mouth to say something. To correct her? Scold her? To ask why she felt the need to tell me that she thinks I am pretty.

But my words do not come. Only her words are here. They are hanging in the stale, sanitized room. When I leave, they come with me. Words are like that. They follow, linger, stay a while. Here I am, carrying what is not mine.

Heavy.

morbid

Meaning disturbing, weird, unpleasant, abnormal, unhealthy. Might as well call my body gruesome, hideous, abhorrent, offensive, dreadful, unwholesome, ghastly. Might as well call me unnatural, shocking.

Call my body macabre and look away. Judge me, fear me. Tell me to be afraid of what I am, tell me to fear what has become of my body. Tell me it's a disease but treat me like it's a choice.

Comment on my appearance.

But tell yourself it's about my health.

mississippi avenue

Driving home from the doctor's appointment, I roll all the windows down so Portland's summer breeze can kiss and hold me the whole way home. Being on Mississippi Avenue makes me nostalgic. There is no remnant of what used to be, but I remember.

This was the street Honey used to tell us to be careful walking on, block after block of boarded-up promises—bungalow houses hidden behind unruly grass as wild as Aunt Aretha's fro back in the day. Every few blocks a group of men standing at their post like birds huddled on a power line. Their *yo momma* jokes funnier than any stand-up comedian's set. They always gave a head nod, always asked how Honey was doing. Feared by folks who didn't know better, loved by every elder who needed help carrying her Safeway bags inside, every elder who needed an arm to lean on while climbing the stairs of her old porch when the banister just wasn't enough.

I still live on this side of town. On principle.

I'm the only Black homeowner on my block. For so long *they* hated it over here. Chased us out, then *they* came running.

bridge city

The Willamette River splits the city in two. There are twelve ways to cross the river.

St. John's Bridge. St. John's Railroad Bridge. Fremont Bridge. Broadway Bridge. Steel Bridge. Burnside Bridge. Morrison Bridge. Hawthorne Bridge. Marquam Bridge. Tilikum Crossing. Ross Island Bridge. Sellwood Bridge.

Bridges. A guarantee that you will be supported from here to there. The tangible promise a city makes that it will unite its places, unite its people, link them together, offer many ways to connect, many ways to go and come, to send out, welcome in.

play another slow jam

On my drive home, I pass the block with all the new construction. Once again, the neighborhood is changing. The other day, Aaliyah pointed out a boarded-up storefront. Something always closing, opening. We tried to remember what was there. It took us the whole drive home before finally Aaliyah shouted out, *The Mexican restaurant! That was the new Mexican place we kept saying we were going to try. We didn't even go yet and it's already gone.* I wonder what it's going to be and what happened to the people who worked there.

I am home, and just as I pull into the driveway, New Edition's "If It Isn't Love" comes on the radio so I stay in the car to listen. There's a new DJ at KBOO Radio and for two hours he plays nothing but R&B. He introduced this set saying, *Let me take it old-school for you.*

The next song is Troop's remake of "All I Do Is Think of You." I call Malcolm, put the phone on speaker.

He answers. *Hello?*

... (All I do is think of you)

(Day and night) day and night, that's all I do...

I let it play before I turn it down. *How's your day going?*

Better now. You? he asks.

Same. I turn the radio back up. We listen and as the song fades, I tell Malcolm, *I just wanted to say hello.*

Love you.

Love you too.

As soon as I come inside, Honey bombards me with

questions: *Are you okay, Lena? What did the doctor say? Do you have to go back in for more tests?*

I'm fine, I tell her. *Bladder infection.* I kiss her on her cheek. The older I get, the more I look like Honey, except she carries her weight in her hips and butt. Hardly a stomach to see. She keeps her hair short and natural. She is a low-maintenance kind of woman. Clear nail polish, bare lips, the only jewelry she wears is her wedding ring and the diamond studs Dad gave her when they were dating. In her simplicity she is regal. Every time my mother steps into a room, people sit up straight. *Thanks for watching Aaliyah,* I say. *Where is she?*

You know where she is. Your twin is in her favorite place, doing her favorite thing.

I laugh. Honey calls Aaliyah my twin because our baby pictures are practically identical. I go upstairs to Aaliyah's bedroom. Just before I open the door, I stop and listen. She is playing with her dolls. Her playtime is a production, always. Full dress-up with props, nothing simple or small.

Aaliyah is pretending to be me right now, mocking a conversation she must've overheard. She puts my voice on, then Kendra's, who she calls Auntie even though Kendra and I aren't blood.

Kendra girl, you looking good. You losing weight or something?

I hope not. Girl, I want to keep aaall of this. Don't nobody want a bone but a dog.

But don't nobody want slop but a pig!

I put my hand on the knob, and just before I walk in Aaliyah keeps Kendra's voice going, saying, *And you ought to know. You know Malcolm loves every curve on you. You two ain't even gonna see the ocean, long as you been making him wait. You gonna be surfboardin' alright!*

I open the door. *Aaliyah! Watch your mouth! Do you even know what you're talking about?*

The innocence in her eyes when she says, *I'm just playing with my dolls, Momma.*

Well, it's time to clean up. Honey is about to leave. Come say goodbye.

Aaliyah's plump hands put away her dolls. She is so careful with them, the way a mother is when she is laying a baby down to sleep. She says goodbye to them and we head downstairs. I walk behind her and want to tell her to hold on to something, the rail, my hand. But she doesn't need to, I know. Sometimes I miss those days, when she needed to hold my hand, when she needed my breast feeding her, my arms rocking her. Aaliyah was born nine pounds, fifteen ounces. The best of me, the best of Bryan. A head full of hair, deep brown, and all mine. When she was a baby, strangers would come up to us, tell me she looked like a brown porcelain doll. Because of her size, everyone thought she was older than her actual age. When I'd tell them *She's only two months* or *She's just five . . . Only six,* people would ask, *What are you feeding that baby?*

When we get to the living room, Honey is digging in her purse. She pulls out her car keys. *Alright let me get back to the house. Your father will be wanting dinner soon. Act like he can't eat without me.* She sounds annoyed when she says it, but I know she wouldn't want it any other way. *He's getting Sunday's sermon ready. Been up at the church office all day.* A tinge of worry in her voice. What she's really saying is that Dad is working too hard, too much. He had a heart attack last year, and since then, Honey has been on him to slow down. *You think Malcolm got it in him to be the lead pastor one day?* She has been hinting at this for months, but she's never flat-out asked.

I don't know, I say. When really, I want to say, *I hope not.* It's hard enough living as a pastor's daughter. I don't want to be a pastor's wife.

I thank Honey for watching Aaliyah.

She hugs Aaliyah, says, *It was my pleasure. You know I love spending time with my baby girl.*

Aaliyah says, *Honey, I'm not a baby anymore. You know that, right? I'm only going to be seven for two more months.*

That's right. Our baby girl has a birthday coming up.

I'm almost eight!

Honey smiles. *Well, how about that? Where does the time go? Where does it go?*

baby girl

From a distance, Aaliyah looks older than she is because her chubby body is already developing and blossoming, and already she is taller than most of her friends. And because she's up under me and Honey and Aunt Aretha so much, she can sound older too. Already she knows the power of dragging out *giiiirl*, knows how to shake her head from side to side, saying *That don't make no sense.*

She is an old soul. But still, a girl.

An old soul, but girl enough to still want to play with her dolls and play make-believe, pretending to cook up a feast, bringing me dish after dish, asking me to taste this and sip that. She is not ready to give away her tea set or the play kitchen Honey got for her when she was four.

At first glance, maybe people see a preteen, a more mature girl. But if they get close, look at her deeply, they'll see her plump cheeks and curious eyes, hear the purity of her laugh, witness her naïveté every time she says her prayers at bedtime, so sure that God is going to answer her.

Just the other day, I called to her, *Baby girl, come here!*

She ran down the stairs, came right away, but said, *Mommy, why do you still call me that? You know I'm not a baby anymore.*

But she is, and I want people to understand that. Want older boys not to look at her with wanton gazes, want White teachers to hear the tenor of her voice and not mistake it for attitude or sass, want her curiosity to be seen as innocent as it is. Want her purity protected. Want her girlhood preserved.

I tell Aaliyah, *You're not even in the double digits yet.*

So when I'm ten, I won't be your baby girl anymore?

How about this—I won't call you Baby Girl once you turn ten.

Deal.

But, Aaliyah, you'll always be my baby girl.

age 8

My best friends, always, were Aspen and Kendra.

Our mommas rocked us in their arms on the front pews of Faith and Hope Church. They bonded while swapping stories of babies teething, babies hollering all night, babies crawling and walking and getting into everything.

At eight, we were inseparable. Church, school, playtime on the weekends. Taking turns to ask our mothers if we could spend the night, always wanting a slumber party, always wanting more time together.

Me, the independent one. No brothers or sisters, I learned how to be alone without being lonely. At eight I wanted to be just like my momma, the type of woman who corrected people who introduced her as *the pastor's wife*. She'd always say her name. Made sure people knew it, made them say it.

At eight, Aspen was the thoughtful one. The youngest of twin brothers, she always had someone looking out for her. The daughter of a deacon, she could recite the books of the Bible and could say the Lord's Prayer by heart.

At eight, Kendra was the outspoken one. Always telling it like it is. Always so sure. At eight, Kendra had stopped playing with dolls, stopped making them talk to each other and ride in their Barbie car. Instead, she styled them. Cut and braided their hair. Took their tiny clothes and remixed them into better outfits. Always the one with an eye to take something good and make it even better.

Eight.

Little versions of the selves we didn't see coming.

age 12

At twelve Aspen was aware of injustice. She led a campaign to change the mascot of our school—the silhouette of a Native American warrior. Aspen volunteered as a helper for Sunday School for the little ones. One Sunday, she committed her life to God at the altar. Decided her faith wasn't something to inherit from family and cultural tradition but something she wanted to choose for herself.

At twelve Kendra was aware of sexism. Hated that boys got called on more in class, that their sports teams had bigger crowds at the games, even though our school had the best girls basketball team in the district. At twelve, we played Truth-Dare-Double Dare-Promise-Repeat. Someone dared Kendra to kiss Steven, an eighth grader whose name was always being circled in a heart on some girl's notebook. She did it. Kissed him in front of everyone on the school bus. A big deal kiss with tongue and heads turning, a kiss that lasted and lasted. He wanted to go out with her after that, she turned him down. Said, *it didn't mean anything, it was just a dare.*

At twelve I was aware of my body. The first one to get my period, the first one to wear a real bra, the only one who didn't participate in Run for the Arts: *How many laps can you run to raise money for the school's arts programs?*

None.

At twelve, I realized my body could not do what other bodies could do.

My body could not sit crisscross apple sauce, could not bend over easily to tie my shoes, could not fit comfortably in the middle of two people while riding in the backseat of a car.

Cocooned in the Black community, I never felt ashamed of my body. Was never outright bullied or tormented like fat characters are in movies. No one dumped me in a trash can and rolled me down a flight of stairs. I wasn't ever called *pig* or *whale*. But still, I knew.

At twelve, I overheard a teacher say to another teacher, *One thing about Lena—she's a big girl, but her momma dresses her well. Keeps her clean and well groomed.* I learned then that I was an exception to a rule I didn't know existed, that my fatness somehow defied the norm: pretty for a fat girl.

At twelve I knew my body was not beautiful to others. It was the way people picked body parts to praise:

you have such a pretty face

your hair is so long, so beautiful

I don't remember anyone ever telling me

you are so pretty

you are so beautiful

Maybe Honey. Yes, Honey told me I was beautiful.

Did I believe her? Could I have even understood the magnitude of what she was telling me?

age 13

At thirteen, our bodies changed.
Aspen: Big
Kendra: Bigger
Me: Biggest

age 16

Me: At sixteen, a boy named Bryan moved to Portland, started coming to my church, my school, my house... in the middle of the day, skipping school to sneak kisses. Sixteen was about first love: mixtapes and slow dancing, hand-holding, falling asleep talking on the phone. Spent my teen years in love with Bryan. Back then, sixteen was only joy.

Aspen: At sixteen, Aspen took the purity pledge. Said her soul, mind, and body belonged to Jesus. Sixteen was about commitment. Too many hypocrites in the church, somebody had to live the life that's preached about.

Kendra: At sixteen, Kendra knew how far was far enough without going all the way. Knew what pleasure was, knew how to ask for what she wanted, knew when and how to say no. Tried to teach us to do the same. Sixteen was about experimenting, about setting boundaries and being bold enough to go right up to the line.

age 39

We all turn forty this year.

We are not opposites or just-alikes. More like a buoy for each other.

Me: The director of diversity, equity, and inclusion for Multnomah County Libraries. My style is casual chic. I am known to dress in maxi dresses in the summertime and oversize sweaters and leggings in the fall and winter. When it comes to relationships and dating: no (more) sex before marriage. I've been celibate for three years. The first one of the crew to get married.

Aspen: Founder and executive director at Starshine & Clay, a community space on Alberta Street dedicated to being a safe space for Black Portlanders. Aspen's style is afro-bohemian. She's always got a flowy print draped over her curves. Almost forty and wearing her purity ring on a necklace, close to her heart. Waiting on Jesus to bring her the right person, still.

Kendra: A personal stylist for plus-size women. Kendra is a fashionista for sure, the queen of mix-matching textures and colors that don't normally go together but somehow look good on her. Even her simple looks have a flair to them, and always, she wears a statement piece—a big ring, a bright-colored shoe, a chunky bracelet or necklace. Kendra's dating life can be summed up in two words: single and content. What's love got to do with it? Her motto—she has many: The body needs sex like it needs water. Don't drink out of any ole well, but don't die of thirst either.

whine & wine

It's a tradition Kendra started. Vent and drink our blues away. In our twenties when we thought we were grown, we drank moscato. Impressing ourselves that we'd become liberal Christians, free enough to drink in our shared apartment, but not bold enough to drink in public or in front of our parents. Bryan teased us, said moscato was just fancy sugar water and to let him know when we were ready for a real adult beverage.

Our early thirties were all about cocktails, blended drinks, and sparkling anything. And, still, the teasing from Bryan because to him the only alcohol worth consuming is bourbon or craft beer. With forty around the corner, Kendra has a wine subscription to a local Oregon winery that sends two bottles every month, and the three of us have been known to spend weekends wine tasting in Newberg.

Alright. Who's going first? Aspen asks.

Wait, I say. *Before we start venting, we need to toast to some good news. Aspen, that grant we worked on—we got it.*

What grant? For what? Kendra asks.

Multnomah County Library will be partnering with Starshine & Clay to do a series of events and exhibits about the history of Black folks in Portland.

Congrats! Kendra says.

Aspen is all smiles. *This is going to be so good. So, so good. I just—yes, this is the type of programming I've always wanted to do at Starshine & Clay. This is why we exist.*

I tell Aspen, *As soon as I'm back from Hawaii, let's talk*

and start planning. I've already been researching stories of Black Portlanders and Oregon's Black history.

Kendra says, *I am so proud of you two. Lena, you just revolutionizing things at the library, huh? I mean, they didn't know what they were getting when they hired you to be the diversity director—or whatever it's called. DI? D—?*

DEI. Director of diversity, equity, and inclusion.

Right.

I pour another glass of wine. *I'm trying to get everyone to rethink what it means to curate spaces for the public to feel welcomed, seen, and validated. I have so many ideas,* I tell them. *They keep trying to erase us, but I'm not letting that happen.*

Kendra lifts her glass. *To Black Portland past, present, future.*

Cheers!

And then Kendra clears her throat. *Well, since Lena is all in love and giddy about the wedding and the both of you are doing big things getting grants and changing the world, it looks like I'm the only one who has something to vent about.* Kendra holds up her phone, a dating app open on the screen. *You see what I'm dealing with?* First she shows us the photos and saved conversations of the men she's matched with. Nothing impressive. Then we go through the new possibilities. The first three men she doesn't even let us weigh in on. Swipe left, swipe left, swipe left. No, nope, nah.

We tell her to slow down. Let us see.

Men posing with dogs. Men posing with cars. Men posing with women. Men taking selfies in bathroom mirrors. Men posing with no shirt on. Men posing with sunglasses on. Men posing with lips puckered, offering a kiss. Men posing with dry, chapped lips like they haven't been kissed...ever.

Men posting misspelled words: their/there/they're, we're/were/where, its/it's.

Men posting one-word answers to questions: How do you usually spend your weekend? *Chillin'.*

Men posting cliché answers to questions: What are you looking for in a partner? *Looking for a Queen who's ready for her King.*

Swipe left, swipe left, swipe left. No, nope, nah.

Kendra says, *It is slim pickings out there.*

Aspen and I ask our what-abouts: *Tyrone? Frank? Derek?*

Derek? I didn't tell you? Kendra starts. *First of all, keep in mind we have never been on a date. We met at that concert Aspen and I went to. We exchanged numbers. Had one—only one—phone conversation.*

Right, we say. *We remember,* we say.

And keep in mind in that one—one—conversation he told me his real age.

I don't remember that part, Aspen says. *How old is he?*

He is twenty-one years older than me. Sixty (too-old) years old.

Wait. Derek? The guy at the concert? Watching Aspen trying to understand this is the highlight of the night.

Yes, this dude right here is sixty. Kendra holds up her phone, shows us.

He looks like he's in his mid-forties. Maybe, I say.

Right? So keep that in mind and tell me why this old man calls me with some heavy breathing and carrying on?

Carrying on? Aspen is truly confused.

I said hello. All I hear is heavy breathing. I said hello again, more heavy breathing, then moaning. I said, "Derek?" He said, "Yes, yes…say my name…say my name…" Telling me how sexy my voice is, how he'd been thinking of me.

*And then…then, he says, "I love a BBW. I love a BBW."
And his voice is getting faster and faster and I just—*

I don't mean to laugh at her situation, I really don't.
But there is no holding laughter when it comes. It spills
into the room, and we let it wash over us.

*Old man, fine though you may be, I don't even know
your last name, first of all. Second of all, how you gonna
call already started? How does that work? It's one o'clock in
the afternoon and this is what you're doing? At sixty?*

More laughter. More and more.

I might be single forever. I'm just accepting that, Kendra
says. She changes the subject. *Enough about me. Aspen,
you still in a friend-lationship with Travis?*

We laugh, but really, it's not funny anymore. It's
been four months of dates that aren't called dates. Of
good-morning texts, good-night texts, miss-you texts. But
no kissing, no touching, no let's take this to the next level.

Remind me how you two met, Kendra says. *Did Malcolm introduce you?* She sits cross-legged on the sofa, set-
tles in.

*He's one of the program directors at the Portland Art
Museum. We're always at some conference or special event
for community arts spaces. Most times, we're the only
chocolate drops in the room, so we sit together, compare
notes of how white the world of museums can be. Our
friendship started one night at a cocktail reception where
we went off after the boring opening speeches and talked
all night. And then we realized we both knew Malcolm
and we became friends after that. We just…I don't know,
we're friends.*

Kendra says, *You should ask Malcolm what's up with
Travis. If they're friends, Malcolm should know something.*

Kendra and Aspen look at me.

Malcolm hasn't said anything to me, I tell them. *You know how guys are, they don't sit around drinking wine, talking about dating. And if they do, they don't tell the women in their lives what they're saying. I think Malcolm feels like whatever is happening or not happening with Aspen and Travis is not his business.*

Kendra says, *Well, someone needs to say something because this friendship-dating thing is not healthy. Grown men and women can't be platonic friends. I could see if we were talking about someone you grew up with, lost touch, and are reconnecting with, but Travis is new. New men who come into your life need to be coming for a reason and it can't only be to text you "hey."*

He's not just texting her hey, I tell Kendra. I give Aspen a look, telling her to let Kendra know the latest text exchange.

Okay, so yesterday, he sent me lyrics to Boys II Men's "Water Runs Dry."

Kendra gives her a look and says, *What kind of foolishness is happening between you two?*

We have this little thing we do—texting lyrics back and forth of our favorite R&B songs—

I'm just gonna stop you right there. No. Just—no, Aspen. Y'all on the phone playing Name That Tune? I mean—if you want to be dating him, you need to let him know—

Alright, I say, stopping Kendra from telling it like it is. I can see the sadness in Aspen's eyes, maybe shame. *Don't feel bad, Aspen,* I say. *We all do counterproductive things when it comes to dating. Don't make sense that we are so talented and smart and beautiful but can't name what we want in a relationship. Seems like we are powerful and brilliant in so many spaces except when it comes to love.*

Aspen says, *I just wish he would tell me what this is, how he feels.*

Kendra finishes the last sip of red. *You don't have to*

wait for him to say something. The question is how do you feel. Stop letting him occupy so much of your heart. What you need to do is start dating someone, get him off your mind. She goes into the kitchen, cuts two apples into slices, and refills a tray with cheese and crackers.

Listen, now, Aspen says. *Don't act like I'm desperate to be dating.*

I know you're not desperate. We can be content being single and also want to be in a relationship, Kendra says.

Well, please tell that to my mom. I think she's more stressed about my dating life than I am. Aspen grabs an apple slice off the tray and looks down at the floor. *She thinks if I lose weight, I'd have more options.*

This is nothing new. Ms. Brown has always been on Aspen about her weight. She used to grab a handful of Aspen's chubby belly and say, *Okay, now, watch yourself. You don't want to get too big.*

Aspen sighs. *Maybe she's right. Maybe Travis just isn't attracted to me because big girls aren't his thing.*

I open a bottle of sparkling water. *No one ever tells a man that he'd have a woman if he just lost weight.*

Right? Kendra says. *Big men are called teddy bears. We're called pigs. They wear their big bellies like a badge of honor, joking about how much they can eat.* She pours a glass of the bubbly water. *No one tells them, "Don't be too successful, don't make too much money, don't get too big."*

Kendra's phone buzzes. She blushes at the sight of the photo flashing on the screen. *Sorry, I have to take this.* She has reverted to a schoolgirl, giddy and smiley. She goes into my bedroom.

Who she getting all gushy about? I ask Aspen.

Girl, who knows. Kendra always has a man—or two— making her smile.

They do more than make her smile.

Aspen laughs. *And look who's talking. You've always had a man too.* She stops laughing. Her tone changes when she says, *I'm not saying I'm not happy for you, I'm just saying I want my blessing too.*

69

We were sixteen and full of Mistic. Drinking from the glass bottles made us feel grown, like we were drinking wine coolers not sugary juice. Our go-to flavors were Bahama Blueberry and Peach Beach. Kendra was stretched out on her bed, the wicker bed frame holding up a squeaky mattress. It was midnight and we should have been asleep, but girls do everything but sleep at slumber parties, so there we were, eating Doritos and drinking our pretend grown drinks, listening to SWV. Aspen was barely keeping her eyes open. She'd been yawning for the past hour but trying to hold on, not wanting to miss anything. She had just wrapped herself in a throw blanket and sat down on the floor, leaning against Kendra's lilac walls, when Kendra blurted out, *Either of you had sex yet?*

Aspen was wide awake now. She leaned forward. *Yet? None of us are married. What kind of question is that?*

Kendra looked at me, rolled her eyes. Sometimes I think she couldn't believe Aspen actually took the Bible to heart, that she really wanted to follow every command, be the perfect Christian girl. She revised her question, *Okay, well, how far have you gone? Kissing? French kissing? Foreplay? Sixty-nine?*

Sixty-nine? Aspen took her blanket off.

What is that? I asked.

Kendra looked at me with shock. *You don't know what sixty-nine means? You and Bryan haven't tried it?*

Bryan and Lena aren't physical with each other. Why are you acting surprised? Aspen said it with such

29

conviction, I didn't have the heart to tell her Bryan and I had done a lot more than kissing. We hadn't had sex yet, but there was heavy petting and touching—his hands wandering up my shirt, mine reaching into his jeans.

Kendra knew. We'd been swapping stories since the time I called her in a panic asking her how to get rid of the hickey Bryan left on my neck. I knew Kendra would know what to do. She was always the one I went to for advice about hair, fashion, sex. She's the one who taught me that wearing shorts under my skirts would prevent chub rub. I had called her in a panic, thinking I had some kind of STD because of the rash between my thighs. *Are you having sex?* she asked. When I told her no, she said, *Then it's probably not an STD*, and when I explained to her what it felt like and looked like, and that the more I walked, the more it burned, she knew what it was right away. I had been walking in the heat in the new denim skirt Kendra picked out for me. She told me about chafing and how to prevent it. She is the one who taught me that big girls like us should wait for the handicap-accessible stall in the restroom because it's bigger and gives more room to move around in. Kendra knew how to move in her big body, how to be comfortable in it, how to navigate space.

That night, she taught me about pleasure. Telling me and Aspen, *Sixty-nine is the position of the bodies. You pleasin' your man, while he's pleasin' you.*

I don't get it, Aspen said.

Kendra gave an extra eye roll. *Aspen, please don't tell me you've never heard of oral sex—giving head—going downtown—*

I know what oral sex is. I just, I don't get why it's called sixty-nine.

Kendra grabbed a pen and notepad from her night-stand. *Draw it*, she said. She handed the pen and paper to Aspen.

Aspen drew the numbers 6 and 9 over and over.

Draw them closer together, I said.

She did and then her eyes bulged out and she looked at me like her whole mind might be on overload.

I wasn't even trying to hide my laugh. I was in tears, not laughing at her but laughing at the whole situation. *The top of the six is one person's head, the bottom of the nine is the other person's head. The round parts—*

Okay, okay. Got it. I got it.

I couldn't tell if Aspen was grossed out, embarrassed, or intrigued. But in that moment, I knew I had made the right decision in not telling her about kissing and touching Bryan. And once Bryan and I did have sex, I didn't tell her. It wasn't until college that she realized I had broken the purity pledge we made in youth group. When she found out I wasn't a virgin, she looked so disappointed, so shocked. *You had sex?* she asked. And the way she emphasized the word *you*, I wasn't sure if she was saying *you* as in *The pastor's daughter is out here living in sin* or *you* as in *How did you get a man and I still don't have one? You* as in *But you are bigger than me*, as in *What do you have that I don't?*

black faith

1862. The first Black church in Portland, First African Methodist Episcopal Zion Church, was once called People's Church. A small group organized and met in Mary Carr's home, which also served as a boardinghouse. Reverend J. O. Lodge was the first pastor.

I think of Mary Carr, take pride in knowing it was a Black woman who created space for folks to gather, to pray, to worship.

1902. Mount Olivet Baptist Church was established by Reverend J. L. Allen. The church was located in Northwest Portland. In 1907 the Ku Klux Klan offered to donate lumber to the church if it moved to the east side.

Mount Olivet agreed and rebuilt on First and Schuyler. What else could they do?

Had they not moved willingly and with promise of enough lumber to rebuild, their church could've burned to the ground.

An old rugged cross blazing in the front yard.

starshine & clay

Aspen became the founder and executive director of the organization five years ago. Working on Alberta Street, right in the neighborhood where we grew up, was her way of holding on to what was. Her way of literally and figuratively taking up space. Opening a Black-owned organization in the heart of a gentrified neighborhood that showcases Black art felt like the best thing to do with the inheritance she received from her grandmother's estate. Her grandmother's house was already paid in full, so she had money to invest and bought the house next door. She combined the two homes to create a sanctuary of self-love, art, and healing.

There used to be a Black-owned art gallery not too far from here on Jackson Avenue, but each year the rent rose and rose, so it had to close. The fact that Aspen owns this property ensures that Starshine & Clay is not at the mercy, whims, or politics of commercial real estate owners. It is here to stay. Besides the art gallery, there are offerings for the community: yoga and dance classes that don't make Black girls or big girls feel out of place, creative spaces for local artists to have studio time, a work-from-home spot for independent folks.

Every time I drive past the building, I beam with pride. We never imagined this when we were little girls, but now we are full of dreams. Every time one comes true, our faith grows for the next.

books

It is no surprise to anyone who knew me as a child that I ended up working in a library. As an only child, books were my friends, they kept me company. In the summertime, before I was old enough to work, I spent hours and hours devouring books at the North Portland Library. I loved nonfiction most. Thought it was fascinating to learn about real people, real places. The obstacles they overcame to be great, the mistakes, the breakthroughs, the moments just before greatness.

I started out as a youth librarian and piloted several programs to address the needs and concerns of Portland's Indigenous and Black communities.

A year ago, I became the director of diversity, equity, and inclusion for Multnomah County Libraries. It was a new position, a revamping and combining of previous initiatives that needed to be streamlined and supported with intention and allocated resources.

At least, that's what I was told in the interview. Public libraries were created to be spaces that welcome everyone, and in one of the whitest cities in America, that welcoming hasn't always been so inclusive. I was told there was a tremendous amount of excitement for this new position and that the staff were eager to collaborate with me and deepen the impact our libraries have across the city. And yes, it is true that I have met teams who have great expectations and enthusiasm, but also there has been resistance and pushback in ways I didn't expect. Some folks don't see a need for this position at all, so supporting nineteen branches—making sure each location prioritizes diversity in hiring, digital equity, and culturally relevant and inclusive programming—has its challenges.

When I first talked with my team about doing Portland: Black, Garrett, who's been working at the library a year longer than me, voiced some concerns that he and a few other colleagues had with the name. They thought it excluded people. He wouldn't tell me who these colleagues were. I had to remind him and whoever *they* were that in just one year, the DEI team has worked with our Indigenous team to strengthen our representation of Indigenous people at the library, added services for our immigrant and refugee communities, and expanded resources and programs in Spanish, Vietnamese, Chinese, and Russian. Our LGBTQIA initiatives are thriving. And soon, we'll be launching a storytelling program for elders with dementia. *I don't think we have to worry about our programs being exclusive,* I told him. *And feel free to send anyone who has questions to me.*

Every day I am getting more and more confident communicating my vision and getting the team to see it with me.

Every day I understand more and more that I am the harvest of my ancestors. Me, a Black woman with one of the top librarian positions in one of the whitest cities in the country. This country, a place where it was once illegal to teach people like me how to read.

beatrice morrow cannady

1930. Twenty-five thousand Black folks living in Oregon.

Beatrice Morrow Cannady was one of them. She moved to Portland in 1912 and married Edward Daniel Cannady, the founder and editor of the *Advocate*, the city's only Black newspaper at the time. She was the assistant editor for twenty-four years and was also a founding member of Portland's NAACP. She used her platform to challenge discrimination and fight for equal rights while keeping her readers informed of KKK activity in Oregon.

On the invitation of NAACP executive secretary James Weldon Johnson, she was invited to give remarks at the association's convention in Los Angeles. Her remarks followed the keynote by W. E. B. Du Bois. She told the audience, *It is the duty of the Negro woman to see that in the home there are histories of her race written by Negro historians . . . so that our youth may grow up with a pride of race which can never be had any other way.*

Beatrice transformed her living room into a reading room and lending library featuring books and artifacts by and about Black people. Her collection had over three hundred volumes on Black history and literature. Her home was frequently visited by Black creatives, activists, and scholars who were traveling west, including Paul Robeson.

Black women were instrumental in laying the foundation for Portland's Black community. Not only do we belong here. We made *here* possible.

date night

Malcolm and I walk into the restaurant, and all eyes are on him because he's tall, and *fiiiine*, and Black, and man, and this is Portland, so everyone (as in everyone White) thinks he's a famous basketball player or someone important. It happens all the time.

Once we walked into an upscale restaurant and the host said, *Right this way, sir,* escorting us to a window table, seating us ahead of all the people who were waiting. We never did figure out who they thought he was, but we enjoyed the star treatment. Malcolm joked that it was the closest thing to reparations we'd ever get.

Malcolm is a sneakerhead from LA. He can name the style and year a shoe came out the way music lovers know classics. He's got that I-don't-try-to-look-this-good vibe going. Everything coordinated but not too matchy.

Everywhere we go, people stare.

And they are staring not just at him but at me. A thin woman looks at me with disgust as I walk these wide hips between tables that are too close together even for the thin server who barely makes it through. It's a maze to get to the wayback of the restaurant. I see three tables at the front, no reservation signs on them. Can we sit there? I want to ask, but I keep walking. The woman scoots out of my way the best she can to give me an inch more. I see her lean in, away from the aisle, making sure I don't bump her.

At the back of the restaurant a man who looks like he might have played football in his younger days is squeezed into a booth, his belly pressed against the table. If he barely fits, I definitely won't.

The hostess holds her arm out. *Here you go. Your server will be right with you.*

Malcolm says, *Can we sit at a table and not a booth? I asked when I made the reservation.*

Oh, I—hold on let me see what I can do. She walks to the front of the restaurant, huddles with her coworker, points to us.

Malcolm takes my hand. *Sorry about this, Lena. I promise I asked for a table.*

I hold his hand tighter.

Let's, uh, come on, let's go back to the front. There were open tables up there, Malcolm says.

We can't walk side by side through the maze of tables, so he lets go of my hand. He motions for me to go first, but I say, *Go ahead.* I don't want him in back of me watching me twist and turn and contort my body just to walk through this space.

I think of the many times Malcolm has tried to show me what a gentleman he is, and I wouldn't—couldn't—let him. When we first started dating, he'd pick me up, open the car door for me to get in, but this big body isn't graceful getting in and out of cars. I was always self-conscious about bending in front of him, of needing to hold on to something for support to get out. There's nothing sexy about that. So I'd say, *You don't have to open the door for me,* and he thought I was that I-don't-want-or-need-a-man-doing-nothing-for-me kind of woman. But really, I was just a big girl uncomfortable in my body.

We make it back to the front.

I'm sorry, we don't have any tables available right now. I can seat you at a booth, or you're welcome to sit at the bar if that's more comfortable.

What about those? Malcolm points to a whole section of tables with no one sitting at them.

That section isn't open yet.

Look, me and my fiancé—

Malcolm, let's just sit at the bar. The bar will be fine.

But—

Malcolm, please.

Lena, I'm not going to give money to an establishment that won't accommodate us. Let's go. He takes my hand, leads me out.

When we get in the car, Malcolm turns on the radio and drives. I don't even ask where we are going. There is a lump in my throat, and I'm not sure what it will become if I open my mouth to speak. It's moments like these that I think about losing weight. Practical reasons. I don't have low self-esteem, no insecurities about if I'm beautiful or not. Most days, I look in the mirror and I like what I see. But then I go to a doctor's appointment and the gown won't fit, or I go to a restaurant, and this happens. These are the moments I loathe my body. Loathe myself for losing and gaining, losing and gaining.

I want to distract myself from this feeling, say something to get us talking. Maybe I can ask him about Travis. But what's the question? *Does your boy like Aspen or no?* Too forward. Maybe I can say something real casual. *Your friend, Travis…is he dating anyone?* I don't ask that either. Malcolm tells me everything. So, if he hasn't brought Travis up, there's nothing to tell or I don't need to know.

I look out of the window, watch the city go by as we head downtown. When Malcolm pulls into the parking garage closest to Pioneer Square, I realize we are going to the food truck pod. One of my favorite sandwich spots is there. Locals call Pioneer Square Portland's living room. There are brick stairs that double as benches, and on sunny days, the square is full of people sitting and eating, walking through, taking photos, or walking with their head down, looking at the names engraved in the bricks—names of donors, names in honor of the dead.

We find a spot, and Malcolm says, *You want the usual?*

You already know. Spicy roasted shrimp sandwich with chipotle avocado mayonnaise. *With truffle fries, please.*

We sit and eat, and my hips are free to take up as much space as they need.

This was our first date. I'll never forget how nervous I was, Malcolm says.

Nervous?

For obvious reasons, he says. *Beautiful, smart woman… daughter of the pastor… daughter of the pastor who was my new boss.* He laughs. *But also, for real, after we made plans, I realized the forecast said chance of rain and I couldn't believe I was taking you on an outdoor date in October. I was still new to the city, didn't know all that talk about Portland rain wasn't an exaggeration.*

I take a bite of my sandwich, offer him some fries. *I was worried about you because you seemed so cold. Kept blowing into your hands. I was like, this California man can't handle fall?*

We laugh.

I am finished eating, and I lay my head on his shoulder. *But it didn't rain.*

It didn't.

And we made plans for a second date.

Trying to act cool about it like I just wanted you to take me to your favorite places so I could learn more about the city. The whole time, I was taking notes. Learning what kind of things you like to do. I studied you, girl. Wanted to be an expert in all things Lena Baker.

We sit till the sun fades, then head back to the car, walking slow.

Malcolm says, *Your dad wants to meet with me. You think this is the "Marriage is serious, you better take care of my daughter" lecture?*

No. I think he's going to ask you if you want to take over soon, be pastor.

Malcolm lets that sink in. *Those are big shoes to fill. I…wow. Are you serious? I'm honored he'd think of me. I…what do you think? Do you think I should say yes?*

He asks me this, but I already know he is going to accept. I see the yes in his eyes.

malcolm

The first time I heard him preach, I thought about how different he was from the preachers I grew up under. He is less fire and brimstone, more grace and mercy.

He moved to Portland from LA five years ago. Aspen and Kendra immediately played matchmakers, but I was on again, off again with Bryan, and it took time and lots of therapy to realize I could do better, that Malcolm was better.

He likes quiet places, the corner of an indie bookstore, a wobbly table at the back of a coffee shop. I didn't want him at first. He thinks he is right most of the time—he is—and it is his knowing that annoys me. How he is not smug about it at all, just a wait-and-see-that-I'm-right kind of person.

He watches television shows and documentaries that teach him facts about insects I've never heard of, and he knows the many types of foliage falling from Oregon's trees.

Before working full time at the church, he worked at a mentoring program for Black boys. He is a surrogate father to so many of the teens in Portland, showing up for basketball games, recitals, and even teacher conferences when needed. Watching him love the young people of our community made me respect him, made me want to know him more.

And I learned, getting to know him, what fuels his commitment to young people, his dedication to showing up for the teens in the community who don't have parents who can. Malcolm grew up bouncing between foster homes. His parents were addicted to drugs and in and out of prison.

I don't know anything about having a close-knit family, like you have, he once told me. When it comes to being raised by always-in-your-business family, Malcolm and I are complete opposites. When I need to make a decision, he jokes with me, *Has the committee weighed in yet?* referring to Honey and Aunt Aretha, Aspen and Kendra.

But then there are the things we have in common. A bond deeper than shared hobbies and music tastes, although he did serenade me with Troop's "All I Do Is Think of You." We had broken up, and this was his grand gesture of wooing me back.

What we have in common is not just places we could live (Atlanta, maybe. Or Baltimore).

What we have in common is wanting to share a life. Not everyone wants to share life with someone. And I mean share what happened at work when nothing happened at work, talk about the best lunch we ever had, admit a fear, learn something new together.

I knew I loved him when I realized we could survive Wednesdays. Wednesdays are nothing days. Anyone can love on a weekend, be around for the exciting, for the thrill. I've dated guys who love me for the big moments. Friday guys. Saturday loves. But love me on a rainy Wednesday afternoon when nothing is on television but reruns, love me when I'm not the life of the party because there is no party, when there is no work promotion to celebrate, no event to dress up for, no lights, no camera.

We have a 2:26 p.m. Wednesday kind of love. Simple, steady.

happily ever after

When I was younger, I wanted to be married because I thought that was what I was supposed to want, was taught that marriage was the next step after college, then children, then some kind of happily ever after that would no doubt have its challenges but would ultimately be worth it, ultimately be the greatest decision I made.

But Aaliyah came before marriage, and she is my happily ever now. Marriage stopped being a prize and morphed into a desire to have a good father for my daughter, to make sure she didn't see men in and out of our home, in and out of her life, in and out of my bed.

When Malcolm first asked me on a date, I told him no. Told him, *I am focused on my daughter.*

You can focus on yourself too, he said. And after many dates and a lot of up-all-night phone calls and first, second, and third, and countless kisses, Malcolm said, *Let me know when you're ready for us to spend time with Aaliyah. I'd love to get to know her when you think the time is right.*

I think that's when I fell deeper in love with him. I fell in love with him because he didn't ask me *if* I'd be ready—he knew it was only a matter of when. And there was no rush. No pressure. I loved him because he wanted to get to know Aaliyah, not just meet her.

I fell in love with him because he understands that I want Aaliyah to grow up and look back on these years with fondness and not despair. He understands that my responsibility is to make sure she is prepared for a world that is sometimes hostile to Black girls, Black women. He understands that loving me requires a love for her.

baptism

Aaliyah made the decision on her own. *I want to get baptized*, she told me. She learned about it in Sunday school months ago and has been talking about it ever since. Dad is the proudest I've ever seen him, baptizing his granddaughter, passing on our family's faith.

Before he dips her in the water, he says a prayer.

He prays not that she masters religion but that she strives to be kind, loving, forgiving. Says, *Your mother named you Aaliyah, which means high, exalted, rising. May you rise always, may nothing and no one ever hold you down.*

sunday supper

After service we gather at Honey's and Dad's for dinner. Aaliyah, the guest of honor, is in a white dress, and already I see her at thirteen, sixteen, eighteen...grown. I want to hold on to these years, these moments. I want her to know the people in this room love her most, love her no matter what. The house is big enough that even with so many of us here, it doesn't feel crowded. Dad did a full renovation not long after I graduated from college, so coming home for me feels both familiar and new.

Honey calls out, *Okay everyone, we're going to serve dinner now. Let's take our seats.* I sit next to Malcolm, but Aaliyah insists on being in the middle of us, so I move down a seat, next to Kendra, across from Aspen, who is sitting next to her dad, Deacon Brown. Ms. Brown is next to him, matching like they do every Sunday. My whole life they have been a real-life fairy tale. Not in the way that they have everything they want, but in the way of things always working out in the end. At the other end of the table are my parents, Aspen's twin brothers Elijah and Isaiah, and Aunt Aretha and her three children. Aunt Aretha owns a soul food restaurant in North Portland. This feast of ribs, chicken, collards, mac and cheese, and potato salad is all because of her.

Honey says, *Thank you all for coming to celebrate Miss Aaliyah. Haven't seen some of you in church for a while, felt like old times.* She looks at Kendra when she says this. Kendra looks away.

It was right at the start of college that Kendra's mother, Ms. Turner, died. Kendra stopped coming to church because hymnals and communion and Hammond organs and fans with King on one side and a funeral home address on the other remind her that her momma is gone, gone. She tried. But every Sunday for a month all she'd do was sit on the last row and cry through the whole service. Folks claiming discernment thought she had The Spirit. Circled around her like they were expecting her to break out in a holy dance, when really she would have preferred they bring her sackcloth and ashes.

Her religion has become friendship.

We are her sanctuary.

But she came today. For Aaliyah, for me. And I can't say I know exactly how she feels, but I imagine that with all of us here—me with my parents, Aspen with her parents—the ache of who's missing must be pulsing. Ms. Turner would have been here. And if it weren't for the doctors who dismissed the Black woman who kept asking, *Are there any more tests you can run?* Ms. Turner would be sitting right next to Kendra, saying *Kendra, girl, when you gonna give me a grandbaby to spoil?* But doctors just saw a poor Black woman, said the pea-sized lump in her breast was merely fatty tissue. Months later, she went back. *Look again. Something's wrong. I know my body, I know my body.*

More months wasted, and then a breast exam showed that the pea-sized tumor was now the size of a Ping-Pong ball.

Stage three breast cancer.

Chemotherapy and radiation was the treatment plan, but more than once, more than three times, so many times, Kendra and her mother arrived at the clinic and were sent away because of broken machines or appointments not listed on the schedule. *We'll have to reschedule your treatment,* they'd say. And then no more rescheduling was needed because the cancer advanced to stage four, and quicker than a clock's tick, Kendra's mother was gone, gone.

Had doctors listened, detected it early, had her insurance been taken at hospitals that always have working machines, that always have enough doctors, she'd still be here.

Ask Kendra how her mother died, and she'll tell you, *My mother didn't die because she was a woman who had breast cancer. Her cause of death was being a poor Black woman who had breast cancer.*

If Ms. Turner were here, she would have made a peach cobbler to celebrate Aaliyah's spiritual awakening. She made peach cobbler for every joyous occasion—and for mourning too. She should be here, she should.

Dad says, *Malcolm, please lead us in prayer.*

We all hold hands as Malcolm prays.

God, we thank you for this day, for bringing us together on this special occasion of the passing down of faith from one generation to the next. I pray that you continue to grow this family's legacy, and I thank you for the blessing they have been to this community. And God, I pray that you bless this food and the hands that prepared it. May the food be a nourishment to our bodies and our conversation be a nourishment to our souls. In Jesus's name, Amen.

After we all have food on our plates, Malcolm says, *So, Aspen, I hear you and Lena are doing a project on the history of Black folks in Portland. I can't wait to bring some of the youth to the exhibit. So many of them have no idea of the rich history of Portland's Black community. I'm still learning, myself.*

Aspen nods. *Yes, I haven't been this passionate about a work project in a long time. And I'm learning so much.* She looks at her parents, says, *I can't believe you two were born and raised in Portland and you've never told me about the sundown laws, the KKK's presence in Oregon, redlining. It's all so infuriating. Sometimes, I just—*

Ms. Brown dabs her mouth with her napkin. *I hope you're being prayerful as you do this. Don't let resentment and anger fill your heart.*

It's important to know, Mom. That's not something I need to pray about. And please know I'm learning how racist Portland is—not was. That history is the foundation of what we're dealing with today. That's what the exhibit is about.

Don't lecture me, Aspen.

Kendra kicks me under the table. Aspen and her mother are known to go at it over the smallest things, and talking about racism in Portland is no small thing, so I brace myself.

Ms. Brown finishes, *I know more than you ever will about racism in Portland. I saw the aftermath of the Vanport Flood firsthand. I know. Don't forget, I grew up right around the corner from Williams Avenue. You are reading books about what I lived, what I survived.*

Deacon Brown whispers, *Baby, just drop it, just—*

Let me finish....All I'm saying is all that digging up of the past can weigh on your soul. Ms. Brown's voice is arresting. The room falls silent, no more forks and knives clanking against Honey's good plates. All of us listening, even Aaliyah, who reaches for my hand, as if she needs to hold on to someone in case this heated discussion turns into a full-out argument.

The work you are doing is fine, Aspen. Admirable, even. But history is a heavy load to carry. It would do you well to think about how to process all that you're learning. And don't forget your faith. It's your faith that's going to help you get through, help you move from a place of despair to healing.

Despair? Who said I'm in a place of despair?

Deacon Brown clears his throat. *Ladies, ladies, not today. Not here, at Pastor's house. We're here to celebrate sweet Aaliyah. Let's not have a social justice debate today, not on the Lord's day.*

We should be able to talk about justice every day, and especially on the Lord's day, Aspen says. Sometimes Aspen is the calm after a storm, sometimes she is the storm. *Mom, you already know how I feel about this.* Then, as if announcing it to everyone, she looks across the entire table, slow and with intention. *I am first and foremost a Black woman. Me being a Christian does not erase my gender or my race.*

Aspen has said this before. Says it so much she should put it on a T-shirt.

A faith that isn't intersectional is a faith I can't believe in.

I am sure Honey and Ms. Brown are both amazed and appalled at who their daughters have become. Our mothers had dreams for us. And while we are fulfilling some of those dreams, our career-centered, race-before-faith, I-don't-need-a-man-but-I-sure-would-like-one attitude is not something they saw coming.

These children, Ms. Brown says to Honey. *They better heed the warning: not all liberation frees you.*

vanport

Portland, 1942.

Black men and women migrated from the south and east to the Pacific Northwest by the thousands. Recruited to work in the shipyards assembling ships for the war effort, they were enticed by the new opportunity.

But redlined neighborhoods left no space for the new Portlanders. Not expecting them to stay after the war, the city constructed temporary public housing, the largest development in the country—named Vanport, because this new city within a city was located between Portland and Vancouver, Washington. The workmanship was sloppy and the homes were built on marshland, protected by dikes to hold back the rage of the Columbia River.

Because who cares about the quality of housing for poor White workers, poor Black workers?

Nice enough is better than nothing.

And then. It happened.

The Vanport Flood.

The aftermath of Portland's snowy winter and a rainy spring raised the levels of the Columbia and Willamette Rivers twenty-three feet.

On Memorial Day, May 30, 1948, the Housing Authority of Portland posted flyers in Vanport:

REMEMBER.
DIKES ARE SAFE AT PRESENT.
YOU WILL BE WARNED IF NECESSARY.

YOU WILL HAVE TIME TO LEAVE.
DON'T GET EXCITED.

The dikes did not hold.

There was no time to leave.

The city within a city washed away.

Eighteen thousand, five hundred residents homeless, one-third of them Black.

The city record says fifteen died. (And I refuse to say *only*; there is no such thing as *only* in reference to a life, a love, gone, gone.)

City gossip spread, saying more people died than were officially reported. Witnesses told stories of seeing hundreds of bodies carried away, said the city quietly disposed of the bodies, didn't want too much backlash, too many questions.

Only fifteen, they said.

Of the displaced, White folks could move into the city—no housing laws against poor White people moving into Portland neighborhoods. But those new Black Portlanders, where could they go?

ms. brown

Before Ms. Brown was the wife of a deacon, a mother to twins, a mother to a daughter who she named Aspen, she was a child being born on May 30, 1948, the day of the Vanport Flood.

At the time of the flood, Ms. Brown's mother was at the hospital, pushing life into this world at a time when so much life was leaving it. Had she not gone into labor the night before, she would have been home when the dikes broke and might have drowned before Ms. Brown was even born. When they left the hospital, they had no place to return to. Their home was destroyed, Vanport a desolate city. Ms. Brown and her parents stayed with a White family who offered to take them in for a few days, but after a while they had to leave, find housing in a red-lined city that didn't want those Black southerners to stay.

All that laboring, all that pushing, all that knowing she was bringing her child into a world that had no place for her, no space for her, a city that refused to be home.

williams avenue

After Vanport, Black Portlanders had only one neighborhood they were allowed to live in: the already overcrowded Albina District.

Nice enough is better than nothing.

No loans from banks for Black residents, but the men had saved up money from working at the shipyards and as porters. Black Portlanders built a new city within the city. Turned Williams Avenue into Black Broadway. Some called it Portland's Harlem, called it home.

Black-owned spaces like the Fraternal Hall, the Citizen Fountain Lunch Restaurant, the Paradise Club, Turnery's Barbecue, Wallace Barbecue, the Keystone Club, Neighborhood Bill's Grocery, and Johnson and Smith's Record Shop were all housed on the tree-lined street.

A paradise, Black.

When I was a little girl, every time Grandma drove through the Albina District, she'd tell me, *Lena, now this you need to know. You need to know this and never forget. You come from a people who know how to make do, you hear me? Everywhere Black people go they make do, figure out how to take better than nothing, make it more than enough.*

searching, searching

I am researching the history of Black Portland and making a list of people we can include in the exhibit. I figured coming to tomorrow's planning meeting with a few names would be better than the team starting from scratch.

The Oregon Historical Society is one of our partners for the exhibit. Their archives have proven to be a treasure. I am overwhelmed with the photos, the articles, the recorded oral histories.

So much history, so many answers to how and why Portland is what it is.

marcus lopez

The first African American to set foot in Oregon, Marcus Lopez was a cabin boy on Captain Robert Gray's ship *Lady Washington* in 1788. His first few days in Oregon were restful and comforting. The Native Americans at Tillamook Bay offered the sailors berries, crabs, and salmon. But when Marcus accused a Tillamook man of stealing his cutlass, things turned deadly. Marcus went after the man but was outnumbered by the man's friends. They killed Marcus and warded off the crewmen of the ship, forcing them to leave immediately. Fur traders named that area Murderers Harbor to acknowledge what happened to the young sailor from Cape Verde.

Marcus Lopez.

He wasn't a resident, but he was here.

Most likely the first Black man on Oregon soil.

He was here, he was here.

oregon, 1865

White folks who wanted an escape from the South at the end of the Civil War made Oregon their home. A state with space and space, rolling hills, and evergreens hovering over the land.

A White utopia.

In the 1900s Oregon got a nickname: the Mississippi of the West.

Fourteen thousand Ku Klux Klansmen made the Pacific Northwest their home.

Nine thousand of the Klansmen lived in Portland.

Lived and worked as politicians, as teachers, as preachers, as doctors, as bankers. They mothered and fathered children, passed their heritage on and on.

shopping while fat

This afternoon, Aspen, Kendra, and I are at the bridal boutique for one last fitting. We meet in the foyer. The three of us talking and talking, probably too loud for a place like this. Aaliyah is here too. My shadow, silent and always with me.

A woman walks over to us and, looking only at Aspen, says, *Here to try on a dress?*

And just like that, we're having a Shopping While Fat moment. I know it is not a coincidence that she only greeted Aspen, the smallest of the three of us.

If this was the first or second, third or fourth, time something like this happened, I would probably not think it, but I know.

Once I went into a clothing store, and before I could get in the door, the clerk was hovering around me like a fly. *Looking for a gift for someone?* she asked, as if I couldn't dare be shopping for me. And it was true—none of the clothes were my size—but I was there for the accessories, not that it should've mattered to her.

I step forward. *I'm the bride. These are my bridesmaids and my flower girl. We're here to do one last fitting.*

Just then the woman who usually helps us walks in from the back room, greeting me by name, offering sparkling rosé.

We go into our separate dressing rooms, Aaliyah with me. Kendra says, *Who am I walking down the aisle with? Have you decided?*

Donovan.

Good Lord, how are we both going to fit down that narrow aisle?

Aaliyah is an explosion of giggles.

Kendra! Aspen scolds her, always the moral compass. But today even more, because Aaliyah is here.

I'm serious. Donovan is a big guy, and I got hips for days. We are going to be a sight to behold squeezing down that aisle.

I tell her, *You two are about the same height, and I think you'll look good together in the pictures. And in real life, actually.*

Aspen says, *Who knows, maybe some sparks will flicker.*

Yes, I say. *Donovan is one of Malcolm's closest friends. I think you two would be good for each other.*

Aaliyah smiles. *And then we'll have another wedding to get dressed up for!*

I hear Kendra come out of her dressing room. Her voice seems farther away, but still, she can be heard. *Absolutely not. He is not my type... sorry to disappoint you, Aaliyah. I don't see another wedding happening no time soon.*

Kendra lists her reasons why Donovan is not a good option: *Can you imagine the two of us sitting in tiny airplane seats side by side? And the sex would be—*

Aaliyah is here! I remind her.

I'm not listening, Aaliyah says, telling on herself. I help her into her dress, send her out so I can get into mine.

When Aaliyah steps out of the dressing room, I hear her say, *Aw, Auntie Kendra, I think you should give him a chance.*

Now, Aaliyah, I can't believe you are turning on me. You're supposed to be on my side.

But Auntie, what's wrong with Donovan? He's nice. Don't you want to marry a nice person?

I call out, *Yes, don't you, Kendra?*

I will not tolerate this line of questioning, Kendra says.

Aaliyah won't let it go. *But what's wrong with him?*

He's not my type, that's all. There's not something wrong with him. I'm just not attracted to him.

But I thought looks don't matter and that what matters is on the inside—

Out of the mouth of babes! Aspen says.

We all laugh.

To be continued, Kendra says. *But let me just say, I am not against dating a big guy. I just think sometimes big women don't get treated like we have a choice, that we can choose. We don't have to say yes to a guy just because he asks.* Then Kendra says, *You hear that, Aaliyah? You don't ever have to say yes to a person who doesn't meet your standards. Dating or friendships—you get to choose who you give your love to.*

Amen to that, I say.

I ask for the attendant to help button my dress. She comes into the dressing room. *Happy with the alterations?*

I think so. We'll see once you button this up. I wait for her to close me up into this white cocoon. It took me months to find a wedding boutique that carried plus-size wedding dresses. The sixth store I went to, I burst into tears in the fitting room, afraid that I wouldn't be able to find anything. The owner of the store told me there were online options, which just made me feel worse. I wanted to feel the silk, try it on with my closest friends and mother waiting in the sitting area for me to come and stand on the pedestal, them staring at me with teary eyes telling me what a beautiful bride I'd be.

That was the fantasy since I was a little girl playing in Honey's clothes, prancing around in her high-heeled shoes, kissing an imaginary groom with my teddy bears and Cabbage Patch doll bearing witness.

Thank God Kendra came to the rescue, telling me about this gem. It's worth the drive to Vancouver.

There we go. What do you think? the woman asks.

I stand and look myself over. *It's perfect.* Sometimes you just know you are glowing. I step out into the hall in all my glory. Aspen, Kendra, and Aaliyah are in their dresses looking at themselves in the oversize three-way mirror. I walk over to them.

They ooh and ahh at me, and I become their echo, give it right back because I am in awe of their splendor. All of us a wonder.

sunday sermon

Daddy's sermon is about the number 40 because soon it'll be the church's fortieth anniversary. It's fascinating to me that my parents were only in their late twenties—and new parents to a baby girl—when they started this church.

Daddy reminds us of the significance of the number, telling us that for forty days and forty nights Noah stayed on the ark he built, protecting his family and two of every land animal from the flood God unleashed to bring punishment to the world.

Moses and the Israelites wandered the desert for forty years.

Before he faced great temptation, Jesus fasted forty days and forty nights in the Judaean Desert.

Forty days passed from Jesus's resurrection to his ascension.

Dad says, *Forty symbolizes the endurance of hardship to get closer to God.*

Today, I am turning forty.

On Saturday, I am getting married.

vintage

When Malcolm asks me what I want for my birthday, I tell him nothing. *The wedding is celebration enough.* He insists, so I tell him, *We haven't been to Vintage in a while. I still haven't been able to find an Al Green record there. Maybe someone has finally traded theirs in.*

Malcolm must be tired of me bringing this up. I've been on a mission to find "Let's Stay Together" for months. And I don't want it brand-new and overpriced. I want one that someone traded in, something old and used that'll fit in with the collection I'm building.

Malcolm promises dessert afterward and drives to Vintage, one of the only places in Portland where you can get reasonably priced vinyl.

When we get to the store, I go straight to the section where Al Green should be. I flip through, and just like every other time, there are no Al Green records. I decide to look for Donny Hathaway. As I look through the records, Al Green's voice is crooning from the store speakers.

The irony, I say to Malcolm, who smiles and takes my hand and begins dancing with me.

The store lights dim, and Malcolm whispers, *Happy Birthday. Guess who finally has your record?*

You planned this? You—

I came months ago and saw they had it and bought it— a 45. "Let's Stay Together" on one side, "I've Never Found a Girl" on the other.

64

He holds me close; our bodies find their groove. We dance for the whole song, and when Al is finished singing, I don't leave his embrace. I let him hold me as he whispers in my ear, *I love you, and for the rest of my life, I want to prove it to you again, and again.*

We kiss, forgetting where we are, not caring if the other customers are watching.

The lights come back up. Malcolm goes to the counter, gets the 45, and thanks the owner for obliging us.

As we walk out of the store, some of the customers clap, a few smile and wave. I hear a woman say to the person standing next to her, *Don't you just love love?*

the bride, the groom

The old wives' tale is that rain on a wedding day is good luck. A knot that becomes wet is very hard to loosen or untie, which means a couple that ties the knot on a rainy day is destined to have a marriage that does not come undone.

It's raining.

Storming, actually. I hope the superstition is true because I don't need one more thing to go wrong today, especially since the caterers for the reception delivered the wedding cake here, to my house, instead of the reception hall. A mix-up with the billing and delivery addresses.

And then my hairstylist called, telling me she is sick—food poisoning—and can't do my hair and makeup.

Kendra has come to save the day. She wanted to do it in the first place, but I wanted to give her a break, let her be pampered for once. She has created a calming vibe. Soft instrumental music, lit candles. My favorite women are all over the house, primping and priming, seeming to have more butterflies in their bellies than I do. Especially Honey, who keeps fussing at Aaliyah, telling her to sit down somewhere and be still so her dress doesn't wrinkle.

Aspen is on the phone with Travis, asking him to come get the cake, to make sure it gets to the reception hall. When she hangs up the phone, Kendra teases, *Your not-boyfriend coming to save the day?*

Aspen rolls her eyes. *That's what friends do.*

I am sitting on a chair engulfed in the cumulus cloud that is my slip while Kendra paints my face.

Aaliyah can't be still and is hovering around us. *When is it going to be my turn?*

Honey scolds us all, *I know y'all are not putting makeup on that child. I don't care if it is a wedding.*

Just lip gloss, Honey, I tell her.

Aaliyah stands in front of the full-length mirror, twirling and twirling, fascinated by the swoosh the bell of her dress makes. Her long braids are pinned up in a princess bun and her petite tiara fits perfectly. I want her to always feel this good, want the smile that is on her face to be the norm, not the exception. She deserves all the good days, she deserves a lifetime of looking in a mirror and being captivated by her reflection.

When it is Aaliyah's turn to sit in the makeup chair, I go into my bedroom, get dressed. I am still barefoot but fully gowned when the doorbell rings.

Malcolm is here.

Aspen says, *You here for the cake? I already called Travis to take care of it.*

I'm here to talk with Lena.

Kendra is the first to say, *That ain't happening.*

Then Aspen, *Bad luck to see the bride before the ceremony.*

It's important, Malcolm says. *I need to talk with her.*

Honey says, *Well, can't you call or text her? She can't come out now. She's getting dressed.*

The thing about a group of women, banding together and in one accord, is that they become a wall, an iron shield.

I hear Kendra say to him, *What could you possibly need to talk to her about at this point—right before the wedding?*

It's important is what Malcolm keeps saying. And I know that tone, that cadence.

I crack the door open, just enough so that my voice can be heard, but I can't be seen. *What's wrong?*

I need to talk to you.

Kendra says, *You can talk to her through the door.*

Malcolm comes closer to the door, steps right up to the crack. I smell his cologne and want so bad to open the door, reach out for him, be in his arms. He just stands there, saying nothing.

Well, what you need to talk about? Kendra asks (yells).

Honey tells everyone, *Let's give them space.*

I hear the shuffling of feet and then silence. A long silence before Malcolm says, *I love you.*

What's wrong?

You are God's gift to me, the best thing that ever happened to me. I believe our lives intersected for a reason.

What's wrong?

And I respect you. And out of that respect and out of my deep love for you, I want to stand before you, our family and friends, and God today with no secrets between us.

What?

Last year, while we had broken up, I...I um...you and I were not together. I didn't think we'd get back together. So, I was just—just doing me, just missing you, trying to fill that void, I guess.

I wait for him to say the words.

I slept with someone. Had sex with someone. Just one person. Just once.

He waits for me to say something. I can't. I focus on breathing. Just breathe, Lena. Breathe.

I, I...you asked. When we started dating again, you asked me if I had been with anyone else and I just...I didn't want to lose you. We were just figuring things out again and I knew she didn't mean anything. Malcolm stops talking.

Breathe, Lena. Just breathe.

I want to stand at the altar with a clean heart today. I should have told you before. I've tried to tell you many, many times. But I just, I couldn't. But Lena, this was a year ago. We weren't together. I didn't cheat on you. I did not—would never—cheat on you.

Breathe, Lena. Just breathe.

Nothing has to change, nothing has changed. I'm still Malcolm. I still love you. I still love us, still want you, still want us.

I open the door, my body enveloped by satin and tulle. What does it matter if he sees me now? Does it matter if I asked him, back then, a year ago, if he'd ever...? Does it matter that he lied and I didn't believe him, but then believed him because why would he lie? Does it matter that it happened when we were broken up? Does it matter that I said it doesn't matter what he did while we were broken up?

I take his breath away, I know. Me in this wedding gown, face painted.

Kendra and Aspen tiptoe in, Kendra whispering, *Um, sorry to interrupt. We've got to get to the church. The car will be here in about five minutes.*

Aspen sees the look on my face and I see her understanding what's happening. She is already crying.

Honey and Aaliyah are here now, walking in just as I say, *There isn't going to be a wedding.*

Lena— Malcolm reaches out for me. I pull away.

Not because he had sex with another woman, but because he lied about it for an entire year. I look at

Malcolm, who can't look at me. *He is not a cheater, he is a liar. And I will not marry a liar.*

And I say it without tears and there is no yelling or cursing and I do not hit or kick or push or slam the door or throw my ring or change out of my dress or move. At all. I do not move from the doorway because I can't. I cannot move and I cannot say another word, so I don't. I do not answer questions, I do not explain.

Aaliyah's tears are coming. I hear it in her shaking voice. *Does this mean you won't be my daddy anymore?*

And then, a flood.

There are too many voices, too many words, too many tears. None from me.

My iron-wall women make demands of Malcolm. *What happened? What's going on? Tell us something. How could you...what were you thinking?* Aspen and Honey bombard him with questions.

Kendra has no questions, just anger. *You seriously waited till now to tell her? No, you cannot talk to her...no, I am not convincing her to change her mind...*

And Aspen and Honey talking at the same time: *Who's telling the guests?...What will we say?...Postponed?... Canceled?...*

And Kendra, yelling, *Leave, Malcolm! You need to go...you need to go now.*

I love you, Lena, Malcolm says before walking out the door.

More words and moving about and making plans. Honey says, *I'll take Aaliyah now. She was already going to be staying with me while they were in Hawaii.* At least something for her is sure and consistent in this moment.

Aspen calls Travis, *Don't worry about the cake.* Then she calls the reception venue to cancel the reservation.

skin & bones

They move about, talking, talking, talking. Words blur and circle around, bees stinging me, paralyzing me.

You need your space right now....Change out of that dress....We'll be back....We love you....You'll get through this....You will be okay...you don't need him....You got us...we got you...

shock

I didn't see it coming.

I saw it coming.

I saw it coming, but he talked me out of it, said he didn't know why I was feeling what I was feeling, said I was paranoid, anxious, worried for nothing.

Shock. Meaning not again. Meaning, Is this really happening? Shock, meaning, Where are my tears? Why can't I move?

Shock. Because of a trauma, a collision, an accident, a jolt, a disturbance, a collapse, an injury. Shock. Because of (un)natural disasters: hurricanes, tsunamis, tornados, earthquakes...breakups.

Shock. As in aftershock. Brace yourself for what comes next.

cake

I cut one thin slice of the top tier, decadent choco-late. It is as good as it was at the taste testing. And that makes me wonder about the second tier, the specialty flavor—the bougie part of us—an Earl Grey sponge with fig filling. The third and biggest tier, vanilla bean cake with marionberry filling, even better than I remember.

Three slices.

Still in my gown, I sit on the floor and eat, my dress spilling out all over the kitchen. The phone is ringing and chiming and alerting me of missed calls, voicemails, and text messages.

I pour milk in a wineglass. A gift given at our engage-ment party.

I sit on the kitchen floor, stare at the grains in the hardwood, remember how proud I was of myself when I purchased my own home, how much I loved this kitchen—the floors, the island, the window at the sink.

An hour later, still in my dress, I make tea. Earl Grey tea with a splash of half-and-half. And another slice of cake. I sit back down on the kitchen floor, let the sweet-ness of the cake and comfort of the tea calm me.

I tell myself over and over, *This will not break you, this will not break you.* I get up to cut myself another slice of cake, then catch myself. I dump the rest of the cake in the trash can. *This will not break you,* I tell myself.

The only thing still intact is the wedding topper. And that, I throw across the room. It shatters.

sunday

My prayer:
God, I believe you are powerful enough
to heal my broken heart.

Why couldn't you be kind enough
to keep it from breaking in the first place?

monday

I want to know who she is, what she looks like. She is forever a part of my story, and I don't even know her name.

I search for her. Look on his Instagram page, scroll, scroll, scroll past the family and friends he's posed with, the same people who gathered at the church, waiting to witness our beginning. I scroll, scroll, refresh, scroll, scroll, and then I am there.

Last year.

We weren't together, and I wasn't on social media much. I search through his time without me.

He didn't post many photos back then. I look through them all. Nothing out of the ordinary. Mostly photos of the city, photos of food, hardly any with people in them. Except two. One—him and his mother on Mother's Day. The other, Malcolm standing with Elijah and Isaiah, Aspen and Kendra, and two women I've never seen before—one is Black, one White. The White woman is bigger than me, the Black woman a twig. The caption says *Happy Birthday to my brothers from another mother.*

It was taken at the twins' birthday celebration. I was invited, but I knew Malcolm would be there, so I stayed home. I study the photo. He's tagged everyone, including the two women I don't know. I think about going to their pages, figuring out who they are. If either of them is dating one of the twins, if either of them slept with Malcolm.

What am I looking for? Why am I looking? If there's something here to find, do I really want to see?

I turn my phone off. Go to bed.

tuesday

No groceries in the house because I am supposed to be in Hawaii. I drive the 15.8 miles it takes to get to Tigard because I don't want to run into anyone on this side of town.

One pound of purple grapes, two Honeycrisp apples, organic brown eggs, whole milk, Tillamook Oregon Strawberry Ice Cream, blackberry Greek yogurt, butter, half-and-half,

(Put the ice cream back)

salmon fillet, chicken breasts,
(Go back, get the ice cream, put it in my cart)

red potatoes, arugula,
(Put the ice cream back)

sourdough bread, frozen broccoli,
(Go back, get the ice cream, put it in my cart)

Tillamook Oregon Strawberry Ice Cream and Old-Fashioned Vanilla too.

wednesday

I want a Wednesday-kind-of-love.

thursday

My neighbor is outside washing his car, blasting music.
KBOO Radio's R&B show.
Our song(s) comes on.
An assault, a torturing.

friday

The light in the kitchen is out. I get a new bulb from the closet, get the stepladder, unscrew the old bulb, and just as I reach to put the new one in, it slips out of my hands, cascades down, and shatters on the floor.

There have been no tears all week. But this?

This is when I come undone.

saturday

text messages: 35 thinking-of-yous, 14 I-love-yous, 11 call-me-when-you-feel-up-to-its, 47 heart emojis, 22 sending-you-lots-of-loves, 19 praying-for-yous, 16 let-me-know-if-you-need-anythings, 9 let-me-know-if-you-want-to-talks, 12 let-me-know-if-you-want-me-to-come-overs, 18 let-me-know-what-you-needs, 2 oh-my-god-what-happened?s, 3 you-good?s, 9 scriptures about God's comfort, 1 I-don't-even-know-what-to-say.

missed calls, no messages: 673

voicemails: 3 just-wanted-to-hear-your-voice, see-if you-are-okays, 7 here-to-talk-if-you-need-mes, 10 Lena...I'm so sorrys, 2 you-haven't-called-me-backs, don't-make-me-come-over-theres, 2 prayers actually prayed, one from Aunt Aretha, one from Honey.

Lord God, I lift up Lena to you asking you to be with her through this situation . . .

the breakup

We were in Malcolm's car, parked outside my house, just getting back from seeing a movie. I don't even remember now what prompted the *Where is this going?* conversation. We'd had it before—several times, actually. Me, the one ready for marriage. Malcolm not so sure.

Are you saying you don't want to be married at all or that you don't want to be married to me?

Lena, come on. I love you. I want you to be my wife... one day. I'm just not ready. Not now.

The conversation went like it always did, Malcolm listing his reasons: *You have a successful career. I'm still figuring things out. I'm working at the church as youth pastor and have my full-time job mentoring the boys, but still don't make enough to support a family. Not the way I want to. I can't give you what you want, what you deserve.*

Do you think I'm rushing us? Forcing you? I asked.

No, not at all. But it's what you want. That's very clear.

So what are you saying?

I'm saying, I need time. And I'm not saying I expect you to wait for me—I just—

You want to break up? You're ending this, ending us?

Let's just—I just need a break. Need to figure some things out and—

Malcolm, if we break up, it's over. There is no break. No time-out. Either we're together, or we're not.

meant to be

It was awkward at first, seeing Malcolm every Sunday, but then I saw him changing. Dad promoted him to full-time youth pastor, which came with a full salary and benefits. He left the mentoring job and started preaching more on Sunday mornings, started looking less stressed and less tired, more satisfied, more fulfilled. Within six months of our breakup, Honey not-so-casually mentioned to me that Dad told her Malcolm had started going to therapy. She was hopeful we'd get back together. I wasn't so sure.

But he came back to me.

And he made good on his promise—got himself together. For himself, for me, for us, for Aaliyah. He came back to me with a plan and with a vision for the years to come. He came back to me with a ring, a commitment.

We started over. And now we've ended.

Again.

grief

Meaning loss, bereavement. Meaning sorrow, sadness. Grief meaning lamenting, mourning.

Sometimes it is waking up and crying before my feet touch the floor, before coffee or muffin, or the birds at the window singing *Good morning*.

Sometimes it is a commercial that makes me laugh, because the two of us always laughed at that commercial.

Sometimes it is staying in, not answering the phone, not being around the people I love who love me back. I can't face them right now. Not because I am embarrassed but because if anyone who truly, truly loves me asks, *How are you?*

I just might tell the truth.

strength

Honey is on the phone, *We're about a block away,* she says. She doesn't have to announce herself. She has a key, but I think she wants to make sure I'm ready, that my tears are all dried up and I can function for Aaliyah. She doesn't say that, of course. What she says is, *You ready for Aaliyah to come home? You need me to keep her for another week? You going to be up and dressed when I drop her off? You got dinner figured out?*

I'm fine.

Because I don't mind keeping her if you need more time. The last thing Aaliyah needs is to see you fall apart.

Of course she says this. Honey hid every emotion from me except happiness, and I think that might be why I feel so guilty when I'm tired, why I apologize for things that are not my fault, why I downplay when I'm angry. I never saw how to handle emotions. How to make space for a feeling, let it be what it needs to be instead of pushing it aside, pretending it's not there. It shows up in other ways, at other times—sometimes months, years, decades later, but always it finds its way, so I might as well welcome it now, let it stay as long as it needs to.

Because what I don't want to do is eat my feelings away, push them down, numb them. I used to be in denial about being an emotional eater. I always saw emotional eating as bingeing, stuffing my face, inhaling everything in sight, completely out of control, with hidden stashes of food all over the house. As long as I wasn't doing that, I told myself I was fine. That I had a healthy relationship with food.

But after my breakup with Bryan, I gained fifty pounds. Not all at once, and not because of eating a whole pizza in one sitting, but because I'd eat a few slices at a time over the course of the day, when I wasn't even hungry, until it was gone. I'd eat when I was sad or frustrated or irritated or insecure or tired. Always treating myself because I had a bad day or rewarding myself for a good day.

During times of celebration or mourning, food is always there for me, with me.

I don't know if it's the same with Honey. She never talks about food or my weight. She never talked about her personal hurt or pain and how she healed from it. Probably because she didn't think it was appropriate to share her struggles, to show any weakness to her daughter.

But maybe daughters need to see how a brokenhearted woman heals. I don't want to teach Aaliyah how to hide her pain, how to cover up.

The doorbell rings. *It's me,* Aaliyah says. Her voice, a salve.

I open the door, hug her before she comes inside. Hold on tighter than I expect to.

I missed you, Momma.

I missed you too.

Honey kisses me on the cheek. Soft. *It's good to put eyes on you. You know I thought to just drop by this past week, but your father said to give you time.* Then she turns to Aaliyah. *Sweetheart, go upstairs and unpack your bag. Give me my sugar before you leave. I might be gone by the time you come back.*

Honey waits for Aaliyah's pitter-patter feet to be a distant echo. *Lena, you sure you okay? You can't do like last time.*

Last time.

Bryan.

I came undone.

I'm fine, Mom. I call her Mom sometimes, when I need her to remember who I need her to be for me.

Honey whispers, *Aaliyah was too young to remember then, but baby girl is older now. She's listening when you don't think she is listening. She knows more than you think she knows. She needs you to be strong, Lena. She needs her mother to be strong.*

What do mothers do when they feel weak?

Am I the only one?

questions

My daughter wants to know if she will ever have a daddy, a real one. My daughter wants to know if I will ever stop crying myself to sleep at night. My daughter wants to know if I want to keep one of her teddy bears with me at bedtime, so I won't be so sad. My daughter wants to know if we are going to Seaside Beach before summer ends, like I promised. My daughter wants to know why I keep saying, *We'll go next weekend,* and never go. My daughter wants to know why she can't have potato chips for a snack. My daughter wants to know why I flushed all the sugar we had in the house down the toilet. My daughter wants to know if all men hurt the women they love. My daughter wants to know if Malcolm is really sorry. My daughter wants to know why I won't forgive Malcolm. My daughter wants to know if she has to forgive people when they apologize. My daughter wants to know if I ever did anything so bad that I didn't deserve forgiveness. My daughter wants to know if I will come outside and play with her in the backyard like I used to. My daughter wants to know why I am drinking smoothies and not eating meals. My daughter wants to know if all girls and women dislike their bodies. My daughter wants to know if *fat* is a bad word. My daughter wants to know if she is fat. My daughter wants to know if I think she looks just like me. My daughter wants to know if I think she's beautiful.

magic & potions

I've started taking appetite suppressants. Aaliyah saw me popping one, asked was I taking medicine. I told her they were my beauty pills, so now every morning while she's taking her vitamin gummy, she makes sure I am taking my beauty pill. She calls her vitamins her *strong* pills, and after she takes her gummy, she flexes her little-girl muscles in the mirror, *I get stronger and stronger every day. See? It's working.*

Now take yours, Momma. Your beauty pill. She watches me take the pill, makes sure I swallow, looks at me, says, *Yours is working, too, Momma. You are so pretty, Momma. It's working real good.*

july

Going back to work. Bracing myself.

Trying to balance it all. I am giving so much to this partnership with Starshine & Clay that by the time I get home, I have nothing left. And Aaliyah needs everything, all of me. But I just don't have enough of me to spread around. And Malcolm keeps calling, texting, sending messages through Aspen and Kendra. Every minute of the day there is something—a boundary to set, a grace to give.

And this means summer is not turning out how I thought it would be.

Week 1: Promise Aaliyah we'll go see the Fourth of July fireworks at Waterfront Park.

Week 2: Apologize to Aaliyah for canceling last week's plans. Promise her we can do something fun this weekend. Whatever she wants: Arcade? Mommy-daughter spa day? Oaks Amusement Park?

She picks spa day and is so excited about getting a manicure. The morning we are supposed to go, I can't get out of bed. Kendra takes her. My promise is only half-broken. At least she still gets to go.

Week 3: Mommy-daughter movie night. I pop the popcorn—the old-fashioned way, like Dad taught me as a girl. There's licorice, lemonade, chocolate pretzels...we are ready. And then, two hours later, Aaliyah is shaking me. *Momma, wake up. The movie is over. Let's go to bed.*

Week 4: Keep forcing myself to get up, get dressed, check things off my list of things to do. There is still living that must happen. A daughter to love, a career to manage, a heart to heal, a life, my life.

august

I have a small birthday party for Aaliyah. Just a few of her friends, and of course Honey and Dad, Aspen and Kendra.

At the end of the night, when I am tucking her in to bed, Aaliyah says, *Momma, guess what I wished for when I blew out the candles? I wished for you and Malcolm to get back together. Do you think it will happen? Do you?*

black, black

The planning committee has gathered today to start working on the logistics for Portland: Black. Aspen has invited Meredith, the director of marketing and promotion at Starshine & Clay. Everything about her is long—her brown hair is down to her waist, her slim body is mostly legs. I have asked Allie to join us too. She heads up our youth programs at the library, and I wanted to make sure we have someone on the planning committee who is actually hands-on with youth. She is the one who keeps me in the know of the latest everything—songs, slang, dances. Every few months she changes her hair color: blue, purple, hot pink, red. Allie has a thin waist and a thick everything else. She is short and dresses in vintage dresses and skirts from the 1950s. She's one of the most beloved staff members at the library. If she's out on vacation, our regular patrons ask for her, miss her. Both Meredith and Allie are White, and I really want to have more Black voices at the table, so I'm thinking we should invite Black Portlanders to a think-tank meeting, ask them for feedback once we come up with something more concrete.

Aspen begins the meeting. *Today we're going to discuss some of the logistics, and Lena has an update on the curation of the exhibit. We just have an hour, so I'll get right to it.*

My cell buzzes. I turn it over, it's Malcolm. I send it to voicemail.

skin & bones

Aspen says, *The last time we met, we decided that opening night of the exhibit will be a party—a throwback to the Black social clubs that existed in Portland during the 1940s. And then we'll offer programming over the year, like panels or a lecture series—*

Meredith cuts Aspen off. *I'm, uh, I don't mean to interrupt, and I know we're not talking about promotion right now, but I just want to express my concern about attendance. Given our location and...well, I, I want to make sure people come.*

Allie says, *Oh, I'm positive people will come. We can support with design and promo material and we can make sure the shops in this area get lots of flyers.*

Meredith nods and says, *Yes, but I mean, well—we need to cast a wide net for outreach, is all I'm saying, so that we get as many people as possible. This neighborhood isn't like it used to be, and I want to make sure we get the word out to, to, um—you know, to the people who this is for.*

Right, Allie says. *I think with both our PR departments working on this, we'll be able to—*

Now I'm the one cutting people off. *I think Meredith means Black people,* I say. I look at Meredith. *Is that what you mean? We need to do specific outreach to Black Portlanders to make sure they know about this and come out, since they don't live over here anymore?*

Yes, yes...that's what I was trying to say.

My phone alerts me again. A text from Malcolm. I ignore it, sit up in my seat. *Okay, Meredith and Allie. I'm just going to be blunt because, well, here's the thing: Black is not a bad word. It is not an offensive word, and if we're going to work together to do a citywide program about Black history in Portland, we—all of us—need to get comfortable saying that word. Black. You can say it. In fact, please say it.*

Meredith's cheeks turn a little red, and Allie, who knows me well, looks pleasantly surprised at my forwardness.

Meredith tells us, *Sorry…I just…I didn't want to offend or make it seem like that's our only audience. Of course I want everyone to come. I just, I know sometimes our space is intimidating, you know? I want everyone to feel welcome, and I also think we might need to consider posting some etiquette guidelines. You know, for…for the Bl— For anyone who isn't used to being in art galleries or spaces like this. You know, like rules about not touching the art, no loud voices—*

I look at Allie, tell her with my eyes that this is the moment she can step in. All the things being learned and discussed in our DEI trainings, all the role-plays and discussions about racial microaggressions, allyship, and antiracism, has to be put into actual practice, or what's the point?

Allie clicks her pen, sets it on the table. *I totally think we should discuss community norms for our events,* she says. *But we don't want to assume that our Black guests—or any guests—won't know proper etiquette, and also maybe we should consider the cultural ways nonwhite people engage with art and not assume that those ways are inappropriate.*

Before Meredith can apologize or clarify, I jump in and say, *And actually, we can return to this. Aspen has scheduled a separate meeting to discuss marketing and promotion. Today, we're going over some of the logistics of what we're actually doing. There'll be nothing to promote if nothing is planned.* I try to say that last part with a smile, like I'm being funny, like I am not offended by what Meredith just implied—that Black people don't know how to act. I look at Aspen, ask her with my eyes, *Why is she here? This the best you got?*

Meredith nods. *Yes, yes. Sorry, my questions can wait… except… sorry, one more thing. I see that Williams Avenue is on the list under places to highlight for the exhibit. I thought we were just covering the Vanport Flood and Alberta Street.*

Williams Avenue is crucial to this project, I say.

Absolutely crucial to Black Portland, Aspen adds.

Oh, I see. I, I know it has some significance, but I want to make sure we're not overloading the exhibit.

Okay, well, let's table that for now. But I'd rather take Alberta Street off and keep Williams, if it comes to that, Aspen says. She facilitates the rest of the meeting. We actually do get a concrete plan on paper.

After the meeting is over, and Meredith and Allie are gone, Aspen says, *She is on my last nerve.* And the way she emphasizes *last,* I know she has run out of patience for the day. Black women only have so many last nerves for folks to get on before, truly, there's just nothing left to give.

You think she's asking questions to waste time and sabotage this? Aspen says. *Or, I don't know, you think she's looking for reasons not to do this?*

I doubt any of that. I think her questions were actually sincere—problematic, some of them, but sincere. She just seems like a White woman who gets to cut people off all the time, take up all the space, and ask any question she has whenever she has it.

Aspen laughs. *Can you believe she couldn't even say the word* Black? *Our whole entire organization is inspired by the words of a Black woman. Our mission is about working with Black artists. I'm so surprised by her. She interviewed so well.*

We laugh and then say the word *Black* several different ways, like it sounds when hesitant White folks say it: *Bl-aaa-ck, B-lackk, Black.*

I grab my purse, walk to the door so we can get out of here.

Aspen says, *She has a point about promotion, though. We have to make sure our churches, nursing homes, and schools get the info.*

True, I tell her. *Ain't that something? We doing outreach to people who used to live over here. Asking them to come visit their new and improved home.*

messages

Malcolm keeps reaching out. It is routine now for me
to delete his voice messages, ignore his texts. Today's tally,
the fewest yet:

Three missed calls.

Nine text messages.

And as I am reading his messages, my phone vibrates
again.

Bryan.

Aaliyah's dad.

I let it ring, send it to voicemail.

Why is he calling me? I ask it out loud, even though no
one is with me. *What does he want?*

bryan

I was eighteen when I realized Bryan wasn't the one for me. We'd been together since freshman year of high school, and back then that felt like forever, felt like we had to stay together and have our perfect ending.

We had spent the day at Lloyd Center Mall, mostly window shopping, but the one thing we could afford was the caramel and cheese popcorn at Joe Brown's. We left the mall, made our way to the Number 8 bus stop, and as soon as we stepped outside, we saw the bus pulling up. Bryan dropped my hand and started running, said, *Come on, let's catch the bus! Come on!* I knew we were too far away to make it, knew my big body couldn't run that fast.

Bryan took a short cut, ran across the flower bed, trampling over spring's fresh tulips. And it wasn't that he didn't understand that his big girlfriend couldn't run fast. It wasn't that he dropped my hand and didn't even look back to realize I wasn't with him. What bothered me most was that he was so unaware of the cobblestone pathway just inches from the grass. He could have run there instead of on the tulips. All that beauty stomped out by negligence and hurry. Nothing else mattered but what he wanted in that moment.

I learned a lot about him that day. Learned that he could crush the most delicate thing and not even notice. Learned that he was selfish and nonchalant with his oblivion.

skin & bones

Bryan's love for me was selfish—it was a love about his needs being met first and foremost. Sometimes it showed up in moments when I just wanted to be held, just wanted to exist together in the sweetness of us, but he almost always wanted passion, wanted our bodies intertwined and me saying his name like his name was the most important thing, like it would save me from drowning.

Bryan is a photographer. Ever since I met him, he's had a camera in his hand. He practically documented our high school years, so much of me he holds. He's never held a traditional job. Even in our college days, he freelanced and worked as a teaching artist for a local community center. But stipends and honorariums don't pay the bills. For most of our twenties I took care of him, of us. Never thought of it as him using me—although Honey did. By the time we were thirty and still living together with no ring, no wedding date, she was done with Bryan. Honey outright demanded I break up with him, said I was taking care of a grown man, said if I let him go, I'd be making space for someone else to come.

And then I got pregnant.

Bryan stayed through the pregnancy, but a week after Aaliyah was born, he told me he was moving to Seattle. He had found a job working for a social justice and art organization. He'd be teaching photography and doing community art installations with youth. I didn't even know he had been looking for a new job, a new city to live in. How could he make this decision without me?

Bryan moved.

But still. I held on. Prayed and held on. Made weekend trips to Seattle and held on. Thought holding on proved to him that I was a good woman, a woman here for all of him, not just the best of him. Mature enough to know that love takes work, that love takes sacrifice, and I loved him enough to leave my family and friends and job if Seattle needed to be our new home.

Soon, he'd tell me. *Soon.*

A long-distance relationship isn't impossible, but it isn't easy. And always there was the threat, the worry, the wondering about another woman. Not because of unfounded paranoia, but because of real proof. Once Aaliyah was potty trained and old enough to spend the weekend with him, he'd tell me, *I just want some daddy-daughter time,* and he'd drive to Portland, spend time with his mom, and take Aaliyah back up I-5. The whole weekend he'd send photos of them, and it always seemed like snapshots from a family vacation I should be at.

Once Aaliyah was old enough to talk and recount what she did at Daddy's in Seattle, I learned why Bryan stopped wanting me to come. Aaliyah always had a story about Daddy's friend(s), always a woman, always spending the night.

We broke up.

Hurt is essential to love. Not in the martyr way but in the human way, in understanding that even lovable people make mistakes. I told myself all the things women say to make us stay too long, love too much. I held on. Told him I forgave him, told him I wanted to work it out, go to counseling. I was willing to do the work.

He's the one who let go. My grip was so tight, I still don't understand how he slipped away. His mom seemed just as crushed as I was. *What man willingly lives in another state, away from his daughter?* she always asks. *I just can't believe he messed up such a good thing. The Bible says he who finds a good wife finds a good thing. You were his good thing!* She doesn't understand how it is that the boy she nursed, the boy she brought to church every Sunday morning, did all the things Christian boys are not supposed to do. Including having a child out of wedlock (and worse, not as a teenager but as a grown man). Always, her refrain: *I raised him better. I raised him better.*

transitions

My mother had a stroke. Bryan's voice is shaking. *I'm sorry to leave this in a voicemail and I know you have a lot going on but I just...I thought you'd want to know. I'm, uh, I'm driving down from Seattle. Passing through Vancouver now and heading straight to Good Sam. I'll, uh, I'll keep you posted.*

And then a long pause.

Lena, she's, uh...she's not...doctors aren't hopeful.

I drop Aaliyah off at Honey's, make my way to the hospital. When I get there, I am told only family are allowed in the room, but then Bryan's sister, Rebecca, tells the woman at the desk, *She's family,* and walks me to the wide doors. We wait to be buzzed in. *Thank you for coming. This is...thank you.* We walk down a long hallway and take so many turns I am sure I will get lost if I try this later without Rebecca. She brings me to the family's private waiting room. *Her room is just across the hall. Do you want to see her?*

I'll wait. I just wanted to be here. I'm just—I'm just here for whatever you all need.

I know most of the relatives. They look at me with surprise, care, and relief. There's an outpouring of hugs and thank-you-for-comings from everyone. I sit down, watch them go in and out of Ms. Coleman's room, two at a time. All of them with tearstained faces.

And then Bryan.

He is here now, and as soon as he enters the room, he asks, *Is she still...is she...?*

Rebecca says, *Yes, yes. I'll take you to her.*

Bryan exhales. And I know he was so afraid that his mother might leave this earth before he made it to the hospital. *Thank you, God. Thank you,* he says. Just as Rebecca takes his hand, he sees me. Our eyes meet, and he looks so surprised that I am here. He walks out of the room. I exhale. If he hadn't made it and his mother died, I don't know if Bryan would forgive himself. Living three hours away is not far at all unless there's a life-or-death emergency.

While Bryan is in Ms. Coleman's room, I make a run to the cafeteria with a list that I've scribbled on the back of a palliative care brochure: three decaf coffees, two bags of Lay's potato chips, a candy bar—anything chocolate but no nuts—and a Coke Zero. Emphasis on zero. *Tastes so much better than that diet mess,* one of his aunts says.

On the elevator, heading back to the family waiting room, I am overwhelmed with memories I haven't thought of in years. The time Ms. Coleman gave me a copy of *Their Eyes Were Watching God*, with notes and questions written in the margins. We started our own two-person book club, engaging in conversations written on pages not meant for our words. The two of us in conversation with Zora, like she was a friend, a sister-girl. I wonder where that book is now. And the copy of *Sister Outsider*. Did she throw them away? Did I? I remember the plastic pitcher always full of Kool-Aid. A permanent stain circled at the rim no matter how hard we scrubbed. She wouldn't let Bryan or Rebecca make Kool-Aid in any other pitcher.

I want something sweet now.

The elevator dings and I get off, try to remember how to get back through the maze. And then another memory, the time when Ms. Coleman caught us having sex in Bryan's bedroom. We were sixteen. I didn't even have to beg her not to tell my parents. I think she knew that while they would probably ban me from seeing Bryan, worse, they would blame her for letting us be there when she wasn't home, they'd say her son was ruining their pure daughter. No good would come out of her saying anything to anyone. It was our secret. Honey still doesn't know. A week after Ms. Coleman caught us, she sat us down, said, *Bryan—you better not get her pregnant, and Lena, you better not let him get you pregnant. It's both of your responsibility. Condoms, the pill, I don't care what you decide, but make sure you're using something. We can't have no babies around here before you two graduate. You understand me?*

We made it through graduation, college even. Maybe that's why Ms. Coleman didn't shame me or judge me when I told her I was pregnant. I was a puddle of tears, hyperventilating, when I told her. *You'll be alright,* she said. *Life is always a gift.*

When I get back to the room, Bryan is sitting next to his aunt. I give her the Coke Zero, pass out the rest of the snacks, and then Bryan stands, walks over to me. *Thank you for being here.*

I don't know what to say, so I just extend my arms, hug him, hold all our yesterdays.

Would you like to see her? Rebecca asks.

It isn't a question. She might as well have said, It's your turn. I walk across the hall with Bryan. And I feel guilty thinking about *us* in this moment, but it is hard not to think that Ms. Coleman could have been (should have been?) my mother-in-law. We step into the room, and I immediately want to turn around, run out. I don't know what I expected to see, how I expected to feel, but this isn't it. Didn't expect my mouth to go dry, didn't expect the thumping in my chest, didn't expect to be too afraid to stand close to the bed, to touch her, talk to her.

I grab Bryan's hand. He probably thinks I am offering him comfort, but really, I need to hold on to something, someone.

memories

The next day, I pick up the phone, almost call Malcolm.
But instead of calling, I scroll through photos of him.

macro microaggressions

It is hard to focus on work, hard to accept that life goes on while someone is dying.

I try to push all of that down so I can focus on what Aspen is saying. Her eyes are lit up. *Look at these! Oh my goodness. Look.*

We look through a stack of black-and-white photos that feel too sacred to hold. Our white-gloved hands handle each picture with such care. Aspen says, *Why didn't we know this history?*

I know, right? I think of what Ms. Brown said about history being heavy. Wonder if she means there's the weight of carrying our ancestors' deferred dreams, wanting to fulfill them, vowing to make them proud. And there's the heaviness that sadness brings, realizing all they endured, all the loss.

Another kind of grief.

Just then Allie and Meredith join us. They went on a lunch run an hour ago. *Sorry we took so long*, Allie says. *The line was out the door.*

Before Allie and Meredith can set up lunch, Aspen says, *Let's eat upstairs in the Baldwin Room.*

Every space at Starshine & Clay is named after a Black legend. Aspen and I walk over to the elevator. Meredith says, *I'm going to walk. Get some steps in.*

Allie hesitates, then joins Meredith. *Yeah, I've been sitting a lot today, need to move more.*

You know, you're right. I need to stop being lazy, Aspen says. She walks over to the stairs.

And now I am walking away from the elevator, because even though they didn't outright say it, I feel like they're judging me. And here's the thing: I don't mind taking the stairs at my own pace, but they all walk fast. Well, fast for me. And they're talking and asking me questions while we walk—and I'm answering and sounding more and more winded with each stair. Beads of sweat drip down my forehead, and after two flights, I stop. I need to catch my breath.

Aspen looks back, says, *You okay?*

Oh, yeah. My, um, my phone is buzzing, someone is calling me. I pull my phone out of my tote, pretend to take a call, saying hello to no one. I keep the act going, silently mouth to Aspen, Meredith, and Allie, *Go ahead. I'll be up soon.*

I hear Meredith say, *I never get service in the stairwell.*

I let them go. Wait until their voices trail off, and when I know they can't hear me, I let out a long sigh. I wipe the sweat from my brow, then continue up the stairs, slower this time, at my own pace.

When I get to the top floor, I go into the bathroom, yank a paper towel out of the dispenser, wet it, and pat my face.

I step into the Baldwin Room and I am overwhelmed by the sunlight spilling through the ceiling-to-floor windows. Meredith is taking the food out of the bag, calling our names and orders. *Grilled chicken bowl—Aspen, this is yours. Beets and goat cheese salad...this one is mine. Let's see, this one is yours, Allie—artichoke-lemon veggie bowl, and last but not least, Lena—chicken avocado sandwich. It came with fries, but I opted for the apple slices. I assumed you wanted something more healthy.*

I wanted the fries, I say.

skin & bones

Meredith says, *Oh, I, ah, I think of fries as my cheat food, something I only splurge on during the weekend.*

I got us dessert, Allie says. *I hope that's okay.* She empties the bag out—an assortment of single-serving baked goods: brownies, peanut butter chocolate bars, and lemon bars. She takes one of the plastic knives from the bag and cuts the dessert into small squares. *This way, we each get a sample of all of them,* she says.

Aspen gets us started. *Thanks for agreeing to a working lunch, ladies. And thanks, Lena, for putting this on the library's account. I'll get it next time.*

Next time? Meredith asks. *All these feasts for lunch, I'm going to have to add some more time to my workout routine. I'm trying to keep my summer body, but if I keep eating like this, no way is that going to happen.*

Can we just start the meeting? Why do we have to talk about food just because we're eating food? Also, I have never known beets and feta to be the cause of weight gain.

Allie and Aspen chime in about their *guilty pleasures* and *sugar weaknesses*. And I am surprised when Aspen says, *I feel you, Meredith, I keep losing and gaining the same ten pounds. I really need more discipline.*

Meredith goes on, *I hear the older you get, the harder it gets to lose weight. In five years, I'll be forty. I want to lose this belly before it's too late for me to keep it off.*

I look at Meredith, who probably wears a size 4 on a bloated day, and can't help but roll my eyes. What belly?

We should start, I say. *I have to get back to the library soon for my next meeting.*

I share some of the stories I have researched on Black pioneers and the history of Black neighborhoods in Oregon. I've made copies of the biographies that will be beside each photo. They look over their handouts as I talk them through my ideas for the exhibit.

We end the meeting with enthusiasm for what's to come and plan our next session. On my way back to the library, all I can think about is what it felt like to have lunch with Aspen, Meredith, and Allie, how they sat there and basically admitted—in my presence—that of all the cares and worries to have in life, their greatest fear is having a body that looks like mine.

belonging

So much of my life has been about fitting in.

Squeezing my body into too-tight spaces.

Adapting my personality to get along, be agreeable.

Always there were reminders that I didn't belong. That the spaces I was trying to fit in weren't made for me.

When I can't fit in a seat, down an aisle, in a bathroom stall, it is a reminder that the space was never intended for a person like me.

When the policy of the workplace is no braids, and when the natural tone of my voice is considered too harsh, and my laugh too loud, the message is that I am too much.

Tonight, while I'm researching Portland's Black pioneers, I see myself in them. Constantly they had to figure out how to navigate this state, this city, and all its spaces that were not created with them in mind. I let them speak to me, teach me how.

jacob vanderpool

In the summer of 1851 Jacob Vanderpool was imprisoned for illegally living in the state of Oregon. A West Indian man, he lived in Oregon City and owned businesses: a saloon, a boardinghouse, a restaurant. He is the only Black person of record to be banished from Oregon because of his race.

He was married to a woman named Eliza. They had three children: twins Amelia and Jane and a son, Martin. Just living their simple Black lives and getting shooed at, swatted like they were nagging flies.

There were others, too, who were pushed out, tried in court under Oregon's exclusion laws.

But some White neighbors petitioned for them to stay. There were instances when White folks stood up for their Black neighbors, said they should have every right as White citizens.

At least someone cared. Someone advocated. I think about Garrett and the mystery colleagues with their so-called concerns. Meredith, with her steadfast solidarity just as potent as her ignorance. And Allie, who sees my Blackness but not my bigness. It all makes me wonder about the motives of White people. What did these White neighbors have to gain? What were their motives? Can any White people—even the good ones, the advocating ones, the I-see-you ones, the Black Lives Matter ones—can any of them be trusted?

oregon, 1857

Constitution, Article II, Section No. 6

"No free negro or mulatto not residing in this state at the time of the adoption of this constitution, shall come, reside or be within this state or hold any real estate, or make any contracts, or maintain any suit therein; and the legislative assembly shall provide by penal laws for the removal by public officers of all such negroes and mulattoes, and for their effectual exclusion from the state, and for the punishment of persons who shall bring them into the state, or employ or harbor them."

It was White men who voted to ban slavery in Oregon. And at the same time, they voted to make it illegal for any new Black folks to take up residence in Oregon. Making it clear they didn't mind Black folks living free. They just didn't want that liberated Blackness next door to them.

allen ervin flowers

One of the early Black Portlanders was Allen Ervin Flowers, a cabin boy on a paddle steamer called the *Brother Jonathon*. He jumped ship in 1865 and hid out in the Portland brush along the river until he knew it was safe to make his way into the city. The miracle he could not have known is that the same ship he jumped off sank near the coast of Eureka, California, on its return trip to Oregon. It is believed that 225 people died.

Allen made a home in Portland and worked as a busboy at the Lincoln Hotel. In 1882 he married Louisa Thatcher. The couple had four boys. In 1885 Allen began working as a porter for the Northern Pacific Railroad.

He was one of the few Black Portlanders who owned land. He built a new road, naming it Northeast Schuyler Street, so that his wife could make her way through the city, pushing her stroller, and have access to Union Avenue. It was the only through street to the river at that time.

Allen and his wife were avid Christians and were members of Bethel African Methodist Episcopal Church, the oldest Black church in the city. It was founded by twenty people in 1889 in the home of a man named Phillip Jenkins. Allen and Louisa served as deacon and deaconess at the church and were very involved in the community. Louisa was also a founding member of the colored YWCA.

They existed. They were here.

Surviving, somehow.

Somehow, surviving.

as long as it takes

Malcolm sends me a text message:

Lena,

I know I hurt you. And I know it's going to take more than my apology to move forward. I want to talk with you, but you're not answering my calls or responding to my text messages. But you also haven't told me not to call, you haven't asked me to leave you alone. So, I'm not leaving you alone. I'm here whenever you're ready. Until you tell me you want me to stop contacting you, I'm going to remind you every day that I am here and I want to work this out.

As long as it takes you to heal & forgive me, I'm here. I'm not going anywhere. You are my forever.

aunt aretha

Honey calls her heavy-handed. Nothing about her is modest. When I was a child and I knew Aunt Aretha was going to do my hair, I knew I'd have to brace myself and hold back my tears. She combed hard, brushed even harder, pulling my hair into the tightest ponytail. When she cooks, she is heavy on the salt, heavy on the butter, heavy on pouring cream in coffee. Even her hugs are mammoth. She envelops, holds on, rocks back and forth. This is how she greets me today. An abundance of love.

It's Saturday evening, and Aunt Aretha is here. She just finished washing Aaliyah's hair for church tomorrow, like she used to do mine. Aunt Aretha says, *Girl, look at all this hair you got on you. My goodness. So long and thick. Just like your momma's was when she was your age. What you want today? Two-strand twists or braids?*

Twists! Aaliyah says.

You want to give me some of this hair? I could cut half your hair off and you'd still have more than enough.

Aaliyah laughs.

Is that a no? Well, how about that smile? You could give me some of that smile and you'd still have enough sun-shine to fill the sky. Aunt Aretha goes on like this, loving on Aaliyah, complimenting her brown skin, her creativity, her playful personality.

And when she is finished with Aaliyah's hair, she goes into the kitchen, says, *Let me get Sunday's supper together,* and starts preparing tomorrow's dinner. For our family Sunday meals, she cooks the night before and warms everything up after service. It's been this way since I was a child.

Usually, the preparation was at Grandma's. We had family dinner on the first Sunday of the month. But then Grandma died, and slowly it was every other month, then twice a year, and now only on Thanksgiving. Earlier this week, Aunt Aretha sent me a text (I was proud of her for finally figuring out how to work her phone) asking me if I would host Sunday supper at my place. *We need to gather again,* she said. And all week, I've been wondering if she has some bad news to share or maybe she wants to check on me, fill my house with food and family. Or maybe we really just need to gather... just because. Family shouldn't need a reason.

Aaliyah, baby, come on over here and learn, Aunt Aretha says. She shows Aaliyah how to shred the cheese, then hands her the grater. *Think you can handle this?* She points to the blocks of cheddar sitting on the counter.

I got it, Aaliyah says with an enthusiastic smile. I realize in this moment that I hardly ever cook with Aaliyah. Breakfast is usually cereal—sometimes eggs—and other than her packed school lunch, we mostly order out.

Aunt Aretha says, *Lena, you hear Gail's daughter is pregnant?*

Cousin Gail in Arkansas? I ask, as if I know several women named Gail.

Chile. She on her third one and ain't even twenty yet. Don't make no sense.

Aaliyah's eyes get big at the number three, but she doesn't look up from her mountain of shredded cheese.

And so it begins. Get Aunt Aretha cooking, and she starts talking and telling all the family business, which

I love when she's reporting on everybody else's drama, but now that I am the one with secrets exposed, I wonder what she is saying about me when I'm not around. Wonder, years from now, will my drama be included in the family lore.

Aunt Aretha stands at the island, prepping the smoked neck bones she bought at the meat market. *You know, Momma never liked eating this kind of food. Called it poor folks' food.*

Really? I ask, setting out a deep pot for her.

Chile, yes. And don't let me cook pig feet. She'd have a fit. Called it slave food. Said back then we had to eat that mess, but now that we can do better, we should. Aunt Aretha laughs. *Your grandma was bougie, you know that right? Loved her, but she was anything but down-to-earth.*

What does bougie mean? Aaliyah asks.

Aunt Aretha doesn't hesitate. *At its worst, it means stuck-up, but it can also mean a person who likes the finer things.*

So eating neck bones and mac and cheese with rice and gravy isn't being bougie?

Not at all, chile. Not at all. Unless you eating at one of those gentrified soul food places that charge an arm, leg, and entire backside for a spoonful of black-eyed peas.

What about king crab legs or smoked salmon?

What you know about all that?

Aaliyah says, *My friend Paige has family in Alaska and they always send crab and salmon. The way she talks about it sounds like it's something special or fancy.*

It is, Aunt Aretha says. *And your great-grandmother loved it. She preferred seafood and fish. Always telling us how it was healthy for you. Momma nagged us all the time about what to eat, what not to eat. Swore eating all this soul food would be the death of us.*

We move about the kitchen, half the food being prepared, the rest already on the stove or in the oven simmering, sizzling, or baking.

Aaliyah says, *Tell me more about Great-Grandma. I
wish I knew her. Was she born here like me?*

Aunt Aretha says, *No, baby, she was born in Arkansas.
Her parents moved to Oregon because her father found
work. Got a job working for the railroad. He convinced the
family that living out west wasn't that bad.* She shakes her
head and sighs. *They were too naive to understand it's bad
for Black folks everywhere.* She takes the bowl of cheese
from Aaliyah, sets it aside, motions for a pot, and fills it
with water.

Aunt Aretha turns to Aaliyah. *My momma and
daddy—your great-grandparents—met at a dance hall and
married two months later. Now that ain't enough time to
know if the heart is in love or in fantasy. My mother didn't
give herself enough time to learn that what my daddy really
wanted was a servant, not a wife. That he wanted sex, not
intimacy. She didn't give herself enough time to know what
she wanted, that she could want.* Then Aunt Aretha turns
and says to me, *Ain't no rush. A woman should be allowed
to take her time when it comes to who she's giving her
heart to.*

Soon, there is a quiet in the kitchen. No more clanking pots, running water, slicing knives. Everything that
needed to be prepared is complete and is cooking. We've
washed and put away the dishes, and now, we wait.

Aaliyah peeks in the oven, watching the cornbread.
*Aunt Aretha, why do you own a soul food restaurant if soul
food kills people?*

I try to explain, *Aaliyah, soul food doesn't kill—*

But Aunt Aretha said that Great-Grandma—

Oh, well, sweetheart, I'm sorry I confused you. Let's

clear this up. First of all, not everything a grandmother or mother says is the truth.

When Aaliyah hears this, she looks at me like she wants me to confirm if this is really how it is.

Aunt Aretha continues, *Momma was right about a lot of things, but she was wrong about that restaurant. That was the best decision I ever made.*

Now, I'm the one with questions. *Grandma didn't want you to open the restaurant?*

Oh, my, not at all. Every time I saw her, she'd say something negative about the restaurant. Or me. You don't remember that? Maybe you were too young.

I pull up memories that have been dormant for years. What first comes to mind is being at a family dinner and hearing Grandma say to Aunt Aretha, *You might have to close that restaurant down if you can't control yourself from eating all the food. Your hips and belly are telling all your business—you supposed to be serving the food, not eating it all.*

The whole family laughed.

I can't remember what Aunt Aretha did.

Or what Honey did.

But I know I laughed too.

The thought of my hips and belly telling on me was hilarious. Would my hips tell how I practiced my sexy walk in the mirror? I was just eight or nine and could hardly walk in Honey's heels and couldn't fully define the word *sexy*, but I knew there was a walk that beautiful, wanted women had. I wanted to master it. Switch, switch, switching down the hallway, looking in the full-length mirror to make sure my hips were swaying the right way. What would my hips say if they could?

It didn't dawn on me then that Grandma was saying Aunt Aretha was gaining weight, spilling out of her clothes, and clearly indulging in her the-boss-eats-free perk. Grandma's words didn't mean much to me back then, but sitting here now with forty years' worth of weight on me, I think about what she was truly saying—that you could lie or be in denial about what you were eating, but the body would always tell the truth.

grandma

Aunt Aretha has been gone for a while now. I am in Aaliyah's room, helping her choose a book. Since she was a baby, it's been a ritual for us to read together on Saturday evenings just before bed. She is old enough to read to me, sounding out the hard words, so proud of herself when she makes it to the end of a paragraph without my help. But sometimes she just wants to listen to me, just wants the story to wash over her and lull her to sleep. We haven't done this since I called off the wedding. It feels good to have some normalcy, to have some quality time.

This one! Aaliyah says.

What about one of the chapter books I brought home from work? You practically know all sixteen of these poems by heart.

Because it's my favorite, she tells me, as she opens *Honey, I Love* by Eloise Greenfield. *Remember when I thought you wrote this for Honey?*

I do.

But then you told me it was written for girls like me.

It was.

We cuddle on the yellow chaise in Aaliyah's reading corner. Just as she is about to start reading out loud, she closes the book and says, *Actually, can you tell me a story instead?*

Sure. You want to make it up with me? We can go back and forth.

No, I want a real story, a true story. Tell me something about Great-Grandma and Honey and Aunt Aretha and you when you were my age. What do you remember?

I pull Aaliyah close, mine stories from my childhood. I'm hardly getting started and already Aaliyah is asleep. I don't wake her right away. Instead, I sit and hold her, close my eyes, and remember all I thought I forgot.

What I remember is the Strawberry Shortcake bike I got for my birthday. It was pink and red with a basket at the front. Red, pink, and white streamers hung from the handlebars, and the banana seat was decorated in strawberries. I rode that bike everywhere. Sometimes I'd collect flowers and put them in my basket. On days when I wanted to leave for a long time and spend the whole day with my friends, I'd sneak snacks from the pantry and store them in the basket so I'd have something to eat while I was out exploring the neighborhood. Twinkies, Hostess apple pie, whatever treats Honey had bought at Safeway.

I remember one day I came back home from my excursion, and Grandma was sitting on the porch with Honey. Before I could even get off the bike, here she came walking over to hug me. When she let me out of her embrace, she saw all the empty wrappers in the basket. The look on her face told me I was in big trouble, but instead of scolding me, she turned around and went off on Honey.

You letting this child eat this junk? When she get diabetes, ain't gonna be nobody to blame but you.

Honey didn't say a word, hardly looked at her mother at all.

I've been wondering what you feedin' this girl. Every time I see her she bigger and bigger. You better get that under control before it's too late.

Grandma took the wrappers out of my basket and walked into the house to throw them away. I heard her mumble to herself, *Better be careful when you take them training wheels off. That bike might not be able to hold her up, all that weight on it.*

I just knew this would be the last day in my life that I'd have anything sweet. I expected Honey to raid the kitchen and throw away anything Grandma deemed unhealthy, but a few days later when we went to the store, she filled the basket with milk and eggs and bread and fresh spinach and chicken to bake and fish to fry and sweet potatoes to roast

and Twinkies and Hostess Apple Pies

and Slice soda and Johnny Apple Seeds and Nerds and Push Pops

and Cookie Crisp cereal and Pop Tarts

and Pepperoni Hot Pockets

and Cheese and Sausage Bagel Bites.

I remember.

I remember feeling caught in the middle of a grandma who wouldn't let me have any of it and a mother who let me have it all.

I remember feeling confused by Grandma's blatant disdain for my body and her palpable affection all at once. What I remember is Grandma reaching into her pocketbook, pulling out a five- or ten- or twenty-dollar bill, telling me to get myself something just for me. I remember her patience with me when I was sounding out words too big for my little-girl vocabulary, but just the right challenge for my curious mind. I remember her buying me books, so I could keep them forever and never have to return them to the library. I remember her nursing me on days I was too sick to go to school and Dad and Honey had to work. Her around-the-clock care included

watching a marathon of soap operas and Oprah Winfrey
at four o'clock, and always ginger ale and saltines—every
Black woman's medicine. What I remember is her miracle hands in my scalp, combing, parting, pressing, barret-
ting. *When you gonna lose this baby fat?* she'd ask. Even
when I was five and six and seven and eight and nine and
ten and sixteen and twenty-one, and not any age close to
being a baby. *You want men to want you, don't you? You
have such a pretty face, got to get the rest of you together.*

Got to get the rest of me together.

I remember wanting to be put together for Grandma.
Always proud to show off an accomplishment, always afraid
to admit I had done something I knew she'd disapprove of.
When I found out I was pregnant, she was the last person
I told. I waited and waited till I couldn't hide my growing
belly anymore. For the longest time, no one knew unless
I told them. Looked like I had just gained more weight. I
never had that perfect round pregnant belly, so it was easy
to hide. When I told Grandma, to my surprise she said,
*Well, Lena, I'm glad you found someone to love you even
with all that weight. I was worried for so long that you'd die
without ever being loved.*

I remember.

Grandma died before Aaliyah was born. She died
without knowing her name, without holding her, without
knowing Bryan would leave me and his daughter to chase
his dream in another state. She died without seeing me
fall apart at his leaving, without seeing me rebuild and
heal.

Just like Honey, I never said anything to Grandma and
neither did Aunt Aretha. Not verbally, anyway. Maybe we
are all responding now. Aunt Aretha with her restaurant
that is thriving and about to open another location out
in Gresham now that Black folks have moved over there.

Renée Watson

Her unapologetic self-love at every size she's been, will be. And Honey, who, with her body that has relatively stayed the same, stayed acceptable to Grandma's standards, and who refuses to judge or make comments on anyone's body. And me, not being tricked by the mirage of love. Me, trying my best to get myself together... for me.

hair

I was always jealous of Kendra's hair. It was thick and could do every Black girl hairstyle. I swore her mom worked as a hairstylist for *Ebony* magazine, the way she'd come to school one day with her hair bone-straight and jet-black, not a nap to be found, and then she'd rock Brandy braids, baby hairs slicked, and every part down her scalp straight like a ruler had been used to measure the gaps between each single. Kendra loved to experiment. She'd dye it, cut it, weave it, perm it, braid it. Always, she was photo-shoot ready. Her hair was not merely her crown, it was fine art, her masterpiece.

Aspen couldn't do much. Not living under Deacon Brown's roof. Everything about her hair was modest. Ms. Brown wouldn't even let her get a perm. She pressed it up until high school, then started getting it flat-ironed. The most creative Aspen could get was choosing how short to cut her bangs or where to part her hair. Usually she parted it on the left and swept her hair over to add a little something, and senior year, when she gained a little weight and her cheeks grew fuller, she parted her hair down the middle so it could drape her face, hide some of the puffiness. She never, ever pulled it into a ponytail, even though her long straight hair would've been stunning swaying from side to side, so long that even when it was pulled up she still had hang time. *My face looks bigger when my hair is pulled back,* she'd said. *Makes me look like a little girl.*

When Kendra realized Aspen had never had a perm, she couldn't stop teasing her. *Girl, everything about you is a virgin.*

Grandma or Aunt Aretha usually washed and styled my hair because Honey's arthritis made her hands weak, and combing through my thick tresses was too much for her. In elementary and middle school, I wore it in ponytails and braids, mostly. In high school I chopped it off, wanted to look like Toni Braxton. Honey hated it, Aunt Aretha loved it. Bryan said he missed running his fingers through my hair when we had sex. I grew it back out in college and started wearing it natural: kinky twist-outs, braid-outs, high puffs, pineapples. Once Grandma said to me, *You like everything big, don't you? Big hair, big hips, big butt.* She was laughing like what she was saying was loving jest, not offensive insult. *Folks sitting behind you can't see over you and folks walking behind you can't get around you.*

training wheels

The library is having a citywide professional development day. A young White woman is leading the workshop, and after all the logistical announcements, she begins the session by saying, *Public libraries and school libraries are under attack. We are here to talk about how to fight legislative censorship and book challenges. It is our hope that today, you all leave feeling empowered and equipped with all you need as you go back to your communities and advocate for liberty and justice for all—especially when it comes to reading.*

And as these things go, it has to start off with get-to-know-you icebreakers with colleagues who work at other branches. We've been asked to partner with someone we don't know well. I don't have much choice, since I am standing at the coffee station and there's only one other person over here who's come for a refill too. I've met him before, so I try to think of his name without looking at his name tag. Before I guess it, he sticks his hand out to me, says, *Lena, right? I'm Blake. We met last month at the mixer. Want to be partners?*

Hi, Blake. Nice to see you again. I pour my coffee, reach for the sugar but then grab Splenda instead and pour a splash of cream. I see Cynthia, a Mexican woman I used to work with before I transferred to this branch. She smiles at me with a knowing look, as if to say, *I'd rather be partnered with you.* I smile back, nod, telepathing my response. *Girl, you know the only two Women of Color can't be in the same group.*

129

Alright everyone, the workshop facilitator says. *We're going to play Two Truths and a Lie.* She goes over the instructions, and already I am checking the clock to see what time it is. We're not even thirty minutes into this workshop, and I'm ready to go home. *Your partner will have to guess the lie*, she says, with too much enthusiasm for a morning meeting.

I go first:

I hate spicy food.

I don't know how to ride a bike without training wheels.

I graduated summa cum laude from the University of Oregon.

Hmm. Blake looks me over, thinking, thinking. He is taking this serious, as if there's some kind of grand prize if he guesses right. He leans back in his chair, runs his left hand through his messy nineties-boy-band hair. *Okay, the lie is that you don't know how to ride a bike. I mean, who doesn't know how to ride a bike? Especially in the Pacific Northwest.*

I smile. *You guessed wrong*, I tell him. *The lie is that I hate spicy food. I actually love it.*

So wait—you really don't know how to ride a bike? What, are you against exercise or something?

He doesn't mean to say it. I can tell because immediately his face turns red and he starts apologizing profusely. *I—um—I didn't mean it like that—*

Like what?

Like, I wasn't saying that a woman your size—I wasn't implying...what I meant was... Blake sighs. *I hope I didn't offend you—*

It's your turn. You should go before we run out of time, I say. Because really, what am I supposed to do in this moment?

Well, hell, I—the only statements I can think of are definitely true: Hi, I'm Blake, and I'm an idiot. Hi, I'm

Blake, and sometimes I don't think before I speak. Hi, I'm Blake, and—

The facilitator is at the front of the room, gently ringing a chime that echoes through the space. *Time to gather back into our full group*, she says. *Please thank your partner before you head back to your seat.*

Blake thanks me and apologizes one more time. His face is still red, his cup still full of the coffee he never took a sip of.

For the first half of the day, I can't focus on anything being said. I am thinking about my Strawberry Shortcake bike and the day Dad tried to get me to ride it without training wheels. Dad came into the living room early one morning while I was watching Saturday-morning cartoons, saying, *Go on and get yourself some breakfast and get dressed so we can get outside. Today's the day you're going to learn to ride your bike without your training wheels.* He was all smiles and so proud of himself for already taking the training wheels off. He had been talking about it for weeks, but I kept saying, *Just one more ride, just one more with them on. I'm scared. I don't want to fall.*

I'll teach you, baby girl. I won't let you fall, he'd say every time. Today, he didn't let me protest. He went into the kitchen, poured me a bowl of Cookie Crisp, and got the milk out of the fridge. Just as *The Smurfs* went off, I finished my cereal and got up to get dressed and ready to go outside. I tried to think of an excuse, but nothing came to mind. I definitely didn't want to lie and say I was sick. That would mean staying inside all day. I was halfway down the hallway to my room when I heard the theme song to *Punky Brewster* come on. *Dad, please? Please can we wait till this goes off?*

One last show, Lena. And then it's me, you, and Miss Strawberry Shortcake.

After *Punky Brewster*, I got up the nerve to go outside and was grateful no one else was out playing. My bike looked different without the training wheels, looked like a big girl's bike. Maybe I would start riding with some of the older girls who lived down the street if I could muster up the courage to learn how.

Alright, here we go, Dad said. *I'm going to hold the back of the bike while you get on.*

I straddled the bike but hardly sat down. Grandma's rebuke had been months ago, but still, it rang loud and clear in my mind. It had been on repeat since the day she said it: *That bike might not be able to hold her up, all that weight on it.*

I couldn't get on.

Lena, just sit down. I got you. I'm holding the bike. Dad was calm and gentle, and I believed that he believed I would be just fine, but I believed Grandma more. I didn't want to break my bike, the gift my parents surprised me with. I didn't want to fall to the ground in front of nosy neighbors peeking out of their windows.

I can't.

Lena, sweetheart, trust me. Just sit down.

I sat down and felt the bike move just a little, and that's when the tears came. *I can't, Dad. Why are you making me do this? I hate this stupid bike. All I wanted to do was watch cartoons today. I don't want to do this.* I wasn't yelling. More like a desperate cry. I got off the bike and ran into the house, praying Honey hadn't heard me disrespect my father. She did not go for that, and the last thing I wanted on a day like today was to be on punishment and get my television privileges revoked.

Honey hadn't heard me, and Dad never said anything to her—or maybe he did, but she never brought it up to me. I stayed inside for the rest of the day, and that night, after eating Honey's meat loaf and mashed potatoes, I got up and went to my room. *What about dessert?* Honey asked.

I don't feel good, I said. It was a lie, and it was the truth. I wasn't sick, but I didn't feel good.

Dad only asked once more if I was sure I didn't want to try again. I told him I was sure. My bike sat in the garage collecting dust for a year, and then on a sunny August day, we had a yard sale, and within ten minutes it sold.

slow

Life's traumas and sagas and hurts and offenses and accomplishments and jubilees don't wait their turn.

All in the same parade they come marching. A music that is both dirge and praise.

I am saying goodbye to Ms. Coleman, slowly, slowly. Letting her go each time I visit the hospital. Preparing myself for the final farewell.

And Malcolm. If not the end of us, the end of my disillusion. No one is perfect.

Slowly, slowly, I release the loves I've been holding on to. I pray God fills these hands. Pray that everything I've been taught about revival and resurrection is true.

fat girl, dance

Aspen's dance class is full tonight. And the most diverse I've ever seen. She's gone back and forth with herself about making this a class exclusively for Women of Color, but then decided it was more important to be intentional about a space for fat women—of all racial backgrounds. There are other programs Starshine & Clay hosts that are for Women of Color only. This hour is about accepting and moving the body, no matter what size it is.

Alright, alright, Aspen says, a little winded. *This was a great session. Let's circle up and prepare to give praise.*

We end every class standing in a circle, and each of us praises a body part we are thankful for. It's my least favorite part of our time together. I always have a hard time coming up with what to say, and without fail, I end up rolling my eyes at someone who doesn't just say something simple but instead goes into a whole ode about their body.

Alright, I need one of you regulars to go first so the newbies learn how to do it, Aspen says.

The White woman next to me goes first. *Praise these hands for being strong enough to pick up my five-month-old daughter. Praise these hands that pat her back gently as she falls asleep in my arms.*

And the Mexican woman next to me says, *Praise these feet that walk me around this beautiful city.*

And then a first-timer says hers, and another, and on and on until I raise my hand. *Praise this heart of mine that keeps beating and that is capable of healing and loving and forgiving.*

A Black woman says, *Yes, girl! Yes!*

And then Kendra says, *Praise my mind for holding information and never letting me forget the Bad Ass Woman I am.*

People actually cheer.

And then a White woman—the one who always talks too much—says, *Okay, sorry...I'm getting emotional... um...okay. It takes a lot for me to say this because usually I hate my belly. Hate how it protrudes and how flabby it is. But I guess we all hate our bellies, don't we?*

Kendra looks at me from across the room and I know she is thinking what I am thinking: What belly? This skinny woman has no belly, and I just can't take these tears. I look down at the floor. Make eye contact with no one because Aspen is always telling me my face tells exactly what I am thinking.

So, I'm going to say it loud and proud today, the woman says. *Praise my belly. Praise my chubby tummy, no matter what the scale says. I've been coming to this class for a while now, and I'm not losing weight at the rate I want, but today, I feel confidence from all of you. We're all accepting our bodies, even the flawed parts.*

There are a few nods of affirmation, but mostly the room is silent.

Well, alright, Aspen says. *Thank you everyone for coming this evening. It's always so good to share space together. See you next week.*

Kendra and I hang back while everyone else leaves. Kendra sees the last person out, locks the door, and immediately starts fussing.

Aspen, I need you to talk to that woman who is always crying and saying offensive things.

Offensive things?

Kendra looks at me, telling me to take over this conversation.

I jump in. *She talks about big bodies like it's the worst thing she wants to have. It's a little inconsiderate, given she's in a room full of women with big bodies.*

The class is for any woman who identifies as—

Girl, you and these terms. I can't, Kendra says. *That woman is White and thin. She is privileged in many ways.*

That doesn't mean that she couldn't use a little self-esteem boost.

But there's a difference, Aspen. Come on—you know there's a difference with her learning to accept herself versus, say, a three-hundred-pound woman learning self-acceptance. Society accepts her. And a bad hair day or a bloated belly is not the same as literally not being able to shop in stores for clothes in your size or not getting jobs or having doctors not treat you with dignity and respect.

Okay, can we just—I don't want to argue. She's a bit much, yes, but what do you want me to do? This is a safe space for every type of body, Aspen says.

I refill my water bottle, take a long sip. *Exactly our point. How is it that she can come to a space created to make big women feel comfortable to move in our bodies, to love our bodies, and yet she talks about having a big body in such a negative way? Like, she's coming to this dance class to work out and lose weight because she literally does not want to look like the rest of us. You don't see that as offensive?*

Aspen doesn't say anything.

I keep talking, making sure my voice doesn't rise, try to sound like we are having a conversation, not a debate. *I just want her to be more aware. You know?*

Kendra agrees. *Especially since the body positivity moment exists because of fat, Black, queer women. Look, body positivity ain't nothing new. It's been here right alongside fat activism since the sixties. I think that's what annoys me about it all. White women and mainstream media have given it a rebranding, and by doing that, the very people the movement was advocating for are silenced and invisible.*

Aspen grabs her keys, signals that she's finished straightening up. We grab our bags, walk to the door. She turns off the lights, sets the alarm, and we leave. On the way to the parking lot, Kendra finishes her point. *All I'm saying is, for all the body positivity talk she does, she sure does say a lot of negative things. I mean, did you hear her say she is learning to love every part of her body, even the flawed parts?*

Yes, Aspen says. *And that's a good thing.*

Maybe, Kendra says. *But I have a big belly. A very big belly, and I don't see my belly—or any big belly—as a flaw at all.*

We are all parked beside each other. We open our doors, get ready to leave, and Kendra yells out, *I've got an article I want you two to read. Check your email. I'll send it when I get home.*

I drive home replaying what happened tonight, thinking maybe me and Kendra overreacted, or maybe we're just tired of the constant bruising our souls endure.

One minute I was simply exhaling and inhaling, moving my body, feeling the strength of my legs and arms, the power of my hips, giving gratitude that this body houses a heart and lungs and kidneys and a brain and memories and talents and fears and joys.

The next minute one sentence from a woman I don't even know pricks me, bumps into me like a stranger who isn't aware of where they're walking. *Flaws and all,* she said. Assuming we all believe our big bodies are flawed.

If it was just this one moment, just a comment here or there that stings a little bit or rubs me the wrong way, that would be one thing.

But it is constant.

Every time I step outside my house, it happens. Words and stares, jokes and passive-aggressive remarks, under-handed compliments.

A constant bombarding.

Mainstream beauty standards knocking into me, bumping into me, hitting the same spot over and over. Making me tender, sore.

But maybe it's not just me. Maybe it's not because I am big and Black and female. Maybe every human feels this way for one reason or another. Maybe we are all just trying to get through the day without our souls getting pushed and knocked and tossed about.

Maybe we are all constantly hurting and mending, hurting and mending.

"how whiteness killed the body positive movement" by kelsey miller

"But no one in this country has suffered so long and so brutally the monstrous effects of fatphobia more than fat Black Americans. Centuries later, it remains an insidious form of white oppression: Black people are redlined and ghettoized into neighborhoods with more pollution and less accessible health care and fewer food options, then have their health problems dismissed by the medical system as simply their own fat faults. The Black death rate from Covid-19 is approximately 3.6 times higher than that of white Americans—a statistic often cited as a direct result of obesity, though there is no data at this point to back up such a claim...

"'The realities of fatphobia extend far beyond what most body positivity rhetoric typically addresses,' wrote Sherronda J. Brown, the managing editor of *Wear Your Voice*, in a searing response piece to Pantaleo's defense. Mainstream body positive advocates denounced fatphobia as an issue of racist and stigmatizing beauty standards, she continued: 'While this is indeed one part of how fatphobia manifests in our lives, it is not its main function....The true function of fatphobia is to dehumanize and debase.' And though it is weaponized as such against fat people of all races, it is inherently anti-Black and innately racist, having been invented and disseminated by white people as a means of denigrating Black people. Our contemporary bias against fat people is the direct descendent of our overt dehumanization of Black people. To hate fat bodies is to hate bodies that seem 'Black.' But crucially, when a white person—especially a white, able-bodied, upper-middle-class, straight, cisgender person with a job at a fancy website—is marginalized by fatphobia, they are also protected from the worst of it by a thick cushion of privilege."

debriefing

Aspen suggests we discuss the article together, so we meet at Kendra's. The walls in her home rival any contemporary museum, showcasing paintings of Black women. Each frame holds a dignity, a power that warms the house, reaches out and embraces you, as if to say, *Welcome sis. Come in, rest awhile.* The biggest piece, a life-size painting of a striking dark-skinned Black woman, greets you as soon as you walk into the house. The woman's hair is natural, and what I love most is that the expression on her face is not intense or soft. It just is. She is a regular woman, fuller than thin, with an everydayness about her.

Kendra had Mediterranean food delivered and has the hummus, pita, lamb, mujadara, and tabouli on her island, so beautifully displayed I don't want to touch anything. There are bergamot candles burning throughout the house and the lights are dimmed just enough—not too bright, not too dark.

Kendra's cropped shirt is black with white letters:

my size is not a movement

She is wearing a high-waisted jean skirt and almost-too-big gold hoop earrings.

Aspen takes a plate, starts with the pita and hummus. *Where'd you get your shirt?* she asks.

One of my favorite plus-size online boutiques.

You believe what it says? Aspen asks.

skin & bones

Well, obviously.

I guess I'm asking why you believe that? Seems like if anything, you'd be wearing a shirt that says, "My size is my brand." Your whole fashion consulting for fat women is based on you being—

No, it's not, though. My brand exists because big women don't have access to fashionable clothes that flatter their bodies.

But okay, what if you lost weight? If you weren't a plus-size woman yourself, you wouldn't be doing this. That's all I'm saying.

But I would, though. That's what I'm saying, Kendra says.

So much for discussing the article. I can already see Aspen and Kendra are going to go back and forth about this for hours. I sit at the island, eat from the bowl of pitted olives.

Kendra sits at the island. Nothing on the plate in front of her. *Big or small, I would still be a fashion consultant.*

I know, but—okay, then, so why won't you lose weight? Isn't fatness part of your whole shtick?

Shtick? Are you—Aspen, I can't with you right now.

Aspen looks at me like she expects me to somehow save her from this conversation, like she expects me to agree with her. I pour a glass of the mint-cucumber lemonade that is probably watered down now because of the melting ice.

Aspen could just stop talking, just leave it alone, but she presses in. *I don't understand why both of you are acting like you don't know what I'm talking about. Both of you have this whole thing about being big and beautiful, being big and stylish, being big and successful. It's very much a part of your identity, and I'm just saying—*

We hear what you're saying, Kendra says. *And I'm saying, yes—I am big and beautiful, big and stylish, big and successful. But most importantly, I'm big and human. Human. I shouldn't have to lose weight in order for people to see my humanity, and no one should have to lose weight just to be able to wear a cute outfit.*

Kendra dishes a few scoops of hummus on her plate, takes one of the sliced pitas, but doesn't eat. *I know we all have our contradictions, but I swear, Aspen, sometimes you can be such a hypocrite.*

Aspen sits at the island. *Hypocrite? Really, Kendra?*

Yes, really. Aren't you the one who is always preaching all that self-love, self-acceptance, everybody's-body-is-worthy-of-love rhetoric?

Yes, and I do believe that. I also think it's important to be healthy and—

Don't do that. Please don't start with the fake I-care-about-your-health comment. This is not about health. And by the way, not that I need to prove anything, but I am healthy—at this size. I don't have high blood pressure, diabetes...I exercise, I'm not out here eating everything in sight. And still, I am this size. And I'm okay with that. I'm not like you, Aspen. I actually do love myself—no matter what size I am.

Oh, wow. So now you're saying I don't love myself? I don't even know how we got here and what we're talking about now. You're just trying to be hurtful.

Now Kendra is looking at me, like she wants me to chime in. Both of them wanting me to side with them.

I wipe my hands on my napkin, clear my throat, and say, *As much as you love us, Aspen, you wouldn't want to look like either of us. That's very clear. My body—all of this? I think it scares you that you could one day be this big. I think that's why you are so diligent with your self-care practices. I mean, yes, you get something out of it, but sometimes I wonder if it's motivated by fear.*

skin & bones

I am talking calmly, but Kendra has no grace or patience right now. She crosses her arms, says, *Just because you know all the lingo and you host that yoga-movement class for all sizes, and you say the word* fat *instead of* thick *or* big-boned *or* plus-sized, *doesn't mean that you don't harbor fatphobic biases. And deep down you do not want to be in a too-big body and you are doing everything you can to make sure that doesn't happen because you believe that looking like me or Lena would be the worst thing.*

And all this judgment and self-righteousness and calling my body a brand is because you have to believe that I've made a choice to be this way.

You can't accept that besides lifestyle choices, it's also about genetics and environmental factors, and God knows what else. All of those things play a role.

I think you're terrified. Terrified to admit that maybe—just maybe—the size of our bodies isn't completely in our control, and if that's true, that means you don't have as much control as you think you do.

positivity

A state of having positive beliefs or happy thoughts.

The practice of being or tendency to be positive or optimistic in attitude.

The state of feeling safe, stable, and free from fear or anxiety.

A feeling of self-assurance arising from an appreciation of one's own abilities or qualities.

positive

Marked by or indicating acceptance, approval, or affirmation. Constructive, optimistic, or confident.

The opposite of negative, as in good.

As in, you have such a positive attitude.

As in, be positive, look on the bright side.

Positive as in, the results of the test are good, this is a
good outcome.

Positive as in, a plus sign.

As in thumbs up.

As in yes, yes, yes.

body positivity

Yes to this skin and this hair
and these lopsided breasts
and these wide, wide hips
and these legs that rub together when I walk.

Yes.

Yes to bodies that don't move like other bodies.
Yes to bodies hued in shades no crayon can match.

Yes.

Yes to big bodies doing yoga and dancing
and running and swimming
and being still and doing nothing
and walking up stairs slow or fast
and taking the elevator or escalator
and minding our own fat body business.

Yes.

Yes to eating everything on the plate
and going back for seconds
and yes to eating less when we want to
and yes to enjoying food not as a guilty pleasure
but as the nourishment it is
and yes to enjoying food

not only because it is nourishment
but because it tastes good.

Yes.

Yes to ailing bodies and to bodies
housing beating hearts, still
and in spite of, and even though.

Yes.

Yes always to what can't be seen.
To the heart, to the brain,
to every breath,
even the last.

Yes, yes.

consistency

Aaliyah and I are doing our morning routine, getting ready for the day. *Mommy, did you take your beauty pills? Don't forget.*

I won't, sweetheart. I won't.

I took my strong pills, already, she says. *When do you think they will start working?*

They are already working. You are strong, I tell her. I squeeze her muscles, then gently touch her chest. *Here and here.*

We move about the bathroom, Aaliyah brushing her teeth, me pulling my twists up in a high bun. My phone buzzes against the marble vanity. Aaliyah points at the screen. *It's Malcolm! Malcolm's calling.* She picks up the phone. *Hello? Yes, she's right here.* Aaliyah puts the phone on speaker. *She can hear you now.* She hands me the phone and rushes out into the living room.

Lena? Lena, you there?

I sit on the edge of the bathtub.

Lena?

I'm here.

I—I wanted to say good morning, wanted to, uh… wanted to ask that as you consider forgiving me, will you consider that I've been consistent with you? I have shown up for you, for us. And you've shown up for me.

You showed up for me when I had to preach my first sermon to the congregation on a Sunday morning. Remember how terrified I was? This was not youth group or a teen

150

revival. This was first Sunday, main sanctuary, eleven o'clock in the morning preaching.

I smile at the memory. How he asked me to listen to him practice, how I prayed over him before the service began. I appreciated his vulnerability. He wasn't hiding his fear. And he wasn't so arrogant that he assumed he'd be great, so lazy that he just put it all on his own charisma or on God's anointing. He took it seriously, cared enough to prepare himself. Malcolm has consistently shown me that he is not careless about the things he loves, the gifts God has given him.

Malcolm says, *And you were there after my car accident. Nursed me back to myself. And I say myself, not just my health. Physical therapy was brutal, and lying in bed not knowing how long it would take to heal, to be normal again, was emotionally debilitating. You were there. You went on walks with me—slow, slow walks—you drove me to and from doctor appointments. You were patient with me, and in your patience, I learned how to persevere and also how to rest. And I learned that healing is a long process.*

Malcolm is quiet, like maybe he is giving me a chance to say something. I don't. I hear Aaliyah in the kitchen pouring cereal and milk, hear the dining chair drag across the hardwood. I'll have to go soon.

Malcolm continues, *And Lena, I've been there for you . . . and for Aaliyah. That night we sat up waiting for her fever to break, taking turns warming chicken noodle soup. That year the library refused to invite you to the annual conference that every other person on your team was attending. Remember we paid for your registration ourselves, bought tickets, and made a work-vacation out of it. You networked and ended up meeting your new boss there.*

And remember the night those raccoons invaded your backyard, how we joked that they were having their own tent revival? But then you started crying because you were terrified, too scared to get out of your car and go inside, so I drove over, walked you to the door.

Malcolm's voice breaks. *And your dad's heart surgery.*

When he says this, the tears that have been waiting, fall.

I was there. We went through that together. And there are no extra points for this. People are supposed to show up for the people they love. This is the kind of love I'm committed to. A for-better-or-for-worse love. Hopefully, we've already experienced the worse. But if not, I'll still be here. Consistently showing up for life with the woman I love. Malcolm takes a deep breath. *I, uh, I know you probably have to go. I just, I just wanted to ask you that—to consider all of me, all of us.*

Malcolm hangs up.

I grab a towel, let it soak my tears.

the parts of love

Honey keeps me telling me, *Don't let Bryan's grief become your grief.* As if I shouldn't be sad that Ms. Coleman is dying, that Aaliyah is losing one of her grandmothers. Sometimes when she says it, I think maybe she is jealous because she knows Ms. Coleman loved me like her own daughter. I feel her wondering why I'm so brokenhearted over this. Feel her saying, *I'm your mother. I'm still here.*

We are sitting outside on the sun porch. The backyard is manicured and bursting with summer flowers. Honey loves her garden. She tends to those flowers like they are her children. It is hot for Portland, but still, every now and then, a breeze comes through, lingers a bit, then leaves.

Have you talked with Malcolm yet? Honey asks.

He calls. I don't respond. He lied to me on multiple occasions. I don't really have anything to say to him.

So what you're telling me is you never loved him?

Never loved him? Why would you even say that? Why do you think I'm so devastated? Of course I loved him. I love him.

Well, forgiveness is a part of love. Now I wouldn't say this about anybody—you and I both know I sure was happy when you finally stopped shedding tears over Bryan. But I tell you what—Malcolm? Malcolm is worth your time and energy. And frankly, it concerns me that you don't see that. Love is an investment. You've got to learn who to give your love to, who to invest in. Honey has her pastor's wife voice on, the one she uses when she teaches Bible study or when she gives words of exhortation at a women's faith conference.

I take a long sip of the iced tea she poured for me.

Okay, I'll leave it alone. But you're going to have to interact with him at some point. He's about to be associate pastor. Your dad is mentoring him to take over the church in two years. Honey smiles when she says this, like this is the fulfillment of a dream she's had for a long time.

The telephone rings, and Honey gets up to go inside to answer it. Even now, my parents have a landline. The same phone number we had growing up. It is the only number I know by heart. I can tell by Honey's joy that Ms. Brown is on the phone. I know the two of them will talk for hours, so I get up, guzzle the rest of my tea, and put our glasses in the sink. While Honey is talking, I kiss her on the cheek, whisper *goodbye*. And leave.

Before I pull out of the driveway, I dig my phone out of my purse, hesitate, then start typing a text to Malcolm. It ends up being more of a letter. I copy it, save it to my Notes app, and delete the text instead of sending it.

I drive home without the radio on.

unsent mail

Malcolm,

I'm not ignoring you because I don't want to talk with you. I just need time to think about what I want, what I need. What's best for Aaliyah. You had a whole year to process and go to counseling and figure yourself out.

You had time.

I need time.

You keep telling me how sorry you are, and I believe you. I believe you when you say you needed and wanted to have the whole truth exposed before we said I do. What bothers me is that somehow you act as if this makes you a hero. But really, it was selfish. It was more about your *guilt* and less about me, or my heart.

But if you are going to love me, if you are going to love me completely, my heart needs to be considered. You have to consider my heart and understand that I have often been told I am too much. Too loud, too sassy, too dark, too big. Too Black. And so even in loving you, I find myself overthinking and adjusting. Shape-shifting to be what you need me to be. Or what I think you need. When I first knew I loved you, I was afraid to say it. Didn't want to come on too strong. Didn't want to be too much.

And just as I did not want to scare you away with my love, with my passion, with my loyalty, I don't want you to get all this hurt and sorrow. I am afraid that it will be too much for you.

But how is it that after what you've done, I'm the one

afraid of isolating you, afraid of making you feel too much shame, afraid of pushing you away? How is it that in my devastation, my instinct is to take care of you?

My love for you is as deep as my anger toward you. Neither erases the other. They are both here. Heavy.

For you to think you could confess to me on the day of our wedding and assume I'd proceed, as if your confession changes nothing, means you overestimated the strength of my love, the strength of my heart. Or maybe you estimated well, but took it for granted.

My love for you is strong, yes.

I am strong, yes.

And I can handle this, work through this.

But should I have to?

Does a Black woman's strength always have to be at the ready and on display?

The magic of my ability to shape-shift and adapt and hold up and support and endure the process of nurturing wound to scar should not be required of me, should not be an unspoken expectation.

I will not take care of you in this moment.

If you love me like you say you do, you will have to take all of this, all of me. There is no quick fix.

My love for you isn't what I'm unsure of.

I am deciding if you deserve it.

I love you.

I love me too.

And I need to do what's best for my heart.

It might be that I still choose you.

But most important, it has to be that I choose me.

Lena

celibacy

The choice to abstain from sex was first a faith choice. Every youth group I attended as a girl somehow mentioned fornication, that it was a sin. There were purity rings and altar calls to pray over the youth, especially the girls—that we'd keep ourselves, save ourselves.

Once I slept with Bryan, I told myself, *Well, at least we're in a relationship.* I pushed the guilt away by telling myself, *We'll be married one day,* so technically I was sleeping with my life partner. Just one person.

But after Bryan and I broke up for real that last time, I decided I wanted to wait. Wanted to take sex out of the equation. Love is already complicated. Sex adds an attachment.

Bryan and I were on again, off again, which means in each other's beds and out of each other's beds for months before I finally let him go. I knew I wanted to be with someone who I loved and who loved me outside of the bedroom, wanted to build a foundation with someone, wanted the relationship to last.

I told myself if the next relationship ends, I'd be able to pull myself away without the yo-yoing because at least there'd be no sexual attachment.

And here I am. Gutted, still.

dreams

For three nights in a row I dream of Malcolm.
Dream of him inside me.
Wake up wet
from tears.

vulnerability

I email Malcolm the letter I wrote.
Hit refresh over and over to see if he replies.

reply

It's Saturday morning and the sky is still waking up. Sunlight stretches long, wide. My phone buzzes, and it's Malcolm asking if he can stop by, bring breakfast and talk.

When he arrives, I am sitting on the porch. The street is still quiet except for my neighbor across the street, who is watering her grass. As soon as I see Malcolm, I think of our last kiss, think of the last time he held my hand. He sits down next to me but keeps his distance. It is so strange not to greet each other with a hug, a kiss. He hands me a coffee with the perfect amount of cream and a breakfast sandwich from one of our go-to spots. Neither of us eats right away.

He sighs deep, like he is bracing himself, like maybe he practiced this or at least has been thinking about what to say. *I'm sorry. For everything. Not just for what happened, but that I kept it from you. And I'm sorry about how and when I told you. That wasn't fair to you. I was so focused on clearing my conscience that I didn't consider you and gave you no time to process everything.*

What do you want? I ask. *You're here apologizing, but what do you want? You need to know if I forgive you?*

I need to know if we can start over. I, I want to start over. I want to answer all your questions, I want to prove to you that I am serious about my love for you. I want to marry you—not, not now, I know. I know that's off the table. But one day. One day I want to make good on my promise to you. He pauses like he expects me to say something, but I can't find any words. Not yet. I am focusing on breathing, breathing.

We sit together, his eyes low, mine watching the White woman across the street. I should know her name by now, but I always mix it up. Ann, I think. Or Ana. She and her partner moved in about six months ago from Corvallis. They seemed almost giddy to be living in Northeast Portland, full of questions about the neighborhood, so excited that the city is made for cyclists. She bikes every day, sometimes to work. The first day they moved in, they had barely unpacked the moving truck and had already stuck a Black Lives Matter sign in the grass.

You're going to be the pastor soon. I don't know why that's the thing that comes out of my mouth at this moment.

You think I shouldn't?

I think you slept with some random woman—a one-night stand—and now you're in training to lead a congregation.

Well, you're skipping some things, Lena. Yes—I had sex with a woman I hardly knew. And I regretted it. Immediately. Not because it was sex before marriage but because it was sex with someone I didn't love and knew I'd never love. I used her. I was wrong on so many levels. And I wanted to be better. But not for you. For me. You and I weren't together, and everything I told you back then about needing to take time for myself to work on me and figure things out—that's what I was doing all that time. I needed to get myself right spiritually. I renewed my faith, I focused on what mattered, I became committed to being a better man. I didn't want to change for you—meaning, telling you and having you checking on me and making sure I repented and that I was right with God was not going to make me repent and get right with God. I had to do it on my own. For me. So I could be my best for us. Believe me when I say I don't take your love for granted. I value you and I know what you're worth. I think, I think what we've built is worth something too, and it's damaged—I damaged it, us—but I don't think we're broken beyond repair.

Ann or Ana waves, not picking up on the vibe that we are not out here enjoying a sunny morning on the porch.

I wave back. *If we start over ... how do we ... ?*

We just start. Malcolm takes my hand. *Like this, by talking. Just talk to me. Let's just start talking again.*

Malcolm! Aaliyah is at the door, talking through the screen. She swings the door open, runs over to Malcolm. They hug, and she sits next to him.

I've missed you, Aaliyah. How are you? What did you do this week?

Aaliyah tells him every detail of this past week. I feel it coming, a wave of emotion. Part of me wants to cuss him out. Most of me wants to cry. I stand up. *We have to get going. I want to take Aaliyah to see Ms. Coleman.* I lower my voice, tell him, *Doctors think it will be any day now.*

I'm sorry to hear that.

Yeah. It's been hard. I stand up and walk toward the door.

Aaliyah gets up, tugging on Malcolm, holding his hands. *When are you coming back over? Can you come over for dinner tomorrow?*

Malcolm looks at me, like a child asking permission to go over a friend's house.

skin & bones

Tomorrow ... tomorrow isn't good. Malcolm will ... he'll come over another time.

Malcolm looks relieved when I say this. Holding on to my words like they are scripture. *Another time?* he says. *That's a start.*

homegoing

Ms. Coleman dies on a Tuesday morning. Bryan is at her side. I don't attend the funeral. I let Aaliyah go with Aspen so she can have closure, say her final goodbye to her grandmother. I already said mine, and besides I think it's more helpful for me to be at her house and prepare for the repast. Guests will be arriving soon. Already, people have been dropping off ham, fried chicken, mac and cheese, too many pasta salads, and every kind of roll you can think of. A few women from the church are here, helping me set up.

Once things are organized, I go upstairs to have a moment to myself. The house feels strange without Ms. Coleman here. Everything looks the same just as it did in high school. Just a fresh coat of paint, but the photos are still hanging where they've always been. I go into Bryan's old room. Aaliyah thinks it's the coolest thing that when she comes to spend the night, she stays in the room her daddy had as a child.

Today, it smells like him. He's been here since Ms. Coleman had the stroke. His cologne fills the room, a mix of oakmoss, musk, and fresh fir. I want to lie in this twin bed, get under the blankets and go back to when love was simple and every single dream seemed possible. It isn't that I had a perfect childhood, or that I was sheltered from life's hardships—growing up a pastor's daughter, I am accustomed to late-night phone calls about traumatic emergencies. I know all about life having unpredictable, heartbreaking, and thrilling moments. But still, I feel

unprepared for this life I am living. No one prepares you
for loss and fear of loss, no one tells you how to hold sorrow while juggling accomplishments and dreams and
worries and memories and what-ifs and maybes and guilt
and hope and pride and motherhood and singleness and
independence and faith and doubt all at once. Make it
look like a practiced juggling act.

I hear the doorbell ring and then voices, voices, voices.
Bryan's laughter carries all the way up the stairs, finds me.
I am glad he is able to laugh. I think of losing my dad or
Honey and immediately tears come. The thing about Ms.
Coleman dying is that it reminds me that my parents will
die one day too.

I follow the laughter. Of course, it leads me to Aspen
and Kendra, who are holding court, telling tales of our
teen years. They go for hours, swapping stories and
memories.

Bryan tells us about the time he got caught mocking
his mom right here in this living room. *I was imitating
the way she had just been fussing at us, making Rebecca
laugh, and what I didn't know was that Mom had walked
back into the room and was standing right behind me,
hand on her hip, asking, "Is that how I sound to you?"*

Mom laughed about it, though, Rebecca finishes. *It
actually got her in a better mood. Bryan, you always put a
smile on her face even when you didn't mean to.*

Those words get us all misty-eyed. He was her only
son, and her love for him was fierce. We eat, laugh some
more, and then slowly the house empties and the energy
shifts like a changing sky. Only the day-ones stay. A
few of his basketball teammates from high school, me,
Aspen, and Kendra. Aaliyah falls asleep on the sofa
in the living room with her cousin, who is two years
younger than her.

We have run out of stories and laughter, and now we sit and sigh and breathe deeply and clear our throats— anything to have some kind of noise in the quiet house. Aspen goes into the kitchen and makes herself busy cleaning up the remnants of the repast. Rebecca joins her.

Kendra breaks through the silence. *I gotta get out of here. Early morning tomorrow.*

When she says this, I am reminded of all the things I have to do tomorrow and this weekend. It doesn't feel right going about a to-do list the day after burying a beloved elder.

Bryan walks Kendra to the door. I am not trying to listen, it's just that the house is mostly empty now and the only sound is coming from the running water and clanking dishes in the kitchen. Bryan says, *Thank you for coming, Kendra. My mom always loved you.*

I hate that I know how you feel right now. I really do, she says.

Any advice?

Just that most people mean well, but nothing they say is going to make you feel better. Not even your closest friends. People move on, people get back to their lives, but your life is forever changed. You will never get over this. It will hurt less and less as time goes on, but it will always hurt.

I walk away so I'm not eavesdropping on their conversation. I go outside to the backyard and sit on the screened-in porch. I think about what Kendra said about grief, about people getting back to their lives. I hope I was there for her when her mother died in the way she needed me to be. I hope I've been the friend I think I am.

homecoming

Bryan comes outside, sits next to me. *Thanks for holding my family down through all of this. I appreciate you.*

I loved your mom. Of course, I'd help in any way.

I, um, I've been thinking that we should talk.

What's . . . what's up?

So, my mom left me the house. Paid the mortgage off years ago, so now I own it outright. And, I—I've decided to move back to Portland.

My first thought is how I longed to hear him say these words when we first broke up. Every phone call, every text, I hoped he'd tell me he changed his mind and was moving back home. And here he is, saying the words so many years and tears later. I think about Ms. Coleman, how she wanted nothing more than for her son to come home so he could be close for family dinners and errand running and stopping by just because.

What makes me smile is thinking about Aaliyah. She'll have her dad at school events and she can see him more than once or twice a month. He's missed out on so much.

Bryan tells me, *I want to reestablish my roots here. Remodel the house and turn my old bedroom into a space for Aaliyah.*

She will be ecstatic about that, I say. *This is—I know it's hard. The loss, the grief. But you coming back for Aaliyah, that's something beautiful coming out of all of this.*

And you, Bryan says. *I'm coming back for you too.*

Bryan—

I don't need to live here to renovate the house and keep it. I could rent it out. I'm coming back for Aaliyah, for you . . . for us. I've thought about this for a while, but you were with Malcolm. And I wasn't going to say anything to mess with that. But, well, that's no longer an issue. Right? I—I'm coming home to start over.

Bryan, I—I'm not ready to date right now. Anyone. But even if I was, I don't think we—

No decisions need to be made now, Bryan says. *I just wanted you to know where I stand. I want us to try again.*

✻   ✻   ✻

I drive the long way home. Aaliyah is in the back seat, listening to me reminisce. *And Kendra and her family used to live there, the house on the corner,* I tell her. *I'd walk to her house and the two of us would walk over to Aspen's.* I drive a block and slow down. *Aspen's house was the one in the middle. The gray one,* I say, pointing.

Aaliyah stares out of the window. I think about how different our childhoods are. At her age, it was common for me to see one of my teachers in the bread aisle at Fred Meyer or Safeway. I could go to church and be singing in the choir next to classmates that I'd see on Monday morning at school. Honey used to joke that shopping at Lloyd Center Mall might as well be going to a family reunion, the way every five minutes she'd have to stop and hug someone and ask about their children, get the updates on the latest happenings.

Portland was a White city, but there was a Black neighborhood. There were five Black families on my block, and three were multigenerational, living under the same roof.

The single-family homes, built in the 1920s, that I grew up around have been renovated into luxury condos and high-end buildings with studio and one-bedroom apartments. It isn't just being priced out of the neighborhood that's the tragedy—it's knowing that developers demolished the gatherings, the coming together that the community brings when a neighborhood is multigenerational, when a neighborhood has all it needs within walking distance. Families aren't moving into these studio apartments, and even the Black families who can afford the high rents have trouble finding space that has more than two bedrooms.

Who was the renovating and upgrading for? Seems like the city only wants single rich folks to live over here. Or maybe young couples with no children.

I think about this often. How I have to schedule playdates for Aaliyah with most of her friends, because they live across town and there is no such thing as dropping by to say hello or walking over at the last minute to invite her friend over. I think about how on our block, the White woman who lives on the corner hardly speaks. I waved at her once, and she turned her head. And then there's the house across from her that the owner rents to Portland State graduate students. There's a revolving door of someone moving in, moving out. To my left is Kathleen, who I've had over for dinner. She travels about two weeks out of the month for her job, so I look out for packages being left at her doorstep.

No elders live on my block anymore. No children, except for Aaliyah. When Black folks talk about things changing over here, we're talking about that too.

I pull up to my house, still processing that Bryan is moving back. He says he's coming back for me, for us. I don't know if I believe him. The possibility of there being an *us* is an overwhelming, daunting thought. For now, I choose to focus on what brings peace of mind, clarity. For now, I think about how proud Ms. Coleman would be, knowing her son is coming back to ensure that the house his momma worked so hard for stays in the family. Decades from now, he'll be one of the ones saying, *They didn't push all of us out.*

march 6, 1919

Oregon Daily Journal, page 5: "Realty Men Intend to Stop Sales of Homes to Negroes and Orientals"

White folks believed that if property was sold to Blacks or Asians, the property values would drop.

The Portland Realty Board agreed and added a provision to its code of ethics that prohibited its realtors from selling homes in predominantly White neighborhoods to Black residents.

unthank park

Unthank always seemed like a strange name to give a park. I never knew it was named after someone. Dr. DeNorval Unthank was a Black doctor and civil rights activist. He was recruited to Oregon by the Union Pacific Railroad because the railroad required Black physicians to tend to their Black workers.

When he purchased his home in 1930 in Ladd's Addition, an upscale White neighborhood, residents of the neighborhood banded together to intimidate him and his wife. Seventy-five neighbors signed a petition to make their contempt known. The windows of his home were shattered, his house was vandalized, and someone left a dead cat on the porch. No matter how many times Dr. Unthank cleaned up the debris, no matter how many times he held his wife in his arms, assuring her that they were safe, that they'd be okay, the neighbors came back and did more damage.

The Unthanks were offered $1,500 to move.

They finally did. Maybe because of the money, maybe to keep their sanity. Maybe even the strong get weary. Maybe wisdom outweighs knowledge. Maybe he knew he deserved to live anywhere, be anywhere.

But maybe more than any of that, he wanted to live.

Maybe he wanted to live.

release

It is two in the morning when the phone rings. The first thing I think is that it must be Honey, calling about Dad. Another heart attack. I think this is the dreaded phone call in the middle of the night that will change my life, but then I see Bryan's name and picture flashing on the screen. I turn the lamp on, sit up.

Hello?

I—I—you said I could call anytime if I needed anything.

And then sobbing.

Bryan's grief is a flood of heavy breathing, panting. The kind of cry one can't control. A cry that forces its way, that overwhelms.

It's okay to cry. Let it out, let it out.

More sobbing.

I want to say something clever in this moment. Want to share some wisdom about love and loss. Maybe a scripture about heaven or a quote about legacy, but instead I just sit with him on the phone. Just take him in.

sunrise

Like a storm fading to drizzle, Bryan's crying is calm now. His breathing is steady and sure. I think maybe he will say something, but there is silence on the other end.

Bryan?

His breathing is deep, loud.

Bryan?

And then a symphony of tiny snores. I smile at the thought of him sleeping on the other end of the line, like we'd do in high school. Two lovebirds so infatuated with each other, we couldn't say good night. I can't count how many times I snuck the phone in my room and talked to Bryan until the moon gave up its spot for the sun. How many times Honey would fuss and be so confused about why the cordless phone hadn't charged overnight. One time, we both fell asleep on the phone and woke up to Ms. Coleman screaming on the line, *It's time to wake up and get ready for school!*

Bryan and I joked that it was the first time we ever spent the night together, that it felt good to wake up and have the other be the first *good morning.*

I fall asleep remembering this, wake up to his voice.

Lena? Lena?

retreat

Today's Whine & Wine is a Saturday brunch. Aspen is wearing a black jumpsuit, her left wrist adorned in thin silver bangles that clank against each other every time she moves. Kendra has on high-waisted jeans with an over-size, off-the-shoulder shirt. Her thick twist-out is perfectly crinkled and folds down her back like an accordion.

I am so tempted to take out my phone, see if Bryan has responded. I left him a message this morning, checking on him, making sure he's okay, but then the girls showed up, so I don't know if he wrote back. I try to focus, be present. I can check on him after Kendra and Aspen leave.

We have finished the chocolate croissants, and most of the fruit platter is gone. Kendra's famous mini-English-muffin, bacon, egg, and cheese sliders were devoured, as always. And there's only a spoonful left of Aspen's hash browns. Aaliyah ate with us, and now she is upstairs in her room. She's quiet, so either she's watching a movie or she's eavesdropping, like I used to when Honey and Aunt Aretha would talk. *We're out of wine already?* Kendra asks.

No, there's more white in the fridge—and champagne too. I can make mimosas, I say.

Girl, yes. You know I love a Lena-mimosa. Why didn't we start with that? Kendra says.

I walk into the kitchen, being careful not to step on my flowing floor-length dress. Any other Saturday, I'd be in jeans, but I have to come correct whenever we're all together. I make the mimosas with pineapple juice instead of orange. This makes me think of Malcolm and how once he had it this way, he never liked mimosas with orange juice again. It is funny the things I remember about us, about him, at random times.

I am surprised he hasn't come up yet, but I'm glad because asking about Malcolm would make me think of Bryan. His sobbing, his reaching out to me, his moving back to Portland. He is on my mind in ways he hasn't been in a long time. For so many years he was a priority, he occupied so much of my heart, and after letting him go, our interactions have become scarce, and only about Aaliyah. To think of him and check to see if his family needs anything as they grieve their matriarch feels like a betrayal of my heart. It has softened. Years ago, he became the bad guy, someone to get over, but now I want to take care of him, want him to know I'm here if he needs me.

I push these feelings down, don't mention them to anyone, especially not to Kendra and Aspen, who nursed me to health after he left me so brokenhearted. I take a deep breath, go back into the living room, and hand the drinks to Kendra and Aspen.

Kendra takes a long sip of her mimosa and says, *You'll both be happy to know that I accepted the request to go on a date with Donovan.* She says it so formally, so dry.

Do tell, do tell, I say. *Details please.*

Not much to tell yet—he kept reaching out, and so I was just like, why not? And I said yes. We're meeting up tomorrow. We're going to walk the Esplanade and then have dinner somewhere downtown.

She is trying to sound casual, but I see a glimmer of excitement in her eyes. I don't bother her about it. But I notice.

Aspen says, *Well, I'm glad you are giving him a chance. I think this is going to lead to something good.*

Kendra says, *We'll see. What's up with you? Any update on Travis?*

Well, Aspen says. *There is, actually. I took your advice and made myself unavailable. I stopped responding to his texts. I've seen him at work-related events. He flirts, but, you know, he's clearly not trying to date me.*

Well, on to the next one, Kendra says. *I've been telling you, Aspen, you should try online dating. Sure, there will be lots of nos, but there will be plenty of maybes and a few good yeses too.*

Maybe, Aspen says. *I'm considering it. But I don't want to be on the ones where the woman has to make the first move. I'm horrible at pickup lines. I'd rather try one that plays matchmaker. I don't mind answering a thousand questions so the algorithm can sort through the nonsense and send me actual potential matches.*

I know the perfect one for you, Kendra says. *Just let me know when you're ready.*

the agreement

Aspen asks, *Do you two have your tickets to the Fat Girl Wellness Conference?*

No, I say.

Kendra shakes her head. *I told you I'm not going to that foolishness.*

Aspen sounds so disappointed when she says, *I'm gonna have to go all by myself?*

We don't answer.

How about this? Aspen says. *Lena and I will get on one of those dating apps if Kendra comes to the conference.*

Kendra says, *Absolutely not.*

And how you speaking for me? I say. *I am not doing online dating.*

Aspen pleads her case. *Lena, we both want relationships, right? You've been singing the blues about Malcolm. Maybe putting yourself out there—just for fun—will be a good thing.*

A palate cleanser, Kendra says. *Fun and light.*

I shake my head. *Really, Kendra, now you're siding with Aspen? How did I get involved anyway? This is about you not going. Not me.*

Kendra says, *I would think about it if the name wasn't so horrible. I mean, come on—Fat Girl Wellness Conference. That's a no for me. You know I don't like those we-took-the-word-back movements.*

But don't you think it would be good to go to the networking hour? You could get so many new clients. You know how many plus-size women would love to have a consultation with a personal stylist? Aspen is good. She has always been able to persuade people to give her what she wants. In high school she was on the debate team and took our school to the state competition. She looks at me. *You have to come too. This is a group affair.*

I don't even have the energy to argue with you, I tell her. *I'll go if Kendra goes.*

I only say this because Kendra is so adamant about not going, but then she gives in, says, *Well, I guess it would be good to meet people and try to get a few new clients. Alright, okay.* She goes into the kitchen, pours pineapple juice in her wineglass, no champagne. *Well, get your phone out, Aspen, let's set up your profile.* Then Kendra looks at me. *You, too, Lena. A deal is a deal.*

compatible

I am in bed, wide awake. Nighttime is the worst. The past, the present, the future—it all feels overwhelming. I keep replaying memories with Malcolm and then thinking about work and Garrett and Meredith and Dad and the church. I sit up against the headboard, turn on the lamp, grab my phone, and play word games till I get bored. Then I scroll through social media, liking posts and bookmarking articles I want to come back to. Then I open the dating app. I haven't looked since I set it up with Aspen and Kendra. Maybe I should give it a try—just have fun and get my mind off Malcolm. And Bryan. I have more matches than I thought I would, but only three seem interesting. The first guy is Kent. I send him a message. *Prince or Michael?* Five minutes later, he writes back *both*. I try to think of something witty to say, and just as I am typing out another question, I get a notification that I have a new match. I click on the message to see the profile.

Bryan's deep smile is beaming on my screen.

We've been matched.

reverse

The morning light is a gentle whisper. I try hard to stay in bed, sleep in, but my body is conditioned to wake up early. Aaliyah spent the night with her friend Paige. The two of them are becoming inseparable and I'm glad Aaliyah has a new friend. Since she's having a sleepover, I have the weekend to myself. I sit up in bed, grab my phone, and check the dating app again, as if I need proof that what I saw last night was real and not something I made up. I check my matches and see Bryan's name and photo. I stare at the screen, reading all the ways the app has found us compatible. Part of me thinks it's quite hilarious. I have the urge to call Honey, tell her, *See, I wasn't completely wrong about Bryan. Even the experts think there's potential.*

My phone buzzes in my hand, and Bryan's face flashes on my screen. I hesitate to pick up but decide to answer. *Hey.*

So, you ready now, I see.

I don't respond.

When I asked you about starting over, you said you weren't ready—

And you said you came back for me. But clearly you are back to meet multiple women and—

I'm going on dates. That's what single people do. You told me you weren't ready to even think about dating. Anyone. So, yeah, I'm meeting people. And now that you're ready, this is me—again—asking to take you out on a date. Let's meet up today—Aaliyah is with her friend, right?

Bryan—

We can keep it simple. A short and sweet coffee date. Me and you. Eleven o'clock at Daily Blend.

There is a long silence.

Not today. I can't. Aaliyah's with Paige because I have plans with Kendra and Aspen.

So, you will let me take you out on a date. Just not today? Bryan—

I let you go once, Lena. I'm not—

I'll think about it. I'm not saying no. Just—I'll think about it.

I hang up the phone, get ready for the conference. I mostly avoid looking at myself in the mirror. I can hardly recognize who this woman is, why she's willing to go backward after coming so far.

inclusivity

It's the day of the conference, and Kendra seems more excited about being here than I thought she would. She looks like she's going to a chic midday fashion show, not an all-day conference at the convention center. I don't even think she tried hard to look this good. It just comes natural to her. I can't count how many times I have stood in front of my closet and asked, What would Kendra wear?

We are standing with Aspen at the merch booth.

This tote is cute. I might actually use it. It's a good size and fits over my big arms. Kendra drapes her shoulder with the bag. *I hate those cheap bags conferences usually give out that can hardly carry a thing and with a strap that barely goes over my pinkie toe.*

I laugh. *Right? And at least here the T-shirts will fit.* I say this just as I see a woman twice my size walking past us. She is wearing the conference shirt, and it looks loose on her, like maybe she could have even gone a size smaller.

Aspen opens her conference folder, pulls out the schedule. *Let's go sit over there and make a plan for the day. There are so many good sessions happening.* We sit together on the couches that are coupled with armchairs in an area that looks like it was put together for attendees who might need to rest their feet, charge their phone, or just take a break.

As we're talking the schedule over and deciding what to attend, a White woman comes over to us, says, *Hi, uh, hello. Welcome.*

Hello, we say in unison.

I just wanted to welcome you to come on over and join us so you're not sitting over here all by yourselves. The woman points to a group of White women—her friends, I think—who all wave and smile at us and scoot over, making room.

Oh, um, we're fine, I say. *We're—we're not sitting alone or by ourselves. We're together.*

The woman gives me a confused look.

Aspen jumps in, says, *But thank you for welcoming us. I'm Aspen. This is Kendra, that's Lena. We're excited to be here. Are you one of the leaders?*

Oh, no. Just a fellow fatty. Sure you don't want to join us?

We're good, thank you. Kendra says. Her smile looks genuine, but I know her. It's not.

When the woman walks away, we all try to keep our laughs in, not to roll our eyes.

I whisper, *I mean, look around—there are groups of people sitting together, or all by theirselves, as she would call it. But they're all White, so she hasn't gone over to them.*

We stand out, Kendra says. *Us Black women sitting over here by ourselves... but together.*

We laugh.

An announcement is made that sessions will begin in ten minutes. We decide to all go to the same session: Fashionably Fat. The description says it's a panel about plus-size clothing, the politics of fashion, and how to push for more accessible sizes at mainstream clothing stores.

As we wait for the elevator, I read a sign taped to the wall that reads SCENT-FREE ZONE. The elevator dings, and the door slides open. *I hope that doesn't include deodorant. Every zone needs to be a deodorant zone,* Kendra says.

I hear someone behind us laugh. I turn and smile at her. Aspen says, *It really is a thing. Some scents irritate people or cause a serious reaction, so it's just best that we all are scent-free.*

But if you stink, you're not scent-free. Funk is a scent, Kendra says. She is laughing but I know she means it.

Once we step off the elevator, we enter a sea of big bodies. I don't think I've ever been in a space where so many people are the same size as—and even bigger than—me. And there's a wider age range than I expected. But there's no surprise that most of the people here are White. It's Portland, after all. Still, I wonder why there wasn't more buy-in from the Black community. Either we didn't know about this event, or we knew but didn't think this was for us.

I've been in this convention center countless times for conferences and workshops. But something is different today. When I smile at a stranger, they return the smile. There's a warmth and the common courtesy of stepping aside or saying excuse me when passing by that is happening today, which I have never experienced. Most times I walk through spaces feeling invisible, or if I'm visible, it's made clear that my body is in the way. People walking behind me often huff and puff until they can find a way to get around me, when they could just say *Excuse me* and I would step aside. I have literally smiled at people, said hello, only to be given a blank stare like I'm not even standing there. But today is different.

Our room is at the end of the hall, I think, Aspen says. She leads us down the hallway. We pass the other rooms, and I look at the offerings happening right now. There's a Healthy at Every Size nutrition workshop, and one called Fat Bodies on the Screen & Stage.

We get to the room. Kendra steps back from the door and lets a group go in front of us. *Oh hell no. Nah, y'all can go in. I'm good.*

What's wrong? Aspen asks.

This is so redundant. Do you see this sign?

I look on the door and taped to it is a handwritten sign: FAT BODIES WELCOMED HERE.

Aspen reads the sign. *What's the problem? It's just welcoming everyone.*

I don't need permission to enter a room that's already a part of this conference. Why do you think they put that sign here and not on any other door to any other workshop?

Aspen doesn't answer, and neither do I. Not because I don't get Kendra's point. I just know this isn't a question she expects us to respond to. She is in full monologue mode.

I paid good money to come to this. I don't need extra permission to enter the workshop on fashion and beauty. I know I am welcomed here. My badge says so.

Kendra, I think you're taking it the wrong way. We should just go in—come on, like you said, we paid our good money. Aspen opens the door. The session hasn't started yet, and people are mingling.

A greeter meets us at the door. *Welcome.*

Aspen says, *Are you . . . are you in charge of this session, by any chance?*

I helped plan it, yes. The woman smiles a proud smile, not knowing what is coming.

Do you mind explaining the purpose of the sign on the door? My friend—well, we're wondering why the extra welcome?

Oh, yes. We just wanted to put everyone at ease. So often conversations about fashion and beauty are so uncomfortable or are set aside for thin bodies and so we just wanted

*to make sure that everyone felt safe to come into the space
and engage, no matter what size.*

This answer seems to appease Aspen. Kendra rolls her
eyes and goes to find a seat. I give the woman a pass. She
is young. I can tell. Not more than twenty-five, probably.
I can see the earnestness in her eyes, hear it in the chipper way she says *Welcome!* to each and every person that
comes in.

We look for seats. The convention center's chairs are
interlocked so they can't be moved to create space, to
be more comfortable. *Um, I need to sit on an aisle,* I say.
*Maybe we should sit toward the back, so we can spread out
a bit.* I might take up a chair and a half. Kendra too.

Kendra says, *See, this is the problem. So woke, and yet
didn't think to have chairs that everybody's body would feel
comfortable in. But they put a sign on the door telling us
everybody is welcomed.* She sucks her teeth, loud.

We settle in for the panel.

As the panelists walk onto the stage, I notice that all
five of them—including the moderator—are White. I
don't even notice their sizes until Kendra whispers, *They
sure are on the thin side of fat. Of course they were chosen
to talk about fashion. They can still shop in mainstream
stores. I'm definitely live-tweeting this.*

She takes her phone out, starts typing.

not that fat

Oh my God, I'm trending. Kendra holds her phone out to me. The hashtag she started, #NotThatFat, is being used by other women at the conference.

What started out as critiquing the moderators, the accessible signs, and the not-so-accessible spaces, has now become a hashtag people are using to share personal stories.

I guess when this conference decided to have fat panelists, they meant fat but #NotThatFat.

These seats are made for bodies that are #NotThatFat.

So basically, this conference is a fat-accepting space but only for people who are #NotThatFat.

As a person who is fat but #NotThatFat, I want to say that I think this conference could have been more diverse.

I told my doctor I wanted to lose weight. He told me I was #NotThatFat. Um, I wanted to lose weight because of health reasons, not to be skinny.

My ex dumped me because I had gained weight. When we met, I was thick. He likes big-boned women, but with bodies that are #NotThatFat.

skin & bones

I'll be glad when clothing stores admit that their plus-size sections are for thin-fat bodies. Their advertisements should say Shop Here if You're #NotThatFat.

@KendraTheStylist, thank you for speaking up and speaking out. I relate to so much that's being said. #NotThatFat.

viral, visceral

It only takes a day. Just twenty-four hours, and already Kendra has been getting invites for interviews and appearances on podcasts and a local morning news station. Her website crashed after someone tweeted that she does fashion consulting for plus-size people. The woman's post got shared on Instagram too.

That's where I saw the photo.

At first I scrolled right past it, but then I went back. The photo is of a White woman, slightly larger than me, next to Kendra, frozen in that selfie-bestie pose that people automatically fall into when taking a picture of themselves. I know her. Well, I don't know her, but I recognize her. I try to think of where I've seen her before, but I can't call a memory to mind. I click on her name and go to her account. I scroll and scroll and scroll, and then I see it. The photo I saw on Malcolm's Instagram page of him, Elijah, Isaiah, Aspen, and Kendra for the twins' birthday party. I don't know why my stomach twists into knots, but it does. Who is she? And why is she making me feel this way?

constance

It's not our official Whine & Wine night, and even though we're together now, we're already planning our next meetup. *Let's do something outdoors—a hike through Mount Tabor Park, maybe,* Aspen says.

A hike or a walk? Kendra asks.

Somewhere in the middle. Aspen has been with me all day, mostly lamenting over Travis. He is still sending mixed signals. *But on a good note,* she says, *I am getting some good options with that app Kendra made me get on. I've got a coffee date tomorrow and a video call this weekend.*

I notice Kendra is on her phone, again. She's here but not here. *Kendra-the-Superstar, do you hear this? Aspen has two low-key dates set up. Aren't you proud of her?*

Oh, huh? Sorry—I'm—

Texting, Aspen says with unmasked disdain.

Constance is trying to coordinate an appointment, and I just got an invite to write an essay for a new fashion magazine.

Constance?! Aspen asks. More disdain.

Kendra looks like she didn't mean to say what she just said. *She's a client.* She says it a second time: *Just a client.* This time she says it like it should be the last thing said on the matter. She pours more wine, and just when she has started to tell us about the other opportunities coming to her, I ask a question.

Who is Constance?

She's a client of mine. It was her tweet about me being her stylist that got me all that attention and made me go viral. Kendra tries to answer in a casual voice, but it's the trying that catches my attention. I feel queasy, and I don't know why.

Constance. The woman whose tweet brought all this attention to Kendra. Constance. The woman in the photo I saw on Instagram. I don't even know what makes me ask the next question. The words are coming out of me before I know what I'm saying.

How do you know her?

She's an indie singer, Kendra says. *I'm the personal stylist for her shows and whatnot.*

Then, as if she just can't hold it in anymore, Aspen says, *She's a friend of Elijah and Isaiah. She's the woman Malcolm slept with.*

Really, Aspen? Kendra puts her glass of wine down.

I pick mine up.

Someone needed to tell her, Kendra. Clearly you weren't going to.

There's nothing to tell. They had a one-night stand. Why does Lena need to know her name?

Oh, it's not about knowing her name. It's about knowing that one of her best friends is working with her. That one of her best friends has become friends with her.

I might as well not even be here, the way the two of them are going back and forth, talking about me and not to me.

We are not friends. She's my client, Kendra says. She scoots forward, talks with less edge in her voice but still with an attitude like she doesn't want to explain. *We all met at the same time. She got my info and hired me to be her stylist. I didn't know she got Malcolm's number that night, and I definitely didn't know he was going to sleep with her.*

But you found out at some point, and you didn't tell me? You continued to work with her?

What was telling you going to do? You two were broken up. It wasn't my place to say anything.

It was your place, Aspen says.

Kendra rolls her eyes. *Aspen, this really isn't any of your business—*

It is my business. This sisterhood—the three of us—we are each other's business. And that's what I've been saying ever since I found out. How you gonna work with someone who slept with your best friend's man?

Key word—work. It's business.

You are so selfish. Just so—

You gonna pay my bills? I'll stop having Constance as a client when you start paying my rent. Kendra stands up, dumps her wine in the sink, and puts her oversize sweater on.

And so now you're leaving? Does anything ever change? We're not in high school anymore, Kendra. You think it's okay to leave right now and not even talk this through with Lena?

Kendra takes her keys out of her purse. *You are not Lena's mother or guardian or conscience. She can speak for herself, and if she has a problem with me, she can let me know, and then and only then will I talk about anything regarding Constance—*

You knew Malcolm slept with another woman, and you didn't tell me? You knew. And now you're friends with the woman who slept with him?

We are not friends, Lena. She is one of my clients. I only communicate with her when she's going on tour or has a special event.

Well, friend or client, I hope she is paying you a lot of money. I hope whatever clout you get from working with her is worth the decades of friendship you exchanged it for.

kendra

Kendra is equally generous and selfish. She's the friend who will pay the bill at the restaurant without you noticing. She's the friend who will stay up all night helping you undo your micro-twists, she'll comb it out and wash it and get you ready for your next protective style. She's the pick-you-up-from-the-airport, help-you-pack, help-you-move, help-you-unpack friend. She's the one who will go with you to Lamaze class, the one who will rub your back, tell you to push when you are delivering life into this world. She's the friend who gives just-because gifts and thinking-of-you flowers.

And

she's also the friend who will cancel plans with you if something more interesting comes up. The kind of friend who always tells it like it is, but not always with tenderness or grace. She's the friend who thinks she is always right. The kind of friend who believes that if her intentions weren't to hurt you, there's nothing to apologize for.

That she chose her client over our friendship both shocks me and doesn't surprise me at all.

freshman year, high school

We were all trying on different personas. Figuring out how to turn our teen selves into women, how to have just enough tenderness, just enough sass, just enough Jesus. How to be best friends but have our individuality.

For the talent show we danced to a Destiny's Child song, and even though we won first place, there wasn't any celebration backstage. The rousing applause kept Kendra on the stage, bowing and blowing kisses as if she were really Beyoncé.

Aspen was annoyed. And what made it even worse was that the biggest fan was a boy Aspen was crushing on. She saw him pushing up on Kendra later after school, and Kendra was not backing away. Aspen confronted her right there in the middle of the hallway. And instead of Kendra talking to her, she grabbed her coat out of her locker, slammed it shut, and walked away. With the boy. The boy who is so insignificant now, I can't even remember his name. What I remember is that day changed things between us. Forever put me in the middle of Kendra and Aspen.

Aspen retells the story from time to time when she's irritated at Kendra for whatever new offense has happened. The thing she always says when she talks about why she was so upset way back then is that it wasn't about the boy, it was about the friendship.

There's just some things friends don't do, she always says. *There's just some things friends don't do.*

origin story

Our solidarity was cemented the day we took a field trip to the zoo in the fifth grade. The school bus was loud and rowdy and everything a school bus should be. A boy at the back of the bus, named Dion, called Aspen *Asphalt* because of her dark skin. We could barely spell *asphalt*, but we knew it wasn't a compliment. Especially when all of Dion's sidekicks chimed in with oohs and ahhs and said, *That's a sting! He's stingin'*. Kendra started up first, got all up in Dion's face and told him someone with teeth that bucked and shoes that raggedy shouldn't be talking about no one. And I reminded him that his momma and sisters were dark just like Aspen, and so what was he even saying? We told Aspen not to worry about that bucked-tooth, raggedy-shoe-wearing boy and said *Come sit with us*, and somehow we made room for the three of us to sit on that green school-bus seat. The pleather was sweaty and clinging to the bare parts of our legs because we were wearing shorts. When we got to the zoo, we stuck together all day, and when Kendra realized she forgot her lunch, Aspen and I shared the lunches our mothers made. We never declared it, never had BFF bracelets, but we knew. We'd always be there for each other. Always.

betrayal

Yes, the betrayal of my best friend and my fiancé. But also the betrayal of my heart, my mind.

The feeling of relief that Constance is fat like me, proof that Malcolm sleeping with her wasn't about my weight, my body. The feeling of anger, jealousy that Constance is White. A reminder that White women are seen as a prize, the ultimate accomplishment.

All the work I did to love my body, my Blackness, torn apart with the knowledge of him sleeping with another woman. I know it's not about me. I know. I know her fatness and Whiteness does not, should not, matter.

But.

Even though I know. I know. I know. Still, there are decades of beauty standards and a lifetime of insecurities and always the wanting to know why and how.

Why did this happen, how can I fix this?

If I figure out why, maybe I can fix it,

fix him, fix us. If the answer is me,

I can fix me...for him, for us.

But I know.

The answer is not me, and what I have to work on is letting go of the notion that my hips or hair texture or skin tone could ever make a man love or leave me. What I need to work on is getting these emotions and my mind to align.

sunday sermon

Dad reads from several scriptures today. I don't open my Bible and follow along. I just close my eyes, listen.

Ephesians 4:32: Be kind and compassionate to one another, forgiving each other, just as in Christ God forgave you.

Proverbs 17:9: Love prospers when a fault is forgiven, but dwelling on it separates close friends.

forgiving

So much written about what forgiveness is,
who we should forgive, why we should forgive.
But nothing about how.

back-to-school shopping

Honey likes to be at the mall early, right when it opens. She insisted on picking us up, and I already know she's not going to let me pay for anything. This is our ritual. Ever since Aaliyah's first year of school, we've gone shopping, the three of us, picking out school clothes and then having lunch at Red Robin. The mall is waking up, still quiet and not crowded. Most of the food court is closed except for a smoothie place and the coffee shop on the lower level.

Alright, what are we looking for first? Tops? Honey asks. She looks through the racks. Aaliyah points to shirts that she likes.

I think we're in the wrong section, I say. *We need to be over there.* I point to the plus-size section for girls.

Lena, this section is fine, Honey says.

I give Honey a look. Can't she look at Aaliyah and see she's gained weight since last school year?

Mom, I want to try this on, Aaliyah says.

I can tell it won't fit. It's not stretchable and will hug her belly. *Sweetheart, let's see if they have it in another size.* I say *another* instead of bigger because I don't want Aaliyah to have a complex about clothes and shopping.

Just let the girl try it on. If it doesn't fit, it doesn't fit. That's the point of trying on clothes.

But it's not.

Honey doesn't get it because she has always been able to walk into a store and have many, many options. I have already surveyed the plus-size section for girls, and it is much smaller compared to this side of the store. And those clothes aren't as cute—not for a little girl. They are plain, as if big girls don't want to look their age and be fashionable.

Aaliyah is already walking to the fitting room before I can say anything. She has three shirts in her hand and a pair of jeans.

I give in, tell her, *Call out if you need help.*

Okay.

While we wait, Honey says, *She'll probably need a couple pair of shoes, too, right?*

Uh-huh.

Have you talked with Malcolm yet?

Yes, actually.

Oh, well, good. Why didn't you tell me? How did it go? Are you two going to work it out?

Mom. Not now. I call out to Aaliyah, *You okay in there? Need any help?*

No, Aaliyah says. *I don't need help.* I hear a sniff. A long, hard sniff, like she is sucking in an ocean.

I walk over to the door. *Sweetheart,* I whisper. *Let me in.*

Honey is behind me. *What's wrong, baby girl? What's the matter?*

Mom. Just—can you step back?

Aaliyah slowly opens the door. The shirts and jeans are scattered on the floor. *Nothing fits me,* she says. She is only wearing her tank top and underwear.

These clothes don't fit, but there are other options. There are clothes that fit you, I tell her.

But I like these.

I know. But we can find some cute clothes in your size. It's going to be alright.

Honey knocks on the door. *You two okay in there? Aaliyah, what's wrong, baby?*

I don't answer. Tears crawl down Aaliyah's face. I wipe them, kiss her on her forehead. *Get dressed, and we'll go to another store, okay?*

I step out of the dressing room, and before Honey can say anything, I begin. *Please don't ask her any questions. Please. We're going to look for shoes, go to one more clothing store, and if we don't find anything there, I'm going to look online. I do most of my shopping online these days anyway. More options.* I take my phone out, text Kendra to ask her if she has recommendations for Aaliyah.

Lena, I think you're making a big deal out of this. She just needs to try a larger size. What's the problem? Honey walks back over to the racks and starts looking for a bigger size.

That's the largest size in girls. The plus-size section doesn't have any of the things she tried on. We're going to look for shoes, then one more store, then home.

Well, what about lunch? is all Honey says.

comfort food

Aaliyah is ecstatic about her new shoes. If I'd let her, she'd wear them out of the mall. And thank God we found her a few new tops. She still needs more, and new jeans, too, but at least she is not leaving the mall empty-handed.

In the car she says, *Are we still going to Red Robin?*

I don't say anything, but Honey says, *Of course we are, that's the tradition.*

We sit at a half booth, half table. Honey and Aaliyah next to each other. The server comes and takes our drink orders, then asks, *And would you like fries as you wait?*

Aaliyah says yes right away. *With ranch dipping sauce, please.*

When the server brings the basket of steak fries to the table, I tell Aaliyah, *Don't eat too many. You won't have room for your lunch.*

Honey says, A *few fries ain't never hurt nobody.* She scoots the basket closer to Aaliyah.

Mom!

Well, Lena, come on. It's just steak fries. Let's just eat and enjoy our meal.

Aaliyah, you can have a few. Okay? Fries are food you can only have in moderation. Do you remember what that word means? I ask.

Only a little bit and not all the time, Aaliyah says as she puts one of the steak fries in her mouth. It is dripping with ranch dressing.

203

Exactly, I say. We order, we eat. I hardly talk for the rest of the afternoon. I just eat and listen to Aaliyah's laugh. She's moved on from her tears and has a smile on her face, and that's all that matters. Honey is telling tall tales of her childhood and joking about Dad and how they've known each other more than half their lives. The server brings a refill of fries. They come and come like bottomless drinks at other restaurants.

Honey says, *And what do you want for dessert, Aaliyah?*

I don't object, let Honey love her granddaughter the only way she knows how.

turning ten

My first joint birthday party with Kendra and Aspen was the year we turned ten. I knew we'd have fun celebrating together because we were able to be silly with each other, laugh uncontrollably at the corniest things, and enjoy regular birthday parties—not like the popular-girl clique at school who had spa days and horseback riding excursions on their birthdays.

Turning ten was also when I realized that Honey and Dad didn't always see eye to eye. That Dad was gentle with his opinions, but that he certainly had them when it came to raising me and letting me eat whatever I want.

We were at Farrell's Ice Cream Parlour, and everything about this day was a big deal because we were turning double digits, and it was also a big deal because Phillip was there and I had the biggest crush on Phillip and he was sitting right across from me. Soon I'd be out of elementary school, and maybe we could have our first kiss once we were in middle school. Back then, I thought middle school was all about getting a locker, having your first kiss, and getting the monthly visitor Honey and Aunt Aretha kept talking about.

My favorite part about going to Farrell's was the self-playing piano. I loved watching the keys move and crank out a tune, and I imagined a ghost was there playing, which freaked Kendra out. She always rushed past, hardly even looking at the music machine.

Kendra loved that the servers all wore period clothing and straw boater hats from the 1900s.

We all got a kick out of the menus that looked like tabloid-style newspapers. But the absolute best part was ordering the Portland Zoo Ice Cream Sundae. It was meant to be shared, and most customers ordered it for parties. I loved it because it was delivered by two servers running frantically throughout the restaurant, carrying it on a stretcher, with ambulance sirens sounding off, before they brought it to your table. It was more than a sundae—the trough had five flavors of ice cream, three sherbet flavors, five toppings, three bananas cut and placed throughout the gigantic bowl, and one big strip of whipped cream wrapped around the edge of the bowl, decorating the ice cream. Toasted almonds, animal crackers, and sprinkles topped it off like a crown, making it the best ice cream treat to a ten-year-old.

Farrell's bragging rights was that it was the biggest ice cream sundae in the Pacific Northwest. It weighed eight and a half pounds.

For birthday parties too small to get the Portland Zoo sundae, a smaller free sundae arrived at the table, with the fanfare of a big marching drum banging to announce a birthday was being celebrated. Sometimes, if you went to Farrell's on the weekend, you could hardly enjoy your food because every five minutes a drum was pounding or a siren was sounding off.

I remember this birthday for all these reasons, but mostly because turning ten meant realizing my chubby baby fat would soon be fat fat. Not something cuteness could camouflage.

Before the ice cream came with all its commotion, we ate dinner. I remember looking over the menu, trying to decide if I wanted a cheeseburger or hot dog. I noticed something written at the bottom of the menu: ANYTHING WORTH EATING HAS CALORIES.

I pointed to it, asking Honey, *What does this mean?*

She turned the menu over, said, *It means eat what you want.*

I told her I wanted a cheeseburger, steak fries, and a cherry Coke.

I heard Dad say to Honey, *You shouldn't let her eat all of that. She's having ice cream later.*

Honey shrugged her shoulders. *I agree with Farrell's,* she said, pointing at the slogan on the menu. She read it out loud: *Anything Worth Eating Has Calories.*

But Honey, this is a bit much, don't you think? Dad was whispering, but I could hear every word.

It's her birthday. Honey gave Dad a look. The one she usually gave me when I kept pressing her on something.

How many times had Dad talked with Honey about what I ate, how much I ate?

Dad shook his head. *She's getting older, sweetheart. Baby fat is different from fat fat.*

I forgot about that moment till just now. Maybe because at the time I didn't even know what that statement meant, or maybe because I knew what it meant, but I couldn't bear knowing that the man I loved the most, the man who first loved me, was saying it.

love, disguised

My mother loves me unconditionally. She never ever talked about my weight when I was a kid. Never put me on a diet. She has watched my body go up and down, down and up, my entire life. Always, she's called me beautiful.

I don't question her love for me.

I know she loves me. I also know that sometimes denial looks like love.

personal stylist

I thought Kendra was going to text a few links to give me shopping options for Aaliyah, but instead she invites us over, says she has clothes for Aaliyah to try on. I hesitate to go, but I know I need to swallow my pride, take her offer. When we arrive at Kendra's, she takes us downstairs to her basement. It is part workspace, part dressing room. Today she has racks out with different clothes for Aaliyah to try on: a casual rack with jeans, sweatshirts, and T-shirts, a rack full of skirts and dresses that can be dressed up or down, and a rack with jackets, sweaters, and coats.

Thank you for doing this, I say. We haven't spoken since I found out about Constance. We don't say much now. Just focus on Aaliyah, who is walking through the room, shuffling through the clothes with her hand, admiring them, feeling the different fabrics.

All this is for you to try on, Kendra says. *I picked out some items I think you'd like and that I think will look good on you. Today, you're just going to play dress-up, okay? I don't want you to worry about the size on the tag. Focus on what feels good on you, what looks good on you. Got it?*

Got it, Aaliyah says.

Let's start here. Kendra points to the casual rack.

While Aaliyah tries on clothes, Kendra tries to ease the tension between us. She plays music, calling out to Aaliyah, *These are the songs your mom and I grew up on.* She does a little shimmy-shake and says to me, *Can you*

*believe we're at an age where we're talking to younger peo-
ple, saying, "Now this is good music"?*

I smile to be polite, but really, I don't feel like talking
or listening to her oldies-but-goodies playlist.

Aaliyah tries on clothes. Some are too big, too small,
most fit just right. She's picked out six outfits, a sweater,
and a coat. *I get to have all of these?* she asks.

Yes, Kendra says. She looks at me and mouths, *This is
on me.* I try to protest, give her something to pay for all of
this but she refuses. *It shouldn't be so expensive to dress a
plus-size girl. And it definitely shouldn't be so hard to find
clothes. This is my gift.*

Thank you, Auntie Kendra. Aaliyah wraps Kendra in
a hug.

*Thank me by doing good in school this year. We got you
looking good, now you have to do your best to be good.
Okay?*

Promise.

*Okay, now before you go, you have to model your out-
fits for us,* Kendra says. *We need to do a fashion show
real quick. Gotta make sure you know how to strut down
the hallways at school,* Kendra says. Aaliyah goes back
into the dressing room and Kendra switches the playlist to something more upbeat. Alright, show us what
you got.

Aaliyah comes out, glorious giggles spilling out of her.
She walks sheepishly across the room.

Own it, girl. Own it, Kendra says. Kendra walks next to
Aaliyah, hand on her hip. Aaliyah follows her lead, and
they strut and pose.

I take out my phone to capture video and take photos, getting into the playtime like I'm a real photographer.
Look at me, Miss Aaliyah. Over here, over here.

skin & bones

Aaliyah poses and holds, poses and holds.

Kendra looks at me, smiles a knowing smile, completely understanding how much Aaliyah needed this, how much I appreciate her for this, how much I love her for this. How I always will.

october

Fall snuck up on me. All of a sudden the leaves are turning and the air is a comfort, a soft hand reaching out to hold mine. Today, I am walking the Tilikum Bridge. It feels like I'm sky-walking, eye-level with the tops of trees. The gold and red leaves make Portland a regal forest. When I was a child, I loved basking in the beauty of the yellow, red, and orange foliage spilling to the ground like confetti. But then, around age ten, I learned that changing leaves were dying leaves, learned that sometimes death is beautiful, that sometimes beauty is deceiving.

I told Honey that fall made me sad. Everywhere I looked, things were dying. Honey told me fall is about change, not death. That fallen leaves represent letting go. She is masterful at twisting the truth just enough to keep it true.

halloween

Aaliyah wants to be an angel for Halloween. At least she didn't say princess. Honey has taken on the task of getting the costume together, which I'm thankful for. The thing no one tells you about being a mother is that sometimes you don't know how, don't have the energy, don't know what you're doing. Honey is making the costume, putting all kinds of extra tender loving care into it. She knows the size the wings should be, how to make sure they are a sophisticated silver—not too shiny, not too platinum. She knows how to make them just the right size—not so big that they overwhelm and become a distraction for Aaliyah and her classmates, but big enough that they are a sight to behold, something to ooh and ahh about. I am not good at that kind of mommying. I can't sew, don't know anything about picking out the right kind of materials for angel wings. But I am paying for everything, and I am going to be sure and take lots of pictures and brag to my coworkers and show Aaliyah, my brown angel, off to anyone and everyone. And I will tell her she is majestic just like real angels. That she is holy, holy. And I will hope—pray—that this kind of mommying is enough.

new beginnings

After making sure Honey has everything she needs, I drive over to Bryan's to help him with Aaliyah's room. He painted last week, and today we are arranging the new furniture and putting up the art and decorations.

When I pull up to the house, I sit out in the car for a moment, staring at the newly cut grass and thinking how happy Ms. Coleman would be to have Bryan home taking care of things. Already, he has fixed the gate that would always stay half-open no matter how hard you pulled down on the lever. Already he has power-washed the siding, making it look like it has a fresh coat of paint.

I get out of the car, ring the doorbell. Bryan opens the door. *Hey, love. Thanks for helping with this,* he says. He walks me over to the dining room table and shows me the designs for each room of the house. *What do you think?* Bryan smells like the cedar-vetiver candle in my bedroom. Every time he walks past me, I get a whiff of home.

He talks me through the different rooms, highlighting the changes that will be his favorite additions. *But I'm definitely keeping the integrity of the house. Keeping that arc there,* he says, pointing to the entryway from the living and dining rooms. *And keeping the crown molding, for sure.*

I'm so glad you're keeping the house.

Yeah, half a mil is hard to say no to, but I want to have something to pass down to Aaliyah. Plus, I don't want these

White folks to have the whole block. Besides the Turner family across the street, Mom was the last one holding out.

I have never heard Bryan talk about passing down anything. He isn't usually a think-ahead kind of person.

We spend the afternoon fixing up Aaliyah's room. Besides painting, he's had new hardwood floors installed, and he's put her bed together. I've spent most of the day working on organizing her closet and dresser and hanging art. Now I'm organizing books on the bookshelf Bryan just put together.

My back is to the door, but I know he has come back into the room, even though I didn't hear his footsteps, even though he is silent and just standing there. *What's wrong?* I ask.

Nothing. I'm just—I'm glad you're here. Wish it was different circumstances, but I'm glad you're here. This, this feels right.

I put another book on the bookshelf and turn around to face him. *What does that mean—this feels right?*

It means I'm ready to do this. Finally, things feel...right, like we can start again, start over. Bryan walks over to me, standing so close his scent holds me.

I turn around, keep putting books on the shelf. I am transported to being sixteen again, in this same room, butterflies and sweaty palms.

You just gonna act like I'm not standing here pouring my heart out to you?

Bryan, really? Pouring your heart out? I don't face him, just keep putting books on the shelf. *I needed to hear this eight years ago when you left me holding our one-month-old daughter, talking about you needed to do you. What do you want me to say? I can't even think about being in a relationship right now. With anyone. You coming back to Portland has nothing to do with me.*

I turn around, look at Bryan, this older version of the boy I once loved.

Yeah, there was a time when I was too immature for you, Bryan says. *By the time I figured things out, you were with Malcolm. It wasn't my place to say nothing to you to mess that up. That ain't me. But now? Seem like he out the picture.*

Bryan steps close to me. *Is he? Out of the picture?* He takes the book I'm holding out of my hand, tosses it on the bed. And he kisses me.

I pull away. *Bryan, I—I'm not ready for—*

Just kiss me. He kisses me again, wraps me in his arms. I lean in. Every kiss we've had since we were fifteen, sixteen, seventeen...is tangled in this moment. His lips feel familiar and new. A history I know, a history I am learning.

daily blend

I agree to go on a date with Bryan. We meet at Daily Blend on Jackson Avenue. It used to be a bungalow owned by a Black woman whose house was a safe space for kids in the neighborhood. This house was always one of my favorites. I fantasized about having a house with a wraparound porch big enough to hold guests who were over for a summer soiree.

I walk up the steps to Daily Blend, find a seat at the window. I am ten minutes early. Bryan arrives at exactly eleven o'clock. He comes to the table, gives me a hug, and asks, *What can I get you?*

He orders our drinks, and we share a thick slice of warm banana nut bread. Every time I look at him, I see our past and the future I thought we'd have.

So, tell me something about yourself, he says. *Isn't that how first dates are supposed to start off?*

I laugh.

Seriously, he says. *Talk to me.*

I take a bite of the loaf, a sip of my coffee. *What do you want me to say?*

Bryan smiles, his shoulders ease. *I don't know. I feel like I know you, but I don't. All we ever talk about now is Aaliyah. There's got to be other things going on with you. I want to know. How's work? Them White people treating you right?*

Work is good. I mean, yes—some of my White colleagues are . . . well, let's just say challenging. But I mean, every job has its challenges.

217

And you've never been one to back down from a challenge. Bryan's smile is intoxicating. *You don't back down from anything. I don't know if those White people at the library know who they hired when they brought you on.*

Listen. They're about to find out. With all this book banning and erasing of history—there's a lot I'm trying to do. Libraries should be at the front of the resistance, but I'm dealing with some people who just want to carry on as usual and hold on to failed systems and outdated program ideas.

Uh-oh. You about to shake things up. You've always been a rebel. Do they know that? Bryan starts laughing. *Like that time you, Aspen, and Kendra led a protest at church. At. Church.*

You remember that?

Bryan nods. *Of course. Legendary times.*

Well, we were tired of being forced to wear skirts and dresses in the sanctuary all the time. I mean, it was such an outdated, ridiculous rule. We could wear pants at home, at school, everywhere and anywhere except in the church building. How silly was that?

Old-school tradition.

I haven't thought about that protest in years. There were about fifteen of us, all high school students, fed up with sexist treatment that was so normalized at church. We planned our protest to happen on youth Sunday. When we stood to sing our first song, all us girls unzipped our choir robes to reveal we were wearing shorts, jeans, sweatpants. *I'll never forget the look on people's faces when instead of singing, we started chanting, "You see our clothes, God sees our hearts!"*

Bryan and I laugh so hard, the woman at the next table looks over and smiles, seeing the good time we are having.

skin & bones

Who came up with that slogan? Bryan asks.

Kendra, I think.

Bryan shakes his head. *I was proud of you, though—it took a lot of courage to be the pastor's daughter and stage a protest in the middle of Sunday-morning service. And I always agreed. If we could wear pants in the sanctuary, why couldn't the girls?*

You know why. It was all about being a temptation to the men of the church. I roll my eyes. Of course, no one ever said this to me, but that's what I always believed. *Monitoring our bodies was never about God and modesty. It was about control and manipulation. And instead of telling the men in the church to control their desires, they tried to control our bodies.*

Bryan shakes his head. *Well, you were heard loud and clear. They changed the rule. My mom was on your side, and so were the other women of the church. I remember her defending you when someone said you were rebellious. She was like, "So was Jesus."*

See, I always loved your momma. She was the best. The. Best. I am not used to talking about Ms. Coleman in the past tense. I don't think I ever will be. I get back to our reminiscing, don't want the mention of his mom to bring sadness. *Yeah, we got the rule changed. Those were good times.*

Very good times. Bryan splits the last piece of bread and motions for me to take half.

I think my dad always wanted to be more progressive, but back then he let the elders influence his decisions more than he should have. I drink the last of my coffee, look at the clock on the wall. I thought I'd only stay an hour. We've been here for two.

From what my mom would tell me, seems like he's changed a lot over the years. How is he?

I swallow the lump in my throat. Just the question makes my heart ache. *He's, I don't think he's well. He's—don't repeat this to anyone—*

I won't. I won't. Bryan pushes his cup away, sits up straighter.

He's stepping down soon.

What? Really? Why?

He says he's tired.

Do you know who he's going to turn the church over to?

It's not, I don't think it's a final decision. But, um, Malcolm. He'll most likely turn the church over to Malcolm.

Here I am bringing up an ex on a date with an ex. Here Bryan is looking at me like it's really sinking in that Malcolm is a permanent stay in my family regardless of if I'm married to him or not. I can't be sure, but Bryan's probably thinking how that was once the dream for us. Ms. Coleman always said Bryan would be a good pastor because he would really tend to the people and not to tradition. Bryan left the church before that ever became a possibility. I don't even think he goes on obligatory holidays.

Bryan brushes crumbs from the table onto the napkin in his hand. *I promised a short date. You ready to head out?*

Yes, I should get going, I say. *Thanks for this. It was nice.* I walk toward the door, say goodbye even though I could stay longer.

angel

Honey's angel wings are perfection. Aaliyah is practically floating down the sidewalk. We're with Honey going door to door of local businesses on Alberta Street for Halloween candy when a boy calls out, *You're too fat to be an angel! How are you going to fly to heaven?*

At first I think maybe Aaliyah doesn't hear the boy, but once she squeezes my hand and scoots closer to me, I know there is no shielding her from the word assaults coming at her.

Honey says, *Just ignore him.*

But I stop walking. *You don't have to ignore bullies,* I say to Aaliyah. *Sometimes it's okay to tell them to shut the hell up.*

Lena! Honey would clutch her pearls if she was wearing them. But instead she reaches out for Aaliyah, grabs her from me like she needs to protect her from my crassness.

I call out to the little boy, *My daughter is not too fat to be an angel. She can be anything she wants to be. She is beautiful just as she is.*

He walks faster, scurrying to the adult that he's with. Honey huffs and puffs in embarrassment.

Aaliyah looks at me with confusion and maybe even disbelief in her eyes, *Mommy, do you really believe that? That I'm beautiful?*

Yes, of course. You are beautiful just the way you are.

playdate

Aaliyah and Paige have become inseparable, and every weekend one is asking to spend the night at the other's house. It's my turn, and I am loving the echo of giggles ricocheting off the walls, bouncing from room to room.

Ladies, dinner will be ready in a few minutes. Clean up and wash your hands, please. I've made spaghetti, Aaliyah's favorite.

We gather at the dinner table, and just before we begin eating, Aaliyah goes to the fridge and takes out three cans of soda. *Mom, you forgot to put out drinks.*

Oh, thanks, sweetheart. I sure did. I forgot all about those.

Aaliyah gives us each a glass and soda. I watch her be a good host as she cracks open the can for Paige. *Oh, I can't have soda,* Paige says. *My mom says it's not good for you.*

Aaliyah pours the soda in her glass instead. *We only have it once in a while. For a treat,* she says.

Oh, well, no thank you, Paige says. *Can I have water?*

How is this little girl making me feel pressured not to drink soda in my own house?

Aaliyah gives Paige a glass of water. As we eat, I notice that Aaliyah doesn't drink one sip of her soda.

So tell me, how is school? I ask.

Paige is eager to fill me in on her favorite subjects, her favorite games to play at recess, and which days are the good menu days in the cafeteria. Then she says, *And we have lots of friends: Kemi, Shayla, Gina, Taylor. They*

*are our best friends. Nora used to be, but we don't like her
anymore.*

Aaliyah's eyes shift to the floor, then, finally, she takes
a sip of soda from her glass.

Who is Nora? I ask. *I don't think I've met her.*

*Nora used to sit next to Aaliyah, but Ms. Burdoff moved
her to another table group because she was bullying Aaliyah.*

She wasn't bullying me. She was just being mean.

Same thing, Paige says.

I do my best to keep my face calm. On the inside I am
cursing and screaming and wondering why Aaliyah never
mentioned a girl named Nora who is being mean, and I
am definitely making a mental note to reach out to her
teacher. It got bad enough that Nora had to be moved,
and I am just now hearing about this?

But on the outside? On the outside my face is calm,
and I try really hard to make my voice soothing. *Aaliyah,
how was she being mean? What did she do?*

Aaliyah takes another drink of soda, this time more
like a gulp. She looks at Paige, giving her permission to
tell me.

Paige says, *Well, it all started when Ms. Burdoff brought
in her favorite books from when she was a little girl.*

Aaliyah chimes in, *She called them classics. George
and Martha.*

Immediately, I know where this is going, and I can feel
tears stinging my eyes.

Paige tells me, *When Ms. Burdoff showed the class the
books, two big hippos were on the cover, and Nora said the
girl hippo looked like Aaliyah and the whole class laughed.
She's always talking about Aaliyah's hair and sometimes
she says not nice things because Aaliyah's skin is dark. But
me, Kemi, Shayla, Gina, and Taylor don't laugh at her*

mean jokes. We stand up for Aaliyah, and that's how we all became best friends.

Is Nora White? I ask.

Aaliyah nods, Paige says, *Yes.*

Now I am drinking my soda too. Swallow, gulp, gulp. Inhale, exhale. *Well,* I say, *I am so glad Aaliyah has good friends like you.* I want to say so much more, but if I do, these tears are going to spill out of me. I want to hold Aaliyah in my arms, never let her out of my embrace. But for now, I reach out for her hand, squeeze it tight, tight.

oregon, 1867

There were no laws that banned Black children from public schools, but still, when William Brown, a Black shoemaker from Maryland, sent his children to school, they were sent home. He petitioned to have his children admitted into school, but the board of directors feared that if they started to let Black children into their schools, White taxpayers would withdraw their money and stop supporting public schools.

It cost $2.25 for each student, per quarter, to attend school. Even though Black parents could and would pay this tax, they were given a proposal that stated: *We will give colored people $2.25 for each child they keep out of our schools. You can use that money to get a house and have your own school, hire your own teacher.*

Black parents countered, *Give us $800. Pay for the rent, pay all the bills, pay the salary of our teacher.*

The school was named the Colored School, and opened in the fall of 1867 on the corner of Southwest Fourth and Columbia Street. Ms. Abbie J. Young was chosen to be the teacher. She made $650 a year, teaching twenty-one boys and five girls.

The Colored School closed in the spring of 1872 after the board changed their minds, decided to pull their funding. Local voters passed a law that approved integration, and the following year, Black students were admitted to local schools.

A deep gratitude for Mrs. Abbie J. Young grows and

grows. I am reminded that it is this kind of strength and audacity that was left as my inheritance.

And then I think of the descendants of the White people who opposed integration, who felt so entitled, so outraged at the thought of their White children being educated with Black children, think about what they left behind—their bigotry, their hate, their fear.

This too is an inheritance passed down, and down, and down.

self-portrait

Thank you for making time to meet with me, Ms. Burdoff.
I sit in a chair next to Ms. Burdoff's desk. The thanking is
only to be cordial. Only to start off on a good note, because
she has no idea what's coming for her. It took her too long
to return my emails and schedule this meeting. I was
just about to get the principal involved when she finally
emailed me back and let me know that she's been out sick.

*Before we get into your concerns, I must say, Aaliyah
is such a gem. I just love having her in my class. She is so
kind to her classmates and so smart. She's really excelling
in math and reading,* Ms. Burdoff says.

*I'm glad to hear that Aaliyah is doing well, given the
bullying that has been happening.*

*Yes, um, that's . . . um, that's resolved now, for the most
part.*

For the most part?

Well, I moved the girl—

Nora.

*Yes, Nora. I moved Nora to a different table group, and
things have seemed better since then.*

*Seemed better? Have you checked in to ask Aaliyah if
things are, in fact, better? Have you informed Nora's parents that she was rude and disrespectful to my child? Did
you let the substitute know that they should look out for
Aaliyah because there have been issues with Nora?*

*Well, no, I didn't contact Nora's parents. I felt I had it
under control, and if things had escalated, I would have—*

You called me at the beginning of the school year because Aaliyah couldn't stop laughing in class at a student who you even admitted is funny but needs to rein it in. You called me to tell me my child laughs a lot, but didn't think to call me when she was compared to a hippopotamus? You didn't think to call Nora's parents to tell them their child was being inappropriate?

Ms. Burdoff's face turns red, and she shifts in her seat.

Nora has teased my daughter nonstop, making fun of her weight and her hair. Now, I am sure you understand that this behavior from anyone should not be tolerated, but I will point out the obvious here—Nora is a White girl making fun of a Black girl's body. It is unacceptable, and her parents need to know what's going on, and there needs to be a consequence for her beyond just moving to a different desk.

I, um, I can definitely have a talk with Nora's parents. I didn't know it had escalated.

I'd like you to check in with Aaliyah weekly to see how things are going. I will too, of course, but, Ms. Burdoff, you are with my daughter more hours out of the day than I am. Your immediate response to what's happening is important. She needs to know—and the other students in the class need to know—that this is not okay. That you will not tolerate racist bullying and body shaming. I don't expect you to love her like I do, but I do ask that you see her, look out for her, make sure she is in an environment where she can learn without feeling degraded and shamed. Can you do that?

I, I can. And I apologize. I see now that I could have—should have—handled this better. I am learning.

I can't afford for my daughter to be your case study. Please do better. I stand. Thank you for taking time. I hope you are fully on the mend.

Yes, yes, I am. Thank you.

Ms. Burdoff walks me to the door. Before she opens it, she says, *Oh! I almost forgot to give this to you. I had students do self-portraits a while back for our Who Am I? unit. Aaliyah is quite the visual artist. She made two. One of just her and one of your family.* She hands me Aaliyah's drawings. *I told everyone they could take these home now that we are in a new unit, but Aaliyah's is still here. I thought you might want to see it.*

Thank you.

I walk out of the building and get into my car. Before I drive off, I look at Aaliyah's self-portraits. The one on top is labeled "My Family," and under the title, she's drawn herself in the middle of me and a man who I assume is Malcolm, given the perfectly drawn goatee. I almost tear up at the sight, thinking how she is still holding on to hope. But then, the image that makes my heart drop. Aaliyah's self-portrait is a drawing of a very thin girl filled in with tan pencil. Her hair is straight and long, and she looks nothing, nothing like the beautiful big, brown girl she really is.

aaliyah

When Aaliyah was in the second grade, I went to her school for a parent-teacher conference. Her teacher, whose blond hair was pulled up in a messy I-did-this-on-purpose-but-want-it-to-look-casual bun, said to me, *I really enjoy having Aaliyah in class. She's so good at sharing with her classmates, and I can always count on her to volunteer when I ask for a little helper. But I have to say, she can be a little sassy at times—*

Sassy? What do you mean by that?

Well, she questions everything—

So she's curious?

I wouldn't say curious. More like combative, always challenging something I'm saying or interrupting, without raising her hand, to ask a question. Just the other day, I was teaching about the life cycle of plants, and Aaliyah could hardly let me teach. She kept interrupting me to tell me she already knew all about seeds and germination and roots—

Yeah, she gardens with her grandmother and I've given her books about plants because she's fascinated by them. I think maybe she was just excited. I tried to sound even. No inflection in my voice, no attitude. No sass. *My daughter knows to be respectful, but I can see how her enthusiasm made her forget to raise her hand.*

Oh, it's not just about her raising her hand. It's that she always wants to share what she knows, what she's already learned, or a book she's reading. It's disruptive and can be intimidating to the other children.

I was stunned that Aaliyah's engagement was being taken as disrespect. Before I could gather myself, gather my words, the teacher was standing and reaching out her hand to shake mine. Her next appointment had arrived.

I left and drove to a bookstore. I bought Aaliyah more books on plants and gardening, and the whole way home, I promised myself that I would nurture Aaliyah's zeal for learning, encourage her to read and study and ask questions and share her knowledge.

Wondering the whole way home why the brilliance and boldness of Black girls is so often seen as defiance.

black girls

We are Black girls—the kind of Black that is not exotic or unique. Our Black is self-explanatory. No one asks where we are from, there is no wondering what I am. My Black is as common as Portland's rain, as regular as morning coffee. Black like fish frys and chicken dinners sold out of church basements to raise money for the Pastor's Aide Society. Black. Our skin a badge of honor, a covering, a shield.

brown tourmaline

I spend the evening researching things that are brown and beautiful. Decide that I will buy Aaliyah a gem, something she can wear around her neck. Brown tourmaline. The deepest brown I can find. Something to anchor her, something that symbolizes my love for her. A physical reminder that her skin is glorious, complex, one of a kind.

skin tones

Portland's Urban League had two initiatives. They advocated for Black people to be hired in establishments that only hired White people, and in the few businesses that hired Black workers, they fought for these positions to be more than housekeeping jobs. They deliberately fought for light-skinned Black folks to get hired as elevator operators, and their plan mostly worked. White folks found Black Portlanders with light skin to be less threatening, more like them.

But there were some businesses that preferred to hire dark-skinned workers. *So there'd be no mistaking,* they said. So there'd be no wondering who was doing the serving, the tending, who was less than.

another time

But Mom, you promised, is all Aaliyah keeps saying to me. *You said Malcolm could come over another time. Today is another time. You promised.*

That promise was a placeholder. A prayer that she'd forget. But I should have known she wouldn't forget. And neither has Malcolm. He asked if the three of us could go out somewhere—dinner or a movie. Maybe both. I've been putting it off for weeks, and now Aaliyah is asking.

Okay. Let's go see a movie. I choose movie because at least I don't have to talk to him, face him from across a table. At least something can distract us from us.

Aaliyah and I meet Malcolm at the theater. He has already purchased the tickets and the largest bucket of popcorn. He kisses Aaliyah on her forehead and reaches toward me, out of habit, I think, but then hesitates. *Hey,* he says.

Hey.

Aaliyah leads the way to our row. She sits in the middle of us, holds the tub of popcorn so we all can dig in. The seats recline, so I lean back as far as I can. It feels like old times. We fit together like we've never been apart. I don't know what I expected, but nothing about this is awkward or forced. It's just the three of us, the way it used to be. Maybe the way it's supposed to be.

After we leave the theater and head to our cars, Aaliyah says, *Malcolm, are you going to come over for a Scrabble rematch?*

Malcolm smiles. *Oh, you ready for this? You sure you ready?*

Um, the question is, are you ready? I beat you last time, remember?

Malcolm laughs. *You always beat me, and honestly, I'm beginning to think the game is rigged.*

You're not letting me win because I'm only a child, are you? I hate when adults do that.

Aaliyah, sweetheart. I love you to the moon and back. But I promise you, you will never have to worry about me letting you win. Kid or no kid. I play for bragging rights. And I've got all kinds of new words to try out on you.

Aaliyah shakes her head. *It doesn't matter what words you want to try out. It only matters what letters you get and your strategy for placing the tiles in the right spot.*

So you say, so you say. I'm not going to take advice from my opponent.

You're going to lose again, just saying.

We all laugh at this because we know it's true. When we make it to my car, Malcolm turns to me, whispers, *So, ah, is it cool if I come through?*

Yes, I'd like that.

You should play with us, he says.

I know my lane. That's your thing with her. It's a good thing. I get into the car, wait for Malcolm to get to his, and he follows me home. When we get to the house, I go into the kitchen, take out what I need to make nachos. After we eat, Malcolm and Aaliyah play the longest game of Scrabble ever because he keeps challenging words and making her recite the definition. I love hearing her giggles every time she proves him wrong. Yes, it feels like old times, like old times. Like a Saturday morning when you slip on a worn T-shirt that's tattered a bit, maybe not the perfect fit, but still just right, just right.

skin & bones

After Aaliyah beats Malcolm in their last round, she puts the game away and Malcolm goes over to the record player and looks through my growing collection. *What you in the mood for?* he calls out.

Aaliyah runs over to him. *Something we can dance to.*

Oh, you got moves to show me? Since when?

I can dance! Aaliyah says. She starts moving before the record spins.

Let me teach you a little something about that old Old School. The music comes on and Malcolm sings along with the Emotions' "The Best of My Love." He comes into the kitchen, reaches over me and turns the water off. He pulls me to him. *Come on, those dishes can wait.* He brings me into the living room where Aaliyah is bopping and twirling. We join in with her, the three of us dancing and singing and making so much noise, the neighbors must think a party is going on, must be wondering what new joy has come.

unexpected

Two weeks after Malcolm takes us to the movies, we make plans to meet up for lunch and a playdate with his niece Bree, who is the same age as Aaliyah. We're going to a fun center where kids jump fearlessly on trampolines, dive into an ocean of foam balls, and play arcade games, only taking breaks to eat a slice of pizza and gulp a swig of soda. Malcolm offered to pick us up, since it's across town and he knows I hate driving on I-5 South because of the Terwilliger curves.

The doorbell rings. I call out to Aaliyah, tell her to answer the door. And then I hear the bass of Bryan's voice booming through the house.

Bryan? I come downstairs. *What are you—is everything okay?*

Things are fine. Sorry to pop up unannounced. I just thought I'd hang out with Aaliyah today. Get some daddy-daughter time in.

Bryan, we have plans…we're, we're about to leave. Just as I say this, I look out the window and see Malcolm walking up the steps.

What plans you got today? Bryan asks. He has an ease to his charm, and even though I am irritated with him, I can't ignore what his presence does to me, how our attraction to each other is always a simmering pot on the back burner.

You really need to call in advance and make a plan if you want to see Aaliyah.

I gotta make an appointment to see my own daughter?
Bryan is trying to play it off like he's joking, but I know he is annoyed with me.

Um, yes. She has a playdate with a friend. I open the door.

Bryan sees Malcolm, says, *Oh, I see what it is—you have a playdate.*

Malcolm stands at the door. Even though I am holding the screen door open, he doesn't come inside. *You good?* he asks me.

Everything's fine, I tell him.

Alright, I'll be in the car, he tells me. He nods at Bryan, Bryan nods back.

As Malcolm walks away, Bryan says, *What was that supposed to mean—you good? What you tell that man that got him asking if you good just because he sees me? I should be the one asking you if you're okay. Why is he even here—*

Bryan, we are not doing this today. I have to go. Malcolm is waiting. His niece is having a birthday party. We're going.

So you haven't cut ties with his family?

His family is my family. Aaliyah looks at Malcolm like—

Don't say it. I swear to God. Don't call that man her father. Look, I ain't perfect, but I'm trying to make up for when my best wasn't good enough. But at the end of the day, I'm her father. And I'm glad she got a relationship with him or whatever, but he will never replace me. And you shouldn't be encouraging him to.

No one is trying to replace you. He's just been here. Always. And the fact that he still makes an effort to be in her life even though we're not together tells me a lot about his character.

And what is that supposed to mean?

You and I broke up, and it's like you broke up with your daughter. So don't come here now trying to act like you didn't abandon both of us. Don't come here making demands on my time, her time, or her affection, I say. We have to go.

I can't even say hello to her? Really?

I call for Aaliyah to come down, and she appears so quick, I realize she must've been sitting on the stairs listening the whole time. She puts her coat on, says hi to Bryan so casually that if you didn't know us, you wouldn't know that was her father, that she carries his sense of humor, his insistence.

All you got is hi for me? I don't get a hug?

I almost reach out for her, tell her she doesn't ever have to hug anyone unless she wants to, especially a man. But she is already in his embrace, being rocked back and forth.

Aaliyah walks to Malcolm's car.

I stay behind, tell Bryan, *This is new for us. We need to figure out how to do this—parent her—*

Mom! We're going to be late. Come on.

I—I need to go. We'll talk later, I tell Bryan. I close and lock the door, head to Malcolm's car.

Bryan gently grabs my arm, turns me to him. *This ain't just about coparenting. Yeah, we need to figure that out, but like I said, I'm staying for you. I want you. If I need to move on, just tell me.*

I open my mouth to answer him, but no words come out. I join Aaliyah at the bottom of the driveway. We get into Malcolm's car. When she says hello to him, she sounds like a daughter coming home.

chosen family

Sometimes Aaliyah calls him Malcolm, sometimes Daddy. The words have become interchangeable for her. The first time she called Malcolm Daddy, I reacted like she said a curse word. I caught myself before I chastised her too harshly. It's just that it took me by surprise, made it clear that she did not have a connection with the man whose blood runs through her veins. I knew this would hurt Bryan. But how could he blame her? He became a once-a-month father who lived three hours away. She knows him mostly through photos and recycled stories of our better days.

One day, I overheard her playing with Paige. She called Malcolm Daddy and Paige told her, *He's not your real daddy*, emphasis on *real*. Aaliyah said, *He's going to marry my momma one day, so soon he will be my real daddy. But anyway, his love for me is real, like a daddy's love should be, so that's why I call him Daddy now. I don't have to wait till the wedding.*

father, dad

As in that boy looks just like his father, as in they love him like a father, as in anyone can be a father but not everyone is a dad.

Dad as in provider.

Dad as in protector.

Dad, as in, *Shh…don't tell your momma* when we broke her rules of bedtime to stay up late to watch reruns of *I Love Lucy* and *The Honeymooners*. Two peas in a pod. Dad, as in the one who taught me how to drive and parallel park, how to check my oil, change a tire.

Dad, who is the first man who told me he loved me, the first man who showed me he loved me. Dad, as in when you have a good one, every man you love after him is held to a high, high standard.

Dad, as in girl-dad, as in nobody better mess with his baby girl. As in, no matter how old I get,

I will always be his baby girl, always Daddy's girl.

old-time religion

Kendra is at church today. She comes every now and then when she gets tired of Honey and Ms. Brown saying *Missed you last Sunday*. We sit together, next to Aspen, who is sitting too close to the front for either of our preferences. Just after praise and worship, Dad steps to the podium and says a few pleasantries and announcements, then says, *We're going to be blessed with a solo from Sister Laila, and after that, we'll hear from our guest minister, Pastor Richie.*

Kendra leans in to me. *Your dad isn't preaching today? You know I love his sermons. Why didn't you tell me?*

I didn't know, I whisper.

Kendra sighs. *Would it be rude if I left now?*

We laugh.

Aspen mumbles, *I can hear you two, just for the record.*

And just like that we are the twelve-year-old girls who used to pass notes during service, talking too much and too loud. Always Aspen the one to put us in our place so we wouldn't get in trouble.

Five minutes into Pastor Richie's remarks, and I'm wondering if maybe instead of a preacher he wanted to be a stand-up comedian, the way he is making jokes and serving punch lines instead of sticking to the scripture. His sermon sounds more like the dirty dozens than a sermon—stinging and clowning from the pulpit.

The Bible says, Faith without works is dead. Amen?

That's right! Preach! The congregation hypes him with affirmation.

243

And I know some of you are not going to want to hear this, but I have to tell it like it is. Some of you women out there praying and fasting and vision boarding for your man to come, when really what you need to do is get yourself on a treadmill.

There's laughter from most people, but I can see Honey give Dad a disapproving look.

The preacher wipes his sweat, steps back from the podium like he wants those words to marinate in the room. A spiritual mic drop. *Oh, it's getting quiet in here, not too many Amens on that, but that's okay. Faith without works is dead. You want a man? You better get your house in order, and by house, I mean your temple. God calls us to take care of our bodies.*

There are amens, but not as many as before. The guest pastor takes a sip of his water and says, *Oh, yeah, I'm goin' there. You see, some of us got solutions at our fingertips. We waitin' on God, and he's waiting on us.*

Are we really going to sit through this? Kendra asks.

And married women, I'm talking to you too. You praying for a good marriage but always talking about you got a headache when it's time to do what it takes to cultivate a happy marriage. You better take a Tylenol and—

Alright now. Okay, Pastor Richie, Dad says. He clears his throat. *Watch yourself, now.*

Pastor Richie keeps going.

Dad stands. He says, *Watch yourself, brotha. Amen?* I have never seen Dad admonish someone from the pulpit. Never seen him not have a united front with ministers and deacons and the elders of the church. When church folks found out I was pregnant, the gossip, judgments, and shunning overwhelmed me. *Dad, why don't you say something? Defend me?* I'd ask. He told me he was taking care of it, that some things need to be handled behind closed doors. But today, today he is not waiting to debrief or check in with any auxiliary board to see what they think.

Okay, uh, I see I need to bring this to a close, Pastor Richie says. *I'm going to bring this to a close. Let us pray.*

The congregation stands with bowed heads, closed eyes. Except me. Except Dad. We stay seated and are staring at each other. There's a look in Dad's eyes that I've never seen before. An apology? Regret? Maybe.

But definitely there are tears, definitely tears.

saved by grace

I never felt pressured into going to church. I loved getting dressed up and making my rounds to all the old ladies who had peppermint and butterscotch candies at the ready to hand out like trick-or-treat goodies. I loved singing in the choir, except in the summer, because choir robes were just too hot and hid my cute summer dresses. I loved listening to Ms. Dixon sing her solos and couldn't wait to see what Ms. Turner was wearing. I loved memorizing scriptures and reciting them for the congregation, always trying to outshine Aspen and Kendra when it was my turn but rooting for them whenever they were at the mic.

Daddy always preached, *It don't matter what you do in this building. What matters is how you live your life outside these four walls.*

Maybe that's why church became more and more disappointing the older I became. By middle school I knew too much about deacons beating their wives, about musicians sleeping around, about women gossiping and rolling their eyes at Honey just because she existed. I knew all about the ways folk talk about love and forgiveness and come as you are but push anything and anyone different away. Saw how single mothers were shunned when their big bellies were showing, but those girls who had abortions, those girls popping morning-after pills? No one ever knew. Where was the discernment then?

skin & bones

I asked Honey about it all. How the church could be such a place of hypocrisy. How she could keep going when we knew so much, too much.

Of course, Honey had an answer. *There is no perfect church because we are all imperfect people.* One time I heard her on the front porch talking to Aunt Aretha, who was all upset about the latest church scandal. She kept saying she was leaving the church. Honey said, *You leaving your job too? You taking your kids out of school too?*

Aunt Aretha seemed puzzled. Didn't say anything.

Then Honey said, *We are committed to places with visions and missions, and none of them live up to those values all the time. If you want a perfect place, you'll never be a part of any community. Find a church that is healthy, one that is going to grow and evolve and strive to be Christ-like. If you're looking for a congregation that's never going to have issues—you're setting yourself up for disappointment.*

sunday sermon

Next Sunday, Dad is back in the pulpit. He asks us to turn our Bibles to Proverbs 31:30, even though the scripture is showing on the big screen behind him. He is old-school like that, still writes checks to pay his tithes instead of choosing the electronic option, still prefers to have hymnals in the pews even though the lyrics to songs during praise and worship show on the screen.

He reads the scripture in what I call his preacher voice. Deep baritone with dramatic pauses:

Charm is deceptive, and beauty is fleeting; but a woman who fears the Lord is to be praised.

middle class

Before the expansion of the railroad, Black Portlanders had jobs as cooks or domestics. But when the Oregon
Railway and Navigation allocated $1.5 million to develop
the Albina rail center, Black folks became porters and
dining car waiters and worked in the roundhouses. By
1909 there were five new railroad lines running through
the heart of Northeast Portland: Southern Pacific, Santa
Fe, Union Pacific, Northern Pacific, and Great Northern.
This created a new working class of Black Portlanders,
and the Black community was established. Most Black
Portlanders lived west of the Willamette River, near the
railroads.

We found a way to make a way, Grandma used to tell
me. The more I search for us in the pages of Oregon history, the more I find, the more I believe her.

coparenting

This time of year there is more rain than shine. But the sky's daily weeping doesn't keep true Oregonians inside. We embrace the rain, we understand that even nature needs to release, needs to let go.

Bryan is here to pick up Aaliyah. *She's upstairs, finishing packing,* I tell him. They're going on a camping trip with his sister and her children. Something I wouldn't do even if it was dry, but especially not in this weather. But Aaliyah is excited. She's been talking about it nonstop all week.

Bryan sits on the sofa, waiting. I go into the kitchen, take out two cans of seltzer water. *Peach-pear or blackberry?* I ask, holding up the cans.

Cherry Coke, he says, laughing.

I only have soda in the house for something special. Too much sugar. And please don't give Aaliyah any.

Damn, Lena. The girl can't have a little sugar?

Oh, she has plenty of it in other foods. I'm sure she'd rather have ice cream than Cherry Coke. She can't have both.

Aaliyah has come downstairs. *I know, I know. No soda, no candy, and I can have potato chips but only in moderation.*

Bryan holds his arms wide open toward Aaliyah and hugs her. He whispers, *At my place you can have whatever you want. We're stopping at Burgerville on our way home.*

Bryan—I'm serious. Please—

Lena, when she's with you, she's with you. When she's with me, she's with me.

I let it go. One cheeseburger is not going to hurt. Moderation, not deprivation. I keep trying to figure out what the balance is between Grandma's tactics and Honey's. I don't want to scrutinize everything Aaliyah eats, but I need to teach her how to make healthy choices. How to be intentional with what she puts in her body.

Bryan comes over to me, wraps his arms around my waist, and pulls me close. Like I am his, like he is mine. *I love her too,* he says. *I'm going to take good care of our daughter.* He kisses me on my cheek, and I pull away.

Aaliyah might see us—

She ain't never seen two people kiss?

Bryan, you're doing too much.

Well, I just wanted to celebrate. I've some good news to share with two of my favorite girls.

Aaliyah's eyes get big. *What's the news? Tell us, tell us.*

Well, I just found out this morning that I got a really good—and by good I mean great—photography job. I'll be working for an advertising, branding, and design company. I'll be on the team that shoots for all the Nike contracts.

Bryan, this is—this is wonderful. Congratulations.

Congratulations, Aaliyah says. She hugs him tight.

We've got to celebrate, Bryan. This is a big deal. Dinner next weekend?

Oh, are you asking me on a date?

I shake my head, give in to a laugh.

You hear that, Aaliyah? Your mom and I are going on a date next weekend.

Aaliyah doesn't respond. I don't think Bryan catches

it, but I know her expressions. The look she has on her face right now is how she looks when she's not comfortable, when she's anxious. The thought of me and Bryan going out on a date doesn't bring joy to her eyes, but tension.

celebrating

Honey is at my house, watching Aaliyah. I didn't tell her I had a date with Bryan. I'm not telling anyone that we're seeing each other again. Not until I know if it's going to turn into anything serious.

Bryan and I are having dinner at a new steakhouse downtown. The restaurant is on the thirty-fifth floor, with ceiling-to-floor windows. It is the perfect place to celebrate his new job. I purposely got here early so I could choose a table instead of a booth. The server places the drink menu on my table, but I sip on water until Bryan arrives, thinking, Why am I doing this? Do I want this, want him?

Lena? Bryan is standing in front of me. Everything about him debonair. He reaches his arms toward me, and we hug. *How was your day?*

Good, good. You?

Same. He flashes a smile and sits down.

We order drinks and toast. Me, to much success at his new job, him to new beginnings. My phone vibrates in my pocket. I ignore it.

We order our food. Me, grilled salmon with lemon garlic potatoes and broccoli rabe. Him, steak frites, medium rare. *Damn girl, you really serious about being on a diet, huh?*

I'm not on a diet.

Oh, so you just eat this way all the time?

Yes, actually. What kind of question is that?

Bryan looks at me, says, *Well, listen, don't go losing too much weight. You know I like you thick. Don't know what's wrong with them other brothas.*

I used to think this was a compliment. When we were young and in love, Bryan would always tell me how beautiful I was. His comments were always tied to my body. My big butt, my breasts. He never made me feel uncomfortable naked. The first time we made love, I kept pulling the covers over myself, kept trying to hide. He tossed the sheet off the bed, said, *Let me see you. All of you. You're beautiful, all of you.* And I believed him.

And I also believed that he was the only boy who felt that way. The way he couched his adoration in comparison to those other guys, like he should win a trophy for liking a big girl like me.

I didn't know enough back then to know this wasn't love, or at least not the kind of love I wanted.

We finish eating our entrées, order dessert. *So tell me more about this new job.*

It feels like I'm turning a corner professionally, he says. He tells me that he already has an assignment for a photo shoot in LA.

My phone buzzes again. I have been feeling it vibrate on and off for the last half hour. I ignore it.

I ask the question that has to be asked: *So, tell me, why online dating? I'm sure there are plenty of options for you.*

Well, plenty of options. No good choices to be made, though.

Before I can protest, he says, *I see that look you're giving me. I'm serious, it's hard out here. The narrative is that it's just hard for women, but men have it hard too. I usually attract extremes. Women either want to get married on the second date, or they have no plan to get serious and are living that I-don't-need-a-man life.*

Do they actually say that, or are you assuming they feel that way?

Oh, they never ever admit it to me. But men know. We know when a woman has already picked out her wedding dress and the names of her children. That's—that's a complete turnoff for me.

Are you afraid of commitment?

No. I just—I don't want to be a stand-in for someone's fantasy. I want to be with a person I can build with and dream with. If a woman already has everything figured out, why am I there?

Bryan orders another drink. *I felt that with us. There was so much pressure from my family and people at the church to get married only because we had a daughter. No one ever asked if I was ready, or if it was what we wanted. And well, sometimes I wondered if you actually loved me or if you just wanted to be married to someone, to anyone.*

Are you serious? I loved you. And yes, there was pressure from everyone, but there was love too. I admit, I was more needy back then. I thought I needed you to be happy, needed you in order to feel complete. But that doesn't mean the love wasn't there. It was just an immature love.

And now?

Well, now I know better. No man can complete me. I say this all the time: I don't need a man, I want a man. I want partnership, I want companionship. I want—

Okay, I hear you. I do. But that feels like some deep way of trying not to sound needy. Like, okay—maybe it's semantics. But it's like saying I don't need chocolate, I want chocolate. I don't need ice cream, I want ice cream. Well, I want to be needed. I want to be someone's water. We need water, we need it to survive. I want a woman who needs me like she needs water. I don't want to be an option she can do without. Bryan leans back from the table.

We don't speak for a while. I want to ask him what he is thinking, but instead I just let the silence exist. I am thinking of all the things Honey taught me about love. How she always says love is a choice. *Don't marry the person you can't live without. Marry the person you can live with.* Does that mean marry who you want, or marry who you need?

Or both?

emergency

Sorry, I tell him. *Someone keeps calling me.*

Me too, Bryan says.

We both take our phones out.

Dad is calling Bryan.

Honey is calling me.

Mom?

Why haven't you answered our calls? Get to the hospital. We're at Emmanuel. Aaliyah...Aaliyah tried to kill herself.

overdose

I don't remember getting into my car or stopping at red lights or parking in the hospital's garage. Suddenly I am here. Sitting in a private waiting room, listening to the team of doctors and psychologists. Listening to Honey's sobs and Dad's and Aspen's and Malcolm's whispered prayers. Watching Bryan sit and stare off into space, paralyzed with shock. I listen, I listen.

...your daughter overdosed on appetite suppressants...

...her grandmother said she was vomiting...

...passed out in the bathroom...empty bottle of pills next to her...

...We pumped her stomach...

...now we're trying to stop the internal bleeding...

...We'll keep you updated...

waiting

Bryan is pacing, and even from across the room, I can see his chest inflating, his shoulders moving up and down. I walk over to him. *She's going to be alright. We've just got to pray and believe that she's going to be alright.* I put my hand on his shoulder.

Bryan snatches away from me. *Lena, don't—I can't even look at you right now.* He stops pacing only to stand still and yell at me. *What the hell is going on? You got our daughter taking diet pills?*

Do you really think I encouraged her to swallow a bottle of pills?

Well, where is she learning it from? You won't let her eat anything. No soda, no ice cream, you're putting all your issues on her. Are you taking those pills in front of her?

Malcolm stands up and walks over to me. He doesn't say anything, but he stands close.

Bryan steps to him. *You need something?*

It's not about what I need. It's about what Lena needs, and she doesn't need you yelling—

And why are you even here? Aaliyah is not your daughter, and Lena is not your wife.

And yet I got the phone call and showed up before you.

Alright, alright. Dad stands between Bryan and Malcolm. *We're not doing this. We. Are. Not. Doing. This.* He turns to Bryan. *Son, go on outside, get some fresh air.*

One thing about Bryan is that he'd never disrespect my dad. He walks away, mumbling, *Worried about why I got here late ... I was with Lena. The woman who called off your wedding—*

Bryan, enough. Go on a walk, get yourself together. Dad walks with him, making sure he leaves.

I sit down next to Aspen. Malcolm and Honey are across from us. Honey has a wad of tissue in her hand. She looks at me, her eyes distraught, her face confused. *Wait, where were you? Did Bryan say he was with you?*

There's a quick knock at the door, then a group of doctors appear. I stand, hope they've come to give us good news.

update

...concerned about her heart...
...arrhythmia...
...the cardiologist is with her now...
...the next forty-eight hours are critical...

critical

As in severe.

As in grave.

As in dire.

As in Aaliyah's vital signs are unstable and outside the normal limits.

As in the doctors *can't predict how she will fare.*

As in *death may be imminent.*

the village

Bryan and Dad and Honey and Malcolm and Aspen haven't left.

Aunt Aretha is here now, and Rebecca and Deacon Brown, and Ms. Brown, too, and Kendra.

She walks in slow, hugs Honey first, then Aspen. She comes over to me. *I—I hope it's okay that I'm here. Aspen tole me and I just, I wanted to be here.*

Kendra knows what it's like to sit and wait for doctors to tell you if the person you love most has died. She sits next to me, takes my hand.

I look around the room at all this care, all this faith, all this solidarity. It is the only thing keeping me from falling apart.

questions

A nurse comes and tells me I need to come with her. *I can see her now? Can I see her?*

No, ma'am. I'm taking you to speak with the social worker. She has some questions for you.

A fog, thick and blinding. I follow the nurse to a different room, my legs wobbling so bad I walk close to the wall, just in case I faint.

When I step into the room, the woman's face looks familiar. High school? College?

The look on her face tells me she recognizes me too. *Faith and Hope Church, right? Your dad is the pastor?*

Yes, I'm ... the pastor's daughter ... yes, my name is Lena.

Her face relaxes, her voice softens. *LaToya,* she says. *Your dad is a good man. He's worked with us so many times to support families in crisis.*

Yes, um, our church ... there's a program for foster families.

LaToya puts her formal voice back on and starts asking me questions. She takes notes as I talk, which makes me more nervous. I keep checking my phone to see if anyone has called to let me know I can see Aaliyah. Nothing.

LaToya asks if there have been any signs of depression, if I believe Aaliyah would intentionally hurt herself.

No ... not Aaliyah ... She ... I ... I don't think she ... No ... No.

Maybe I should stop there. She asked a yes-or-no question. But I keep talking, tell her all of it. I tell her what's been happening at school, and what happened on

Halloween, and I explain to her our nightly routine of beauty and strong pills.

LaToya's face is stone. Not in a cold way, but in a neutral way. I can't tell if she believes me, if she's judging me.

I—I wasn't home, so I don't know, but I just don't think Aaliyah would intentionally harm herself…I just…I know my child. I know my child.

LaToya jots down notes.

I know my child…

I know my child.

more questions

LaToya speaks to Bryan, then Honey, then Dad.
I want to know what she's asking them.
What they're telling her.
I want to know if she's blaming me,
if they're blaming me.
I want to know
if this is all my fault.
Is this all my fault?

advocate

LaToya asks to speak to Dad again.

After he's gone for an hour, I say out loud, *What is taking her so long? What does she want with him?*

And then another half hour passes. *Should I go check on him?*

Aunt Aretha takes my hand, says, *He knows what he's doing. He's not only your father right now, he's in there being your pastor.*

twelve hours

...nothing has changed...
She's not better or worse...
...we've got the best of the best
taking care of her...She's in good hands...

meditation

The nurse brings us snacks and drinks: water, juice boxes, crackers, cookies. *Help yourself*, she says. There's more in the hospitality room down the hall.

I can't eat anything, but I drink water. *I'll be back. I have my phone with me*, I announce to the room. *I—I just need to get out of this room for a minute. I need to walk.* I step into the hallway, and as soon as I get to the other end, an avalanche of anxiety comes out of me. I can't stop crying, and I can't catch my breath.

I didn't realize anyone had come with me until Malcolm says, *Breathe, just breathe.* He puts his hand on my shoulder. *Breathe, Lena. Focus on your breath.* He walks me over to an open waiting area. We sit, and he doesn't accuse me of not taking care of my daughter, doesn't look at me with disappointment, doesn't judge me at all, he just holds my hand, takes deep breaths with me.

In, out.

In, out.

In, out.

In, out.

In, out.

In, out.

twenty-four hours

Doctor says, *The internal bleeding has stopped...*
but her heartbeat is still irregular...

still waiting

The doctor tells us, *She's still in the ICU, but we'll allow one visitor at a time...*

I stand, walk toward the door.

Not you, ma'am... The social worker is still investigating... you can't go in yet...

My heart collapses. Aspen and Kendra hold me up.

Honey goes instead.

heartbeat

I say it all the time. Aaliyah is my heartbeat. My literal heart living and breathing outside of my body.

I hold my hands to my chest, steady my breath, feel my chest go up and down. Pray her heartbeat syncs with mine.

God, please.

God, please.

God, please.

hauntings

If I have to bury my daughter
I will dress her in white.
And white lilies will drape her white casket.
Already, at eight years old, her obituary
will tell of a life well lived and tell how
creative and funny and smart and inquisitive
and generous and loving she was...
was...is.
I do not want to talk about my daughter
in the past tense. Ever.
I stop myself.
Tell myself, *Don't let your mind go there.*
Come back to yourself, stay here, in this room.
Your daughter needs you praying
and willing her to pull through. Come back
to yourself, stay in this moment.
Breathe.
In, out.
In, out.
In, out.
In.

thirty-six hours

Aaliyah is stable is what the doctor says.
Honey wails, a deep bellowing cry,
drowning out the rest of his words.
...keeping her for observation...
psychologist... evaluation...
...She's going to be okay...
She's going to be okay...

holding on

Finally, they let me see her.

Looking at my baby girl in this bed with tubes and monitors and noisy machines breaks me. She is sedated, not in a coma but not fully alert. I take her hand. *I'm here, baby girl. Mommy is here.*

forty-eight hours

The psychologist has been talking with Aaliyah all morning. And then the social worker meets with her. I haven't slept. Maybe I've eaten. I've definitely had water, coffee. Each hour the fog gets thicker and thicker, the disbelief that this has happened, is happening. Exhaustion and relief and fear all tangled up inside.

When they are finished with Aaliyah, they take me and Bryan into a private room. The psychologist speaks first.

I believe this was an accidental overdose, the psychologist says. *Your daughter expressed that she thought the pills were beauty pills. I don't think she was trying to hurt herself at all . . .*

She took the pills because she wanted to be beautiful.

blame

All of this because she wanted to be beautiful? Who is telling that child she's not beautiful? Honey is crying and yelling, and I feel like I am fifteen again, sneaking back in from seeing Bryan past curfew, being lectured for being a bad daughter—and now a bad mom, a bad everything.

If you can't take care of that child, then she needs to live with me, Honey says.

Dad shakes his head. *Let's not make any rash decisions.*

I'm serious, Lena. She could have died. And who's to say she wasn't trying to ... to ... Oh, I just can't even fathom it. If I had not found her in time. Oh, God. Oh ...

Dad, always the voice of reason says, *The psychologist isn't concerned about Aaliyah being suicidal or depressed—*

But how can she be sure? Honey asks. *Is she sure?*

Honey walks around the room, occasionally stopping at the window, watching Portland's rain waltz to the ground. *From the day Aaliyah was born, I have been on you and Bryan to get yourselves together and—*

Not now, Dad says. *Now is not the time.*

Well, when is the time? That baby could have died, and why in the world are you taking diet pills, Lena? I need some answers. What is going on? Answer me, Lena. How could you let this happen?

I let this happen? Mom, nothing you can say to me will make me feel worse than I already do. Yes, I should have made sure she couldn't get to the pills so easily, and I shouldn't have taken them in front of her or called them beauty pills, but maybe she wouldn't feel so bad about herself if you'd stop giving her whatever she wanted, whenever she wanted, making her gain all that weight.

You cannot be blaming me. This is not my fault.

I'm trying to get Aaliyah to be mindful regarding food. I'm trying to teach her how to eat healthy, and you are not helping.

Lena, I just…Your child almost died because she took pills thinking they'd make her beautiful and the first person you attack is your own mother instead of looking at yourself and asking what you could have done to prevent this.

Dad plays referee, tries to get Honey to sit down next to him. She refuses. She walks over to the door instead. *You are not the daughter I raised.*

No, that's the problem, Mom. I am exactly who you raised. You never taught me about taking care of myself. No boundaries at all with food. Well, that wasn't helpful. I'm trying to be a better mother to Aaliyah than you were to me.

Dad yells at me (and he never yells at anyone). *Alright now, Lena! That's enough. That's enough from both of you.*

what honey says

You *think I didn't notice that year after year your size went up and up when we'd go shopping? I didn't ignore that. I chose to affirm you. I knew there would be enough people pointing out every pound, commenting on your weight. I knew you'd have a lifetime of diets and exercise if you wanted to do that. I knew you could learn that on your own.*

But loving yourself? I taught you that. That took priority. I made sure you were clean, that your hair was done, that your clothes were cute—and fit just right. And what did I say to you every single morning? Huh? What did I say?

I said, "Good morning, beautiful." From the time you were a day old till the day you moved out of my house for college, I woke you up by saying "Good morning, beautiful." Because you are beautiful. And I wanted you to know it, to hear it first from me. I wanted those words to be so embedded in you that you would never, ever doubt it, no matter what or who told you otherwise.

I was not a perfect mother, Lena. I didn't know anything about these fat body movements or whatever you call it, and I didn't have blogs to read because there were no blogs and there were no support groups for mothers with overweight daughters so I am sure I could have done some things differently. But I loved you. I loved you well. That ought to count for something.

silence

No one speaks for the next few hours. We take turns, one at a time, going in and out of Aaliyah's room.

Praying, praying.

mercy

Before I can take Aaliyah home, I have to sign and commit to her care plan.

I promise to get Aaliyah counseling, promise to put all medicine out of reach.

LaToya tells me, *If it weren't for your father being such a well-respected pastor and a proven child advocate, child protection services might've taken Aaliyah away from you.*

Thank God he was able to talk to the social worker, thank God his reputation spoke louder than anything either of us could have said.

Thank God. Thank God. Thank God. Thank God. Thank God. Thank God. Thank God. Thank God.

mandatory

As in required by a law or rule.
As in essential, vital.
In other words:
you have to, you need to.
As in *This is the only way*
to keep your daughter.

therapy, mandatory

Prayer can't fix this.
No anointing oil, no laying on of hands.
Not by itself. Not instead of.
LaToya says, *You and Aaliyah will go together.*
Says, *Don't waste this.*
Says, *Take advantage of the resources you have.*
Tells me, *Everyone doesn't get second chances.*

inheritance

My daughter is broken, and I want to fix her. My daughter is broken, and I want to fix her, but I can't fix her because I am broken too.

I don't know which is harder,
being a Black girl
or raising a Black girl.

Motherhood brings me the most pride and most fear. I am afraid that when Aaliyah grows up, she will spend all her adult days undoing the damage of her childhood. I am afraid that the worst parts of me is all I've given her.

knowing

What I know is that when Aaliyah was born, she was embraced and loved well and cherished. She was held and fed and sung to by all of us—her grandparents, Aunt Aretha, Aspen, Kendra. Me.

At night, I prayed over her, asked God to help me raise her to be a good person, to fulfill whatever purpose she was put on the earth to fulfill. Asked him to give me wisdom. Because sometimes I felt so unsure how to mother. I read all the books on what to expect during pregnancy and what the first few months would be like. And I loved it all. I loved feeling her kick, loved updating Aspen and Kendra after an appointment, *This week she's the size of a pear...a grapefruit...a coconut...a watermelon.* I loved breastfeeding, felt powerful knowing that my body held everything she needed to stay alive.

I knew how to keep her alive.

And she kept growing, and I sent her out into the world, and a classmate bullied her, and a teacher dismissed her, and commercials made it clear that beauty has a size, a hair texture, a skin tone.

And me.

I taught her that too.

And I don't know how to undo what I've done.

Don't know how to keep her spirit alive.

monday

It's our first day home from the hospital. Bryan is here, watching Aaliyah while I take the quickest shower because I am afraid to leave Aaliyah alone. I know she said she wanted to live, but I want to make sure. Want someone's eyes on her at all times. As the water rinses the soap from my body, I let it wash away my tears too.

tuesday

Honey brings us lunch
and flowers and handwritten scriptures
on index cards about peace
and healing and wisdom.
Pray these over her at night while she's sleeping.
Pray them over yourself too.

wednesday

Malcolm sends flowers and a text message with a link
to a playlist.
The first five songs are some of Aaliyah's favorites
and the rest are empowering tunes,
songs by women, about women
who love their bodies,
who use their voices,
who are unashamed
to be exactly who they are.
Aaliyah and I play the music loud and sing along,
let the anthems speak for us until the words take root.

thursday

Aspen takes the day off from work, comes over and spends the day with me and Aaliyah. We watch movies, play board games, paint our nails, eat takeout, and when Aspen notices that I need a break, need a good cry, a short nap, she tells me to go to my room, says, *I'll watch her. I got her. I got you.*

friday

The doorbell rings, and I figure it's Honey, who said she was on her way. When I get to the door, I see Kendra standing there holding a rectangular dish covered in foil. I open the door, stand there.

A peach cobbler. My mom's recipe. Kendra hands me the dessert. Her eyes heavy and tired, like maybe she has been crying. Her face is bare of makeup and her hair is pulled back in a bun. I don't think I've ever seen Kendra look so regular.

I am waiting for her to say more. But she just stands there. She steps forward as if she's going to come inside. I don't move.

Thank you for the cobbler. I'm not feeling up for company right now. She knows it's not true. Aspen's car is parked out front.

Lena, let's talk—

Not right now, Kendra. I have a daughter to tend to. I don't have the capacity for this. You come over here with a dessert and think all is forgiven? No. It doesn't work like that.

Well, then, let's talk. That's—that's why I'm here.

And that's the problem. My daughter almost died, and you've come over to talk about our friendship. Our friendship is the last thing on my mind—

We have four decades of friendship.

And that's exactly why you should've known better. Actually, no, you knew better. You just chose yourself, like you always do.

Really, Lena? I always choose myself? I've never been a good friend to you?

I'm not doing this right now, Kendra. I step back into the house, close the screen door. *Thank you for the cobbler,* I say.

Kendra doesn't move.

I close the door.

therapy

We're in our first therapy session, and right away, I can tell that Aaliyah likes our therapist, Janice. She is maybe sixty. Her salt-and-pepper hair is glorious. Her nails are manicured and polished clear, her navy pantsuit is just stylish enough to be more than conservative but nothing too trendy. She is thin and White, and I wasn't sure if she'd understand our situation, if she'd be able to help us the way we need. But the way Aaliyah warms up to her makes my reservations dissolve. Aaliyah is usually quiet when she's not feeling someone, but today she's talkative and is answering all of Janice's questions without hesitation.

Janice's questions evoke positive answers, and I know she must have a reason for this, but honestly, I thought therapy would be more emotional than this. She must realize I am having second thoughts about this session. She offers a knowing smile and says, *I just have a few more baseline questions and in our next session we will go a little deeper, okay?*

I nod.

Janice says to Aaliyah, *Tell me about your best friend.*

Her name is Paige and we're in the same class and she likes the same music as me and we always laugh at the same thing, even if nobody else thinks it's funny.

What's your favorite subject at school?

I like math the most. And I'm really good at spelling too. My teacher says I should compete in the National Spelling Bee next year.

skin & bones

Well, that's wonderful, Janice says. And then, *Thank you for sharing, Aaliyah. Just one more question and we'll be finished for today. If you could wave a magic wand, what would you change?*

Aaliyah hesitates, and I don't think it's because she doesn't know her answer, I think she's not sure if she should say it out loud. She looks at me, then down at the floor. *Can you repeat the question?* she asks.

Sure. Janice sits up in her chair, crosses her legs, softens her voice. *If you could wave a magic wand, what would you change?*

Aaliyah's voice is barely a whisper. *Me.*

a cleansing

Bryan has been spending the night. Wants to be close to Aaliyah. Wants to support me.

Wants to be here. He sleeps on the sofa, never comes into my room.

Except for tonight.

He is standing at the door, looking at me with desolate eyes. He leans into me, and for a moment I think he is going to kiss me, but instead he collapses into my arms, sobbing.

He has lost his mother, could have lost his daughter.

I hold him, close the door with my foot, hoping Aaliyah doesn't hear her weeping father.

We sit on my bed, his head on my lap.

And now I am breaking, too, and no matter how many deep breaths I try to take, I cannot calm down.

We trade off all night. Crying and holding each other. Crying and holding each other.

between night and morning

We fall asleep, and when I wake up, I can't remember the last thing we said. But here we are, locked in the cuddle our bodies know so well. I sit up, trying not to wake him, but he feels me move, pulls me to him like I am his safety blanket.

And then we kiss. But this kiss feels different. It is a soliloquy. So passionate, so intense, but only for him. He does not force me, but he doesn't caress me, either. Feels like he is releasing all that's been bottled up and I am just here to receive.

Soon, our lips are trembling again. Tears and saliva and fears and grief all releasing, releasing.

It hurts.

It feels good.

I want to stop.

I want more.

I let myself stop overthinking, stop analyzing. Sometimes you just need to be held, to be touched, to be in a familiar place when every single thing around you is foreign territory.

hypocrite?

We do just enough for it not to be sex. An old-fashioned make-out session like the ones we used to have when we were teenagers, before we finally went all the way. He would have, he tried, but I stopped him. Sex with Bryan is not really what I want. And if I let myself see this situation for what it really is, sex with me is not really what he needs.

All these emotions, bottled up.

All these feelings, misplaced.

I wash Bryan's essence off me, let the water cleanse me. And then the question hits me in my gut: *If you get back with Malcolm, are you going to tell him about any of this?*

hope, still

Malcolm is coming over today. Aaliyah has been asking for a Scrabble rematch.

When I open the door, a wave of emotion washes over me. He could be coming over to help me plan a funeral.

Aaliyah comes downstairs, and when she sees him, she runs to hug him.

Hey, baby girl. You ready for a rematch? I've got some words I been waiting to try out on you.

I keep telling you that's why you always lose. You do too much planning. You just have to figure it out as you play. Aaliyah laughs. She runs over to the closet in the hallway, takes out Scrabble, sets it up on the dining room table. *I'll let you go first this time,* she says.

How I only get vowels? Malcolm says. *What am I supposed to do with this?*

Aaliyah is so tickled.

See, you rigged the game. Just like last time. I'm bringing my own Scrabble the next time we play.

Aaliyah laughs harder.

I gotta pass, Malcolm says. *I can't do nothing with this.* He exchanges a few tiles.

Aaliyah shakes her head. Puts her word on the board, counts her score. *That's eight, and because it's a double word, it's sixteen. I'm gonna win,* she says. *I'm gonna win.*

healing

Honey is here. Without Dad. It's the first time she's come over without him since Aaliyah has been out of the hospital. He's been a buffer, a boundary neither of us cross. She mostly goes straight to Aaliyah's room when she gets here, but today, she says, *Can we talk?*

I sit down at the dining room table for some reason instead of the sofa in the living room. Maybe because I still need something between us. We sit across from each other. I lean against the table, let it hold me up.

I'm sorry, Honey says.

It is the first time she's ever apologized to me. I mean, she's said sorry in the way that you say *Oops* or apologize for something you didn't do, like *I'm sorry that happened to you.* But I don't remember her ever owning her part in hurting my feelings.

I shouldn't have said anything to you that night at the hospital. The only thing I should have asked is, How can I help, what do you need? I should have just been there for you and Aaliyah.

Thank you for saying that—

I mean, there's plenty of time to talk about where things went wrong and what needs to happen next. Honey stands up from the table, goes over to the kitchen, and puts water into the teapot.

I take a deep breath, say, *I'm not... I'm not sure we need to talk about what went wrong. I just, I'm focusing on her healing and on making sure she—*

skin & bones

Well, in order for there to be healing, you have to process the pain, assess what happened. You can't just move on from this without addressing—

Mom!

The last time I yelled at my mother I was sixteen and didn't realize that she believed that *Spare the rod, spoil the child* applied to teenagers. She slapped me. And I never disrespected her again, not in that way. I usually walk away when I feel heat rising in my chest, usually say, can we talk about this later? But I don't have any decorum to give. *Aaliyah is my daughter*, I tell her. Emphasis on *my. I got this.*

You do not have this. You do not. And that's okay, Lena. You can ask for help, you have a family, you have friends. What do you need? How can we—

I don't know. I don't know what I need. I don't know what I want. I don't know how things got so . . . I just. I don't know. I am crying now. Again. The kind of cry that mixes snot and tears and shakes your insides at the core.

The teakettle cries with me. Howling and screaming. Honey turns the stove off, doesn't even pour her tea. *Lena, sweetheart, I don't know either. I didn't know how to be a mother to you when you were younger, and I sure don't know how now. Motherhood is figuring it out as you go, doing your best, forgiving yourself and your child. There's just no way to have all the answers. I knew I would never be perfect at mothering, but I vowed I'd get as good at it as I could. That's all I could do. That's all you can do. Your best. So the question is, Are you doing your best for Aaliyah? And if not, well, let's figure out how to get better. And I am asking myself if I am doing my best for you. Me coming here today is me trying.*

I am still a heaving mess of tears. It's all just too much. Too much fear, too much doubt, too much guilt, too much frustration, too much disappointment, too much anger, too much anxiety, too much love.

My love for Aaliyah is overwhelming, all consuming.

And Honey telling me this, it means she knows this feeling, means she must've spent countless nights crying and praying about how to take care of me. I am overwhelmed by that too. Honey's love. Her love that has been given to me the best way she knew how.

Honey comes over to me, wraps me in her arms. Says, *Let it out. Let it all out.* And she cries with me.

lessons my mother taught me

Honey never backed down. Never. Not when I was eight years old and we were out shopping for Easter dresses and the White woman stepped in front of her at Meir & Frank, acting like she was in line before us. She didn't back down at church when the auxiliary board told her she needed to be more pastor's wife and less independent woman. She spoke up, always.

Honey never left the house looking unkept.

I watched Honey cook and clean and wife and teach and friend and daughter and sister and mother. She did it all, balanced her many roles and responsibilities and never complained.

I watched Honey give her money, her time, her husband, to the church. Volunteering, coming early, staying late, raising other people's children, answering the phone all hours of the night to be a comfort in someone's crisis. Being a pastor's wife is a full-time job, around the clock, never-ending.

All the while having questions and doubts. All the while having her own insecurities.

All the while raising me.

how we heal

The next time Honey comes over, she brings Aunt Aretha with her. She called earlier and asked me what I was doing today. When I told her nothing, that Bryan's sister took Aaliyah to the movies, wanted to spend time with her niece and give me a break, she said, *We're coming over. We'll keep you company.* Everyone keeps checking on me, keeps stopping by, calling. I appreciate the concern and for the first time in my life, I accept all the love and care and don't push people away or feel bad for being so fragile.

Honey and Aunt Aretha are in the kitchen making tea and going through my cabinets looking for something sweet. The doorbell rings and when I answer it, Aspen is standing there with a box of my favorite shortbread cookies. *I can either drop these off or stay,* she says.

Might as well come in, join the party. When she comes inside, she is greeted with hugs and kisses from Honey and Aunt Aretha, who are happy to see her but even more thrilled that she comes bearing gifts. They plate the cookies, pour tea, and we go into the living room. Aspen sits down on the sofa, props herself against the charcoal gray throw pillow. *How are you today?*

That's a loaded question, I tell her.

Right. Sorry—I—

It's okay. It's a valid question, just loaded. I'm, uh, I'm here. I sit next to Aspen. *I'm here.*

Aunt Aretha who has never been one to avoid what

needs to be dealt with says, *You feel like talking about Aaliyah or no?*

I appreciate her asking, but I already know what tonight's agenda is. I knew when Honey called that they were not just coming to hang out. This is a check-in.

We can talk, I guess, I say. *I don't, I don't know what to say.*

How's therapy going? Do you feel like it's helping? Aunt Aretha asks.

We've only had one session. Aaliyah seems to like our therapist.

Honey sips her tea, says, *And Aaliyah is still saying it was an accident? She wasn't trying to . . . she didn't intend to hurt herself?*

Yes.

Do you believe her? Aspen asks.

I do. I say the words firm, without hesitation.

Honey asks, *How do you know?*

Because she's like me—I was the same way. Am the same way.

They all look at me, waiting for me to say more.

I didn't grow up with low self-esteem. I'm not saying there aren't people who truly struggle with low self-esteem. I'm just saying I wasn't one of them. I didn't hate my body. Mom, you are right in that you nurtured me and made me feel worthy of love, made me see my beauty. It wasn't until I went out into the world and realized that you were telling me something different at home than what was being told to me when I was away from you. Commercials, passive-aggressive compliments, outright insults—there were all kinds of messages coming at me that were completely opposite of what you were teaching me.

Honey nods like she gets what I'm saying.

Aspen is not so sure. *So you never struggled with low self-esteem?*

Not really—I mean, sure, in my teen years I had those days of looking in the mirror and bemoaning the pimples that had popped up overnight, and I had my fair share of bad hair days or clothes that I wished fit differently. But I think there's a difference between a person having a bad hair day and a person wishing they had different hair. You see what I mean? I just—I didn't start feeling the need to change myself or think of myself as less than until I met a world that told me that who I was and how I looked was not good enough.

I see what you're saying, Aspen says. *Low self-esteem wasn't innately in you—*

Right. It was something that seeped through, something that day after day tried to penetrate the fortress of love and affirmations Honey and Dad had built around me.

Honey looks relieved when I say this. Like she needed me to remember that she tried, how hard she tried. Aunt Aretha sips her tea, perks her lips as if it's too bitter and adds honey. *I keep thinking about the things girls do to be beautiful. That's what gets me. Not only that Aaliyah didn't think she was beautiful but what she was willing to do to become beautiful. Wanted it so bad that she took a whole bottle of pills thinking she could make it happen overnight. And no matter what we've told her about how beautiful she is, still, she sees herself as lacking. Aaliyah has a chorus of women loving her, raising her, nurturing her. And still. Still the voices outside of this circle are louder, stronger.*

Honey goes into the kitchen and returns with more shortbread cookies. *No matter what we as mothers do to love and protect our daughters, there's no saving them from heartbreak.*

skin & bones

So then the question is, how do we heal? Aspen's words hang in the room. Aunt Aretha doesn't answer, Honey doesn't say a word. The silence is not awkward or uncomfortable, instead it is soothing. The kind of silence that doesn't need to be filled with words or noise. The kind of silence that gives us permission to sit and ponder.

The question lingers, unanswered.

How do we heal?

And after more than a moment, after more tea, after more talking, after the tears dry up, after eating the rest of the shortbread cookies, after washing the mugs and plates, after wiping down the counter, after hugs, and just before saying goodbye, Aunt Aretha says, *Ain't this how? Ain't this how?*

beauty's only skin deep

Janice begins today's session saying, *Aaliyah, today, I'd like to talk about the self-portrait you made at school.*

You've seen my self-portrait? Aaliyah asks.

Your mom brought it to me and I thought we could talk about it. Janice slides the thin paper out of her folder and sets it on the coffee table.

Aaliyah looks at me like I betrayed her. *Why do we have to talk about it?*

Well, I wanted us to think about the artistic choices you made. You sure are a good artist. I noticed how you even designed the background with all these lovely flowers. What does that represent?

My teacher told us our self-portraits should show who we are and who we want to be. Some of my friends drew themselves as doctors or firemen. My friend Paige drew herself singing—because she's really, really good at singing and wants to be a famous singer one day—her background is a stage with big lights shining down on her. I filled in all the blank space with flowers and plants because I love working in Honey's garden and I always want to be around beautiful things.

I love that, Janice says. *I can see you put a lot of thought into the background. And what about the person in the middle of the page?*

Aaliyah looks at her artwork, then at me, then at Janice. She fidgets with her hands, says, *That's me. Well, not me right now but it's how I want to look one day and since my teacher said we could draw something that represents who we want to be, I drew her.* Aaliyah looks at me, then at Janice. *Am I in trouble?* she asks.

Janice looks at me, and with her eyes she signals that I need to adjust my body language. Calm down. I can feel myself tearing up. I bite the inside of my lip, press down on my right leg to keep it from shaking.

You're not in trouble at all, Janice says. *I notice you said you drew who you want to be. Let's talk about that.*

I shift in my seat, try to breathe deeply.

What do you want me to tell you? Aaliyah asks.

I jump in. *This doesn't look like you at all, Aaliyah. Why did you—*

Janice cuts me off. *We're just curious about what you drew. Is there a reason why the person on the page doesn't look like you?*

Aaliyah shrugs. *I already told you. I wanted to draw myself as beautiful. And—*

But you are beautiful, Aaliyah. Just as you are. I can't help myself from cutting her off. Janice doesn't stop me. *I tell you that all the time.*

But you don't really believe that, Mommy.

Yes, I do, sweetheart. Your curly hair, your brown skin, your—

None of it is beautiful! Stop lying to me! Aaliyah's eyes are filling with tears. I reach out for her but she pulls away. *You always lie to me.* Aaliyah is yelling and crying and she won't let me console her. She scoots to the other end of the sofa, buries her face in her hands and sobs. *Why do you always lie to me?*

Why are you saying that, sweetheart?

Because you always tell me that I'm beautiful just the way I am but I know you really want me to lose weight... and the things you tell me are the most beautiful about me are things I get teased about at school... and,

and . . . and you take beauty pills every night so doesn't that mean you don't think you're beautiful? And if I look just like you, doesn't that mean you don't think I'm beautiful?

I can't do anything but let my tears run free. I have asked myself over and over again, what could I have done differently? Why doesn't Aaliyah believe me. I tell her every day that she is beautiful, that she is brilliant, that she is a bright light. Aaliyah opening up today in our session makes me remember all the platitudes about actions speaking louder than words. The way I come undone when I realize she's not just listening, she's watching. And she believes everything I've shown her.

Janice looks at me, says, *I think this is a good time to explain to Aaliyah what those pills are.*

I sit closer to Aaliyah, rub her back, hold her in my arms. *Sweetheart, those aren't beauty pills. There's actually no such thing. Those are pills that help Mommy not be so hungry all the time, they help me regulate my appetite—*

So you can lose weight?

So I can be healthy.

You can't be healthy unless you lose weight? Do you have to be skinny to be healthy?

I look at Janice. How do I answer that? Janice just nods, as if to say, You know what to say.

You can be healthy at any size, yes. And you can be any size and be beautiful, yes. Sometimes I conflate the two. It's—it's complicated for me—how big a person is and if they're beautiful and how big a person is and if they're healthy gets all tangled up for me sometimes because of the lessons I've learned about beauty, about health, about food.

I look at Janice, she nods, encouraging me to say more.

But—I'm, I'm working on that. I'm growing and learning still, Aaliyah. I . . . I'm sorry. I should've never called them beauty pills. I should've never taken them in front of you—I'm sorry. I give you mixed messages a lot and I'm— I'm sorry.

I wonder what Grandma would think of me apologizing, of explaining this to my daughter. She was old school and in her mind, any questions from children were signs of defiance. *Because I said so* was often her answer. Or *That ain't for you to know.* I don't want to be at either extreme, saying nothing at all or over-explaining and having kumbaya moments with Aaliyah like we're living in a happily ever after sitcom. But I do want to be human with her, want to communicate openly with her and apologize when I get it wrong. I needed that from Grandma and Honey. I think Aaliyah needs that from me.

Janice says, *I'd like for us to think of new ways to define beauty. Do you understand what I mean by that?*

Kind of, Aaliyah says.

Let me rephrase that—what if there are many ways to be beautiful? Your hair texture and other hair textures, your body size and other sizes…can it all be beautiful? Janice asks. *We keep using the word beautiful. I'd like us to also think about words like original, unique, one-of-a-kind. What do you think about using those words to describe yourself?*

I like those words, Aaliyah says.

And let's think about all the ways a person can be beautiful, all the ways humans are unique and one-of-a-kind. Can it be more than what a person looks like?

Yes, Aaliyah says. *It can be—but not everyone believes that.*

But that's okay, Aaliyah. You have to believe it, I tell her. *This world—your classmates, your teachers, random people walking past you on the street when you're just minding your business—they might not believe that. But you can't let that change what you think of yourself. Baby girl, this world is not made for you, so you have to make the world you want. You've got to carve out space for yourself, define what beauty is for yourself and hold on to your own definition when this world tries to tell you otherwise. And I wish I could tell you the first time you do it will be the last time. But this is something you will always have to do. Define and redefine yourself. Make and remake your world.*

I look over at Janice, thinking maybe she is going to chime in. But she is just sitting back in her chair, just nodding, encouraging me to go on.

Aaliyah says, *I know how beautiful I am on the inside! I'm smart, I'm kind, I'm creative. Mom tells me all the time that all those things make me beautiful. And when I look in the mirror, I see beauty. I like that my hair is fluffy and that my skin is brown like Honey's and Mom's, but sometimes people at school tease me and I know that even though everyone in my family knows I'm special, not everyone else sees it. And that makes me sad,* she says. *Sometimes I don't know who's right. Don't know who to believe.*

what i tell aaliyah

Before I go to bed, I write Aaliyah a letter. I want what we talked about with Janice to be more than words said. Want her to have a tangible reminder to hold on to. I don't know when I'll give it to her. But I know one day she'll need these words.

Dear Aaliyah,

Believe the women who are still able to laugh, even after loss and famine and drought and heartbreak. Trust the ones who know how to nurse a wound, who know something about the time it takes for hurting to heal.

Believe me when I say, you have to hold on tight to yourself. Keep your mind anchored to what you know to be true. The anchor is me, is Honey, is Aunt Aretha, is every Black woman who came before you and survived. They are holding you too. Their know-how, their not-gon'-let-nobody-turn-us-'round. Their loudness, their pride.

Believe those voices above all other voices.

Believe that it's not your responsibility to make anyone see your worth. You just be every bit of brilliance and beauty you are. Just because they don't believe you, don't mean it's not true.

brown skin

Skin as in epidermis, as in cuticle, as in integument. As in protective layer, as in tough and fragile all at once. Skin as in barrier, protecting the body from harm. Skin as in outer shell, as in keeper of the soul, keeper of beauty. Skin, deep.

Skin as in complexion, as in tone and pigmentation, as in dark or light or fair. As in Black folk's skin always being compared to food, something to consume: chocolate, mocha, coffee, caramel. Skin, tasty. Sweet and salty like kettle corn. Skin, black. Like a kettle, like smoke. Skin like ash, like dust. Skin as in transformative, restorative. Skin blemished, skin aged, skin bruised, skin scarred, skin healed.

elephants in the room

Aspen and I are shopping at Saturday Market, not looking for anything specific, just browsing, just catching up. *You talk to Kendra? She asked about you.*

We text here and there. She checks on Aaliyah.

Are you planning to talk to her for real—like an actual conversation?

Not now. I just—there's already so much I'm dealing with. And weren't you the one who was all mad at her and telling her how she is not a true friend? Now you want us to have a kumbaya circle?

Aspen says, *I think you two should talk. I wasn't trying to break up your friendship—our friendship—I just wanted everything out in the open. That's all. We always work through things. I thought this would be like every other time.*

I think I'm done working through things with friends. Like, it's too much work to keep having these heart-to-heart conversations, and nothing really changes. Friendship should not drain you. Loving Kendra shouldn't be so exhausting.

Aspen is not nodding or moaning *hmm-hmm*, like she does when she agrees with me. She stops at a vendor's booth and looks through the handmade jewelry, trying on rings.

What? You disagree?

I think love is always worth fighting for. Even platonic love. We've known each other our whole lives. That's a lifetime of love to throw away. I'm not saying stay in every relationship at all costs. I mean, obviously set boundaries and all, but also, extend grace. There's gotta be a balance, or else we're all going to be living isolated lives 'cause none of us are perfect, Aspen says.

She smiles at the vendor, and we go to the next booth and look through tote bags with quotes about feminism. *I mean, you know I have my issues with Kendra. But I love that girl, and that's why I'm always pointing things out—and she does the same to me. We love each other enough to tell the truth and to ask for what we need.*

Just when I think she's finished, she has more to say. It's like she's been holding all of this in, waiting for a chance for us to talk.

Lena—you are like family to me. For real. So trust me when I say I am telling you this in love. Ever since Bryan, you've become really good at walking away without any conversation. Just ending everything without trying to even see if there's a chance for things to be better. With Bryan, you were at the other extreme, holding on to him at all costs—you gave him a million and one chances. And I'm glad you realized that wasn't healthy, but that doesn't mean everyone else has to be at arm's length like Bryan.

What would it be like if you weren't at either extreme, but somewhere in the middle? Sure, you can heal on your own. But what could it be like to love someone and be hurt by them and heal together?

I know she is telling the truth, so I don't even try to defend myself or make excuses. I am good at walking away and letting relationships end with an ellipsis. Always there are words left unsaid. *I have a feeling you're not just talking about Kendra,* I say. *This is about Malcolm too?*

Aspen gives me a knowing look, says, *Don't let pride or fear keep you from love. You do love Malcolm, don't you?*

Yes, but—

skin & bones

Are you still considering Bryan? This is the first time Aspen has brought him up. She hasn't said anything, even though I showed up at the hospital with him, even though she knows he's spent the night.

We're not—I thought about it, but no—

Because you love Malcolm.

I do, I tell her. *I just don't know if I should. I want to be a good example to Aaliyah. Want her to know she can walk away when someone disrespects her. That marriage shouldn't come at the cost of self-love.*

I hear you, Aspen says. *And you can teach her that, for sure. You can also teach her what forgiveness looks like. You can also show her that love is hard work. That true love—real love—is not only romance and good vibes. You can show her that it takes strength and wisdom to know who to give that energy to.* Aspen stops at a booth with ceramic housewares, looks at the teapots. *But what do I know? Girl, I'm over here still trying to decipher Travis's codes. I'm going on these dates, but I still want there to be more between us. I was seriously replaying the hug he gave me last night over and over in my head, trying to figure out if he held on longer than usual and what it means. So, clearly I do not have all the answers.*

Why is it like this? We always know what to tell someone else. Never got advice for ourselves.

essence

When we arrive at our counseling session, Aaliyah's eyes light up when she sees the art supplies sitting on the table in the middle of the room.

We are going to make another self-portrait, Janice says. *And, Lena, I'd like you to make one too.* She hands each of us a big sheet of paper that has the silhouette of a human heart muscle. Janice tells us, *We say we carry what we love and hold dear in our hearts. I want you to fill this heart up with the things that matter most. Focus on what people can't see, the beauty that's inside. You can write words or draw symbols that describe your talents, your personality, your dreams. You can include the people you love and who love you back. I want the essence of who you are to be the focus, not what you look like.* Janice puts on instrumental music and we start making our portraits.

At first, I am just doing the artmaking activity to be in solidarity with Aaliyah. I can't remember the last time I had colored pencils and crayons and oil pastels at my fingertips. I begin with Aaliyah's name, right at the center, and by the time Janice lowers the music, I have filled every inch of the paper up, not realizing how much time has passed, not realizing how much this activity was not only for Aaliyah, but for me.

I really like yours, Momma.

I like yours too. I think we should frame them, hang them up at home as reminders of all we are, of all we carry.

joy to the world

Everything still feels heavy. My body, my spirit, my love. The smell of evergreen is in the air, and pine too. And holiday songs are serenading me in every store I go into. We even got a dusting of snow a few days ago. And still. Still, it doesn't feel like Christmas.

But Aaliyah is laughing today.

A real laugh.

A belly laugh.

Remember the time your phone rang in church and interrupted the service? she asks. She tells the story to me, saying, *Grandaddy was preaching and all of a sudden Beyoncé was singing.*

So embarrassing, I say. It wasn't one of her Black power songs or heal-the-world songs. This was one of her booty-shaking, drop-it-low songs.

You changed your ringtone after that, Aaliyah reminds me.

Been keeping it simple ever since. Good old-fashioned telephone ring, I say.

And Honey? The look on her face when she realized it was coming from your phone. Aaliyah is an avalanche of laughter.

I am laughing too. Thankful she has some good memories of me, of us.

january 1

No mantras about self-love.
No dieting gimmicks.
Just want to live free.
Just want to be better
at everything: mothering, careering, daughtering, dating, friending, forgiving, healing, resting, celebrating, rejoicing, hoping, dreaming, loving.
Just want to be me.

spotlight

I pull into the parking lot at work the same time as Allie. The sky is barely day, and already Allie is chipper and full of energy. She is waving and smiling and rushing out of her car so we can walk in together.

Oh my goodness. I am so excited about today, she says. Her car door slams, the alarm chirps.

Today is going to be a good day. I feel it. I do. It's not every day the press comes to profile one of our very own. Are you ready?

I'm ready, I say. I am excited but also nervous. Not about what I'll say in the interview, but about what I'm wearing. I miss Kendra—for many reasons—but right now, I miss that we didn't go shopping together to find something for my TV debut. I miss her okaying my hair and makeup, miss her telling me, *You got this, you got this.*

taking up space

The press is here. A feature is being done on Portland: Black. The reporter asks Allie the first question. Allie says, *I appreciate you asking me that question, but I'd like Lena to speak first. None of us need another White woman taking space from a Black woman. You know?*

The reporter turns red. He looks at me, offering an apology in his eyes, nods at me to speak. But Allie keeps on going.

I mean, so many times the people doing the work are Black women. This project would be nothing without Lena's vision and passion and the amazing leadership of Aspen Brown, founder and executive director of Starshine & Clay.

And on and on she talks. About me, with me standing right next to her. And on and on she talks. About what I do when I could just speak for myself. And on, and on, and on.

And me? I don't see myself as an ally, she says. *But a co-conspirator.*

I try not to roll my eyes. Here she is, seeing me but not seeing me at all. Here she is talking about giving me space, while taking up all the space. I clear my throat. *I am really proud of the work we are doing, and I know without a doubt that my ancestors paved the way for me to do this work. This is why I wanted to share their stories. We need to know the rich history, the full history of Black Americans in the Pacific Northwest. Black Portlanders are a part of a legacy that took care of the community, that provided services for young people, that crossed cultural barriers to make sure the needs of the people were addressed. I see the programs we are doing at the library and in partnership with Starshine & Clay as a part of that legacy. And at a time when our stories are being silenced, banned, and attacked, I think it's even more crucial to have these archives and spaces.*

I figure they'll probably edit this part out, but I say it anyway: *And I'd like to add that in order to keep these kinds of programs going, we need more White people with influence, resources, and power to listen more and talk less, to actually do the work, not just talk about doing the work.*

I smile at the camera. Sometimes I am really good at channeling Honey. I feel like her daughter today.

bpp

Portland, 1970.

There was a vital Black Panther Party and Black Beret movement in Portland under the leadership of Kent Ford and R. L. Anderson. Within the group's first year of existence, the Black Panthers hosted a children's breakfast program at Highland United Church of Christ, providing free breakfast each morning for more than 125 children. They also established a dental clinic and provided services for local residents of all races.

Black and White people volunteered for the Black Panther Party's Portland chapter. They existed for ten years.

Every now and then, I'll hear someone say, I remember when... and they tell a story about standing in line for that free breakfast, talk about how going to the dental clinic was the first time they saw a Black dentist.

Living remnants abound.

[black] history

It's early enough in the year that people are still saying Happy New Year. The sky is either dark or darker, and the rain hasn't let up for days. I watch it fall outside my office window. It is a good distraction from the debate that's happening at the weekly team meeting.

The first thing on the agenda is to finalize the list of books to showcase for Black History Month. Garrett starts by saying, *So I was thinking this year we could do something different. These special monthly displays perpetuate the notion that we should only celebrate certain groups during certain months and not year-round. I think we should be intentional about making diverse book displays throughout the year.*

Allie says, *We absolutely should be intentional year-round. I think we've been great at that. However, showcasing Black books during Black History Month is not saying we shouldn't read these books all year, it is highlighting and celebrating Black history, Black culture, and Black creatives. How is that offensive?*

Garrett doesn't answer Allie's questions. Instead, he says, *I just don't know if we need these special months anymore.*

They both look at me, like they want me to be a tie-breaker, like they need the Black woman to make the final decision. I take a moment, let the silence stay a while.

I take a sip of my coffee, say, *Something you should know about me is that I love celebrating my birthday. I*

don't really care much about most holidays. But my birth-
day? That day is all about me, and I go big.

They both look at me with confused faces, as if to ask,
Where is this going?

It always means so much when family and friends
remember my birthday and call or send small gifts of appre-
ciation. I love that. Those same friends and family love me
all year long, and they show it—not just on my birthday.
They do both. I need both. I'd be hurt if they showed me
love all year but didn't acknowledge my birthday. I'd be
confused if they made a big deal about my birthday but
ignored me the rest of the year. Both. This library does both.
We make space for Black voices all year long, we celebrate
and highlight them during Black History Month. It doesn't
have to be either-or.

After the meeting ends, everyone leaves the room
except for Allie. She stays behind, helps me tidy up the
room. *I really respect the way you handle Garrett,* she
says. *I learn so much from you. You could teach a class on*
how to work with sexist men who are dismissive to all the
women.

Oh, is that what this is? I ask. *Sexism?*

Yeah, he treats all the women here like that—talking
over us, thinking his ideas are the best ideas, mansplaining.

Interesting. I've never been sure what his issue is with
me—sexism, racism, or both.

Allie looks at me, like she is considering for the first
time that it could be because I am a Black woman.

I tell her, *Whatever it is, I have to be assertive with*
him—with everyone in this place, actually. If I don't, they'll
just walk all over me.

to ban

To officially prohibit, to banish, to make illegal.
To put an end to, to suppress, as in to silence, to censor.
As in abridge, as in curtail,
as in cut back, diminish,
as in reduce, dwindle, debase.
As in they want us to feel small and insignificant, want to mute our voices, erase our stories, want to trample on the seeds planted by the ancestors, not understanding harvest has already come.

We are walking epistles, and the stories we bear have already been witnessed.

We are walking epistles written in the permanent ink of our ancestors' blood. Our existence a testimony of what was, a prophecy of what's to come.

bones

Bones. The essence, the core, the most deeply ingrained part. As in, to know something in your bones. Bones. The basic design or framework of a thing. As in stripped down to the bare bones.

Bones as in skeleton, as in fossils. Bones as in remnants, as in remains. As in unmarked graves full of the ancestors' essence hundreds of years after their spirits found freedom, after they were gone, gone. Bones as in gone, but still here. Their histories buried just beneath the surface, waiting to tell their story. Bones as in proof. They were here, they were here.

my funny valentine

For Valentine's Day, I take Aaliyah out on a mommy-daughter date. We go to a coffee shop that has an assortment of board games, and we play tic-tac-toe with wooden blocks, and eventually her favorite, Scrabble. I get a brownie, she gets a lemon bar. We split them and wash down the sweetness with hot drinks.

Mom, you want to hear a Valentine knock-knock joke?

Sure.

Knock, knock.

Who's there?

Willoughby.

Willoughby who?

Will-ya-be my Valentine?

Aaliyah laughs so hard, she snorts out her hot chocolate. Her laugh is always the sunrise, always a morning song.

partnering

Aspen and I are ironing out the details for Portland: Black with Meredith and Allie. Before we make final plans, we want to get feedback from the Black community—specifically our elders—to make sure this exhibit is something they'll feel proud of. We've spent most of the meeting going back and forth about what to call the feedback meeting. The only thing we're agreeing on is not to call it a community feedback meeting.

Town hall?

A gathering?

Community circle?

A community conversation?

Community meet & greet?

Think tank?

Sometimes we get so caught up in the semantics that the important details fall by the wayside. It's more important to me to discuss who we are inviting and how we'll get the invitations out. I could care less what we call it. I interrupt the brainstorming and say, *We only have about fifteen minutes left for this meeting. Can we talk about how we plan to get the word out?*

Oh, I think our e-newsletter would be the most efficient way. We can track rsvps that way, Meredith says. *I can also post on social media and include an rsvp link.*

Yeah, that's my concern, I tell them. *A lot of elders aren't on email, so they won't find out about it. I think we will exclude a big part of the community if everything is through email and social media.*

Oh, yes. Good—good point, Meredith says.

Aspen says, *So flyers at churches? And senior living homes?*

Yes, I say. *I think that's where we focus this, and maybe even, instead of asking them to come to us, we go out and share our plan with a few select places and get feedback that way. We don't need to hear every single Black person in Portland, we just want to get input from the community, in a more general sense.*

Well, that sounds great, Meredith chirps. *Goodness, Lena, what do you and Aspen even need us for? You two have it all figured out.*

Here she goes again. I look at Aspen. She looks at the clock. *I want to respect our time,* she says. *We're right at two o'clock. Let's call it a day, and we can email any updates or thoughts.*

We end the meeting. Meredith's question, though said in jest, is playing over and over in my head. What *do* we need them for?

newcomers

After our meeting ends, Meredith invites me to a tapas bar around the corner. *I've really been wanting you to meet my new friend Shay. She and her partner are new to Portland, and I think they could benefit from meeting you.*

Are they Black? I ask.

Well, yes, but I think they should meet you for more reasons than that.

I laugh. *It's not a bad thing. I was just asking. I actually don't mind it at all. I want to meet every Black woman that moves here. Call me the Black Girl Welcoming Committee.*

Meredith laughs at this.

I'm serious. It's hard moving to a new city, especially when you're Black and the city is so White.

Meredith asks Aspen and Allie if they'd like to join us, but both of them have other plans.

I walk with Meredith to the tapas bar and when we get there, two Black women are sitting in the waiting area. Their eyes light up when they see us walk in. Meredith introduces us. *This is Shay, this is Natalie.* We exchange all the pleasantries—hellos, hugs, so-good-to-meet-yous.

Just a few more minutes and your table will be ready, the greeter says.

Meredith says, *Shay, here, sit down. You need to get off your feet.*

It's not until she says this that I notice Shay's baby bump, how she holds her belly like so many pregnant women do.

How far along are you? I ask.

Six months, Natalie answers. *We are so excited.*

And we are so tired of carrying around this basketball belly, Shay says. *I'm at the point now where I can't find any cute clothes to wear.*

Lena, where do you shop? Meredith asks me. *You always have stylish outfits.*

I—well, I don't think where I shop can benefit Shay. She needs maternity clothes.

Of course. I was just thinking maybe plus-size clothes would work too. More room, more stylish.

Shay says, *That's a good point. I never thought of that.* But Natalie gives me a knowing look. Like she is apologizing for Shay, and maybe for Meredith too.

After we are seated, our server appears, asking us for our drink orders. In solidarity with Shay, we all order mocktails. Natalie starts the conversation with her questions about Black Portland—where to get her hair done, where the good restaurants are.

Natalie says, *I don't know how you did it, Lena. Growing up here must've been so hard.* She takes a sip of her lavender lemonade.

Well, I didn't have anything to compare it to. You know? And honestly, there's so much I love about Portland. Even with all the things that could be better, I don't see myself living anywhere else. This is home.

I get that, Shay says. *I grew up in Chicago and we have our fair share of issues too. But home, it is. If it weren't for the job offer from Nike, I don't think we would have ever left.*

Natalie nods. *That's the truth. I came here kicking and screaming. I just—I don't know how long I can do this. The other day a White woman asked me if she could touch my hair, and I just—I didn't even know White people still did that.*

We laugh and laugh. Meredith laughs, too, because even she knows better.

Not that I never dealt with White people back home, but being here makes me realize, I have never been the only. You know? Sure, I had White coworkers but in my daily, personal life? It was Blackity-Black. My neighborhood, my church. I didn't know how much I was going to miss that, Natalie says.

I get that, I tell them. *But there is a Black community here. We're scattered now, all across the city, so there's not necessarily a Black neighborhood anymore, but the community? We haven't let go of that. We're still here, still strong.*

neighbor(hoods)

There has to be an MLK Boulevard, for that is the artery. And also a wing spot where the chicken is worth standing in line for. And also a Caribbean spot that might be open, might not. That might have jerk chicken, might not. And a hair salon where women stop by who don't even need their hair done, just come through to say hello, catch up on the latest gossip. There is a barbershop, too, and churches on every corner and that one church that has the best choir, and the best Christmas plays, whose lead musician is doing this and that in the streets but is too good at playing those keys to be reprimanded. And there's the church that gives away school supplies at the Back to School Prayer Night service and hosts coat drives and turkey-dinner deliveries in November. And there's always that one church with all the young folks, which has a New Year's Eve gathering (party) to give the twentysomethings something safe and fun to do. And you might see hair weave blowing down the streets, swirling with the fallen leaves, tangled with deferred dreams, blowing right past the check cashing spot and the liquor store. And also the old drunk who is not as mean or scary as you first thought, and the old woman on her porch—nosy and all-knowing, keeping the toll of births and deaths and the comings and goings of the block. There is music, always: from the church house, the club, a car whose bass is so strong, the cement quakes. And there are fireworks just because (just before and just after the Fourth of July, just before and just after

Labor Day). There is always, always yellow crime tape somewhere blowing in the wind like ribbon dancing from a little girl's ponytails. And makeshift memorials, burned-out candles, dried flowers, and faded photos set up in front of corner stores, under a tree, on a chain-link fence, to honor the dead. And there are car washes in parking lots that are raising funds for a church's youth group and a woman buying chocolate bars for a dollar, telling the child, *Keep the candy, I just wanted to support your cause.* And women tell each other, *Watch out for him, don't walk down that block at night,* and *Girl, did you know Safeway is having a sale on eggs,* and *Girl, you know so-and-so is single now,* and *you know so-and-so is pregnant (again),* and *Girl, so-and-so got up out of here and made a life for himself, didn't he?* And you always know a newcomer, an outsider, because they walk past without speaking and the elders clear their throats, say, *Good morning,* teach folks that 'round here we speak, 'round here, we love.

the new black

We decide to hold two simple focus groups. One at the library and the other at my dad's church. I'm glad there's a mix of young and old here at the library—and new Portlanders are here too. I invited Shay and Natalie, but only Natalie could make it. She is sitting next to Ms. Brown. I forget sometimes just how much Aspen looks like her mother. But the two of them here in the same room makes me see them in each other.

After we've shared our plans, we take a few questions. Most are about logistics—*Is admission free? Will there be refreshments? Is Starshine & Clay wheelchair accessible?* And then a woman who looks like she's barely thirty raises her hand and says, *This isn't a question but a comment. I just want to say that I hope this is just the beginning of something bigger. I mean, it's nice to be nostalgic about the past, but what are we doing about Black Portland now?*

So she does have a question.

Before I can answer, an elder says, *What these women have put together is more than nostalgia to me. This is history—some of it living history—and it's important that it gets the honor it deserves. Our stories are often erased or dwindled down to only Vanport—and there's nothing wrong with talking about Vanport—but Black folks were here before 1948, and we have been an instrumental part of this city—*

Oh, I'm sure that's true. I'm just saying that I think looking at photos and reading biographies has to lead to something more profound. I'm a part of a coalition of

Black Portlanders who have the ear of the mayor and our city councilman, and we're talking about what Black Portland needs and how our community can best be served, the barely-thirty-year-old says.

This has taken a turn, and I'm not sure how to get us back on track. Aspen starts to speak, but her mother jumps in.

Chile, I've lived in Portland my whole life, and I can tell you having the ear of the mayor don't mean nothing if you don't have a heart for the people. And I can tell by the way you cut off one of your elders that you don't have a clue about—

Alright, okay! Aspen stands and gives her mom a look. *We're going to trust that everyone has the community's best interest at heart—*

Well, that's the problem. That's actually not something we should assume, Ms. Brown says.

I know that's right, Honey adds.

A row of elders nod, and I think I even hear someone say, *Amen.*

Honey says, *Some folks just want notoriety, some just want to use our small Black community as practice for the bigger city they want to do real work in. Trust is earned, not given. And I'm curious as to how a coalition is speaking on behalf of a people they haven't even been talking with.*

Ms. Brown cosigns, *We got a new kind of Black person living here now. And I'm not saying this about all the newcomers, but I know some of them coming here doing a whole lot of talking and not even a little bit of listening. They moved here from Brooklyn or Chicago or LA or wherever and think they know. Think they first. But Black folks have been here, long before they could even pronounce Or-e-gone.* Ms. Brown is in a mood today. She turns to the barely-thirty-year-old woman and says, *Some of y'all*

just as presumptuous as some of them White folks. Think
you the first to have ideas about equity and diversity and
what the Black community here needs. Don't let them
White folks isolate you. It would do you some good to know
what's happened here before you get to thinking up what
could be.

So much is running through my mind. I am thinking,
This is good, let them talk, let the discussion be what it
needs to be. When will old Black Portland and new Black
Portland ever be together in one room again to talk this
openly?

The conversation continues, and once I realize it truly
is a dialogue not an argument, I relax a bit. Let it flow.
Now the only thought on my mind is how relieved I am
that neither Meredith or Allie is here to witness this.
Some conversations are for family only. Even a family
that doesn't always see eye-to-eye.

oregon, 1953

Sandwiched between Washington and California, Oregon joined her neighbors as well as the District of Columbia and eighteen other states in banning racial discrimination in public spaces.

1953.

Sometimes we talk about *back then* like it was so long ago. But back then was more like yesterday, a fresh memory, a tender wound, not a scar.

urban renewal,
negro removal

Portland, 1960s and 1970s.

Eighteen thousand Black folks lived in Portland. Eighty percent resided in the Albina District, a community where many Black folks owned their homes, owned businesses.

In the early 1960s, construction of a sports arena and expansion of I-5 leveled 476 homes, mostly owned by Black Portlanders.

City planners could have determined other routes for the freeway, but uprooting working-class White folks and Black families proved to have less resistance. Hundreds lost their homes to highway lanes and ramps.

In the early 1970s, Portland's urban development agency destroyed more than two hundred properties to expand Emmanuel Hospital. The City of Portland condemned, purchased, and demolished these homes and buildings under the name of urban renewal. The agreement promised a new home for every home bulldozed, but those new homes were never built. Three-quarters of the displaced families were Black. Dozens of Black-owned businesses were knocked down.

Every time I drive through this area, I swear I hear the pens signing dotted lines, hear the bulldozing of Black dreams, hear the brick and mortar crumbling, crumbling.

I smell the cigar smoke, the gin. Smell the colognes and perfumes, smell the new paint of a grand opening, the dinner special being boiled and simmered and baked and fried. Taste the bowl of chili and saltine crackers, the barbecue sauce soaked up with cornbread. Taste the Mississippi, the Alabama, the Arkansas, and the Georgia they brought with them.

Taste their salty tears, the aftertaste of their American Pie.

Every time I drive through this part of town, I think about the Black community who remains.

We are the whisper of their oral histories, the whirlwind of nostalgic hope. We are the remnants and dust of each demolished building. We are the splinter festering in the heart of this city, not easily removed.

portland, 1990

Thirty-three thousand, five hundred and thirty Black people lived in Portland, making up about 8 percent of the total population. Nearly 80 percent of Portland's Black residents lived in inner Northeast Portland, with roots reaching to the South, the East Coast, and across oceans.

Honey says it all the time: *There are Black people everywhere, and everywhere we are, we know how to create community. Somehow, someway, without meeting each other, living in different regions, speaking different languages, there is a knowing, a way of being that we all relate to. We are not a monolith, yet even in our individuality, we are one.*

dreaming

Janice asks me and Aaliyah to each make a list of things we want. *It can be simple or extravagant. A combination of both is even better. I'm going to time you. Just two minutes... begin.*

When the two minutes are up, she tells us to turn to each other. *Share three from your list.*

Me:

Travel and attend more work conferences as a guest speaker.

Start a tradition of going on a family vacation once a year.

Grow a garden in the backyard with Aaliyah.

Aaliyah:

Take theater classes at summer camp.

Redo my bedroom at home so I can have a remake like at my dad's...

And can I change one of my answers? I didn't write this down, but my mom made me think of it when she talked about gardening.

Sure, Janice says. *You can say something that's not written down.*

I want to be a— Mommy, what's the word for people who work with plants?

A botanist? I look at Janice for confirmation.

She nods. *Yes, botanists are scientists who specialize in the biology of plants. There are many kinds of jobs that fall under that.* She looks at Aaliyah. *That's a lovely dream to have.*

Aaliyah smiles, says, *Honey always tells me knowing how to make things grow is a superpower.*

familiarity

Bryan is at the door with Aaliyah, who is drunk with sleepiness and can barely keep her eyes open. *She fell asleep in the car,* he tells me. *She is worn out and delirious from all the birthday-party shenanigans with her cousins.*

I kiss Aaliyah on her forehead, walk with her upstairs to put her to bed. When I come back downstairs, Bryan is standing at the door, coat on.

Thanks for taking her for the day, I tell him.

You don't have to thank me for spending time with our daughter.

I'm glad she's getting more time with you, is all. And I love that she spent the day with cousins on your side of the family. It's good for her. I sit on the sofa, tell Bryan, *You can stay a while if you have time. I want to hear about the house—how are the renovations going?*

Bryan sits down, talks me through room by room. *I just wish I had been able to do this while my mom was still living.* He leans his head back on the sofa, slouching his body down. *I miss her, Lena. Being in that house is comforting but also heartbreaking.*

Bryan's sadness fills the room. All the almosts hanging in the air. *We've been through a lot, me and you,* Bryan says. *Real talk, besides my mom, your love has been the most consistent in my life.*

I don't even see it coming, but he kisses me. At first with hesitation, a soft whisper of a kiss. Then, a full shout.

I pull away abruptly. *We can't keep doing this, Bryan.*

He leans in again, his lips pressing in.

We can't—I can't.

So, we're really not even going to try? I came back so we could—

No, Bryan. You didn't come back for me. Your mother died, and you became nostalgic. You're reaching for anything that resembles the past, that makes you think of her. Your grief is not about me—or maybe it is. Maybe you need to grieve what we had. Because we did have something. But you ended it. And we don't have it anymore. It is selfish and arrogant for you to come back to me thinking we could just pick up where we left off. We left off eight years ago. I am not the same woman you walked away from. And this is not to say you are not a good man, Bryan. I see you changing. I see. But I get to choose. And, and I— I don't choose you.

Right. Because you still love him.

Yes, because I still love him, and because you don't love me. This—these feelings we're feeling aren't— We are both grieving. Different losses, yes, but grieving just the same. We are both vulnerable right now, and—

Bryan doesn't let me finish the sentence. Maybe because he can't take one more loss. *You're right,* he says. *You're right.*

I am not slipping back to him.

I am not opening that closed door.

Honey would be proud.

boundaries

The next few times Aaliyah and Bryan spend time together, I drop her off and stay in the car, waiting to make sure she gets inside before I pull off. He does the same when he brings her back to me.

Without even saying it, Aaliyah becomes our safeguard, our buffer.

getting dressed

Tonight is the night. The opening reception of Portland: Black. This morning Kendra sent me a text asking me if I was good, if I needed anything. I told her I was fine, that I was ready. I usually put on three or four outfits before I leave the house. Especially on a night like this, when I am going to be the center of attention, going to have to speak in front of my closest friends, in front of the community, in a fancy dress and not my usual comfortable clothes. First things first are the sleeves. They have to be long or quarter-length, no spaghetti straps and definitely not strapless. Then I turn sideways, make sure my belly doesn't make me look pregnant from the side, make sure there's enough give and room in the middle section. Then I pull up a chair in front of the mirror and sit down. This is the most important part. How do I look sitting down? A dress can look perfect on me when I am standing, but when I sit down it can rise or tighten or get extra loose, all kinds of weird things that put the focus on my stomach and not on my face.

All of this I talked about with Kendra. She knew how to pick clothes out for me that flattered my figure.

And shoes. We never agreed about shoes. I will always choose comfort over sacrifice. Kendra is more committed to being a fashionista. I will be standing most of the night, and these wide feet need to be comfortable. I've pretty much stopped wearing heels, and I don't care what Kendra says—flats can be sexy too. Who made up the rule that women look better with their feet propped up at an obtuse angle?

Just when I finish getting dressed, my phone buzzes. It's a text from Kendra, wishing me good luck tonight. I send a heart back. Progress. Slow, steady.

I stand in the mirror. My casual-formal black dress fitting me perfectly, jewelry in place, makeup not too much but enough to make my eyes pop. I slip into my shoes, take another look, turn to the left, turn to the right. I have been doing this routine my whole life.

portland: black

The gallery looks like a Black history time capsule. Life-size vintage photos of Black Portland pioneers are showcased throughout the space, with short biographies mounted on the wall next to them. The building is full and pulsing with energy. Aspen and I have been doing press all evening, and finally I am walking around, taking it all in, listening especially to Black people—this is for them, after all. Their oohs and ahhs, their astonishment and pride, are confirmation that we needed to do this.

I search the crowd for Aspen. She is working the room, talking with potential funders. Travis is her shadow, and if I didn't know the backstory, I'd definitely think Aspen and Travis were dating. The way he keeps checking on her, asking her if she wants another glass of wine, if she needs anything. The way he leans into her, touching her back gently, whispering something that makes a smile appear on her face. I watch her tell him she'll be back, and she walks away with a guest. I go over to him, step right up behind him, tap him on his shoulder. He turns and smiles. I stand close to him so he hears my gentle but firm whisper: *You need to make your intentions clear with my friend. If you're not interested in her romantically, you need to let her know.*

I don't give him time to respond. I turn around, walk away, saying hello and mingling with the community. I didn't realize Kendra was here until just now, as both of us approach a server who is walking by with a tray of stuffed mushrooms. I didn't think she'd come, but I shouldn't be surprised. This is what Kendra does. She can put aside any tiff, any drama, for the greater good. I know she's thinking that at the end of the day we are sisters.

I smile at her. *I'm glad you're here.* Donovan comes over to us and congratulates me. He puts his arm around Kendra's waist, and I try my best not to react, but I'm sure it's written all over my face that I want to know all the new developments. Before I can say more, Meredith is at the mic beginning the program. Soon she's going to call me up to speak. I forge these hips through the crowd and stand nearby.

Meredith says, *Welcome, everyone. Wow. What an amazing turnout.* Then she pauses and says, *I know most of you are probably wondering, Why is a White woman up here talking at an event like this? But I am one of the organizers of the exhibit. I'm going to get out of the way in just a moment, but first, a few thank-yous.*

She doesn't get the laugh she must've thought was coming. I wonder why White people do that self-deprecating thing when they are in a room full of Black folk. Why they think they need to point out that they are White, as if we don't see it, know it, feel it.

Now that I am near the front, I can see the whole room, and I realize how massive this is, how many people have shown up. My eyes rest on Malcolm. I smile, and we have a whole conversation that no one else can hear. *Meredith needs to sit down* is the gist of what we are thinking.

Finally she calls me up to the mic. I bring up Aspen. We stand together, looking out at the audience—our mothers and fathers, family and friends, beaming with pride. Some of the descendants of the Black Portlanders featured in the photos are here too. I take the mic, start my remarks by saying, *It is very fitting that we are all here standing in a place called Starshine & Clay . . .*

joy, black

The gallery is now a juke joint. The DJ is playing
the perfect mix of R&B throughout the decades, and
the main room is now a dance floor. Donovan and
Kendra are up on each other the way the sky envelops
the moon. Malcolm is mostly hovering near my parents. When he makes it over to me, I reach out for him,
hug him tight. *Malcolm, you came. You're here. I didn't
know if—*

Of course I'd be here. I wasn't going to miss this, he says.
You look stunning, by the way. He looks me over, dramatic
and playful, then says, *I'm so proud of you.*

*Thank you—thank you for being consistent. For show-
ing up.* I take his hand, stand closer to him. If I wasn't in
a room full of people, I'd lean in, kiss him. Instead, we
dance. And being in his arms, I surrender, let myself feel
everything I've been pushing away.

I love him.

I forgive him.

I want him.

And then, because this is a Black gathering, a coming
together of yesterday, today, and tomorrow, there has to
be, needs to be, a Soul Train line. You can tell right away
who the real dancers are, who the cool cats and divas are,
and who feels completely out of their element. But it is all
Black, and it is all beautiful. Arms wave, and hips whine,
and sweat drips, and this is a kind of heaven. Elders dancing alongside the young folk who stand on their shoulders. A whole room of Black sunshine.

black

onyx, obsidian, melanite, coal, tar, cast iron, smoke, soot, storm clouds, ink, oil, blackboards, pepper, sesame, blackberries, coffee, crows, ravens, night, afros, beaded braids, cornrows, du-rags, silk hair bonnets, shea butter for skin, cocoa butter for scars, coconut oil for hair, wide-tooth combs, hair picks, raised fists, dap, the hum of a church organ, the collards at a repast, the solo before the sermon, the hair grease dripping down the edges of foreheads, the plastic butter container saved for tupperware, the eye roll, always the eye roll, putting a handle on an elder's name, the tambourine being passed from hand to hand during a praise break, praise breaks, play cousins, uncles that ain't your uncle, aunties that earned the title because of how much they love you, how much they scold you, playing church, playing dominoes, playing spades, knowing when and how to say *I am not playing with you...you think I'm playing...I am not the one to be played...don't play yourself...you betta stop playing with me,* knowing when and how to say *can't stop/won't stop, nothing can stop us, ain't no stopping us now.*

black spaces

I've been introducing Shay and Natalie to Black women I think they'll connect well with. Today, we are out with Aspen having brunch at Zelle's. I tell them I know there are a lot of new trendy spots in the area, but there's nothing like a classic joint.

Shay asks, *Besides Starshine & Clay, where do Black folks gather?*

My heart aches at the question. *There aren't many spaces anymore,* I tell her. *I mean, well, besides some of the churches, there's not necessarily a space in the city where we all just go and hang out.*

Aspen reminds me, *There's the Soul Restoration Center.*

Oh, yes. Definitely check them out, I say.

But there used to be more places? Shay asks.

Yes, before gentrification sent most of us to Gresham and Vancouver, we had our spaces. Remember Reflections Bookstore? I turn to Aspen, who is nodding and smiling at the mention of the only Black-owned bookstore in Portland. It opened in 1995 and was a beloved gathering space for twelve years before it closed in the changing neighborhood.

Aspen says, *Reflections was so much more than a bookstore. I mean, yes, it was amazing because you could go there and get books by Black authors that just weren't going to be easy to find at mainstream bookstores—*

Black greeting cards too, I add.

Right! But also, they had that coffee shop and the Black art market.

I got so many gifts there for my mom. Honey loves her some Black figurines.

And they had that space in the back where book clubs held meetings and people gave poetry readings for the community.

Dad used that space sometimes for meetings when he wanted to switch things up and get out of the church office. It truly was a space for us, I tell them.

Aspen asks, *And what was the name of the bakery next door? Wasn't there a bakery?*

Oh my goodness yes! Mother Dear's Tasty Pastries—or something like that.

Aspen and I are caught up in our nostalgia. Yes, there used to be a Black Portland. Not just past tense before I was born, but while I was alive, memories that are just beneath the surface of my mind, not always at the ready, but there, there.

remembering

Shay and Natalie want to know more. *Tell us what else you remember,* they say. They hang on our words like we are telling them tales of a magical land from long ago.

Aspen asks me, *Do you remember Northeast Spectrum?*

Oh my goodness. Yes! I look at Shay and Natalie and explain. *Northeast Spectrum was an independent local TV show hosted by Black anchors and journalists who highlighted stories and happenings relevant to Portland's Black community. My mom loved tuning in.*

It had a local vibe but also did some national stories too, Aspen adds.

What happened to it?

No idea, I say.

Natalie seems amazed and maybe relieved that at least there used to be a strong Black presence in Portland. Maybe she is wondering how to bring it back.

Aspen says, *So much of what we're showcasing at Portland: Black is about the early settlers and leaders of Black Portland, but we've seen Portland change with our own eyes. I forget that some of this history didn't happen that long ago.*

my-te-fine

All these memories from my childhood are coming to the surface. Talking about the past has me remembering things I didn't know I remembered. I don't know what brings this to mind, but I am thinking about a time we had a sleepover at Kendra's. We were so excited because her mom said we could have dessert for dinner. Ice cream sundaes with all the fixings.

When she went to the freezer, I was expecting her to pull out a pint of Tillamook ice cream because that's what my mother always had. Or maybe Häagen-Dazs, like when I went over to Aunt Aretha's. But instead she had a half gallon of Fred Meyer's My-Te-Fine vanilla.

Kendra saw me eyeing the cheap store-brand ice cream and said, *It was on sale. We usually get the better kind—*

I love ice cream. Any kind. I'm just wondering why it's called My-Te-Fine.

We got tickled and started saying the phrase over and over: *My-Te-Fine.*

Kendra strutting around the kitchen. *I am my-te-fine. How you doin', Aspen?*

Aspen said, *Oh me? I am my-te-fine. How you doin', Lena?*

Oh, I am definitely my-te-fine.

Still, even now as grown women, every now and then, when someone asks, *How are you today?* One of us gets to laughing and says, *My-te-fine.* And even if the person doesn't get the joke—me, Kendra, and Aspen laugh and laugh.

breaking news

It is seven o'clock in the morning. I wake up to the weather forecast because I fell asleep with the TV on. My eyes are hardly open when the phone rings. I squint, see Honey's name flashing, and panic. *Hello?*

You read today's New York Times *yet?*

No, Honey. Is this really what you're calling about this early in the morning?

Kendra wrote an op-ed for the New York Times. *Ain't that something. I wish her momma was here.*

I sit up in my bed, put Honey on speaker, so I can search my *New York Times* app for Kendra's op-ed. I search her name, and it immediately comes up: "How It Feels to Be Fat Me." Right away I know it was inspired by Zora Neale Hurston's essay "How It Feels to Be Colored Me." I remember when we first read Zora's essays in college, how we devoured her writings and discussed the many layers of her work.

I'm so proud of her, so proud, Honey says. *How are you all celebrating? Have you talked to Aspen yet?*

I, I—no. I haven't. But yeah, we'll definitely have to figure out something. I mean it when I say it, even though I have no idea what I'm going to do, since Kendra and I haven't had a real conversation. I copy the link, text it to Aspen. She immediately responds with exclamation marks and then a heart. Then, a text that says, *I had no idea. Wow. This is amazing.*

At this point, I am not listening to Honey at all, who is giving ideas of how we could celebrate this moment.

Something about framing the article and giving it to Kendra. I am out of bed now and searching my closet for something to wear today.

Aspen sends another text: *This is a big deal.*

I reply: *A very big deal.*

Did you hear me? Lena, you there?

Oh, sorry—yes, I'm here.

I said, make sure you tell Kendra I love her and I am so proud. You girls are so confident and strong. I just love what you have become. Alright, have fun whatever you do tonight. Bye.

Bye.

hot off the press

Honey's enthusiasm makes me teary. The automatic knowing that we would—should—do something tonight, her sincere pride in Kendra like she's her second daughter. This is why I never told Honey about our falling-out. Some things mommas just don't need to know. I catch myself at this thought, think about Aaliyah and all the secret crushes and friend dramas she's destined to keep from me. I push the thought out, head to the shower.

By the time I am out of the shower, Aaliyah is up and eating breakfast.

I make coffee, sit across from her at the dining room table. We exchange good mornings and talk about today's after-school schedule. *We see Ms. Janice today, right?* Aaliyah asks.

Yes, our therapy appointment is right after school. I'll pick you up.

Aaliyah smiles and keeps eating.

The doorbell rings. Aaliyah looks at me, and we both rush to the door. Who in the world is coming over this early?

Honey.

Grandma! Aaliyah opens the door, and they hug like they didn't just see each other two days ago.

Honey has a handful of newspapers in her hand. *Here, I thought you'd want a copy, and there's one for Aspen and whoever else. You young folks read everything on them gadgets, but there's nothing like print. And this, you gotta see in print.* She hands me the newspapers. They are heavy, and the smell of them immediately makes me think of my grandfather, who read the paper every morning with a cup of joe—black, no sugar, no cream. It's always so jarring how smells take you back to a person, a place.

Honey leaves, giving more hugs, saying, *Just wanted to drop those off. You two have a good day.*

When she leaves, Aaliyah is full of questions. *Why did Grandma bring all those newspapers?*

Because Kendra wrote a special essay and an important newspaper decided to publish it.

What did she write about?

She wrote about loving her body, about accepting all of who she is in a world that sometimes doesn't accept her. We sit back at the table, finish breakfast.

Can you read it to me?

I pause for a moment, then say, *Sure. And then you need to get dressed. You can't be late for school.*

I read the essay out loud as Aaliyah eats the rest of her cereal. She listens so intently, feasting on Kendra's words. The essay is so Kendra, so authentically her voice, it feels like she is here with us, talking to us.

I have missed her for weeks now, but in this moment, it's like she is right here with us. Right here offering wisdom and loving us. Telling Aaliyah she is worthy and showing her how to rise.

wine & wine

I show up at Kendra's unannounced at seven o'clock in the evening with a bottle of her favorite wine and a copy of the *New York Times* in my hand. I ring the doorbell, wait, wait, wait.

She answers the door, looking shocked and relieved all at once. *Lena!*

Hey. I, ah—congratulations. I hand her the bottle of wine but don't move forward, just in case she doesn't want me to come in.

She steps back, opens the screen door. *Oh my goodness, this is unexpected. Thank you. You, um, you have time to stay awhile?*

I step inside. Before I get too far into the house, she whispers to me, *Donovan is here.*

I smile like a giddy sixteen-year-old.

I sit in the living room, open the paper. *Girl—you did that! This is so good, Kendra. I am so proud of you.* I tell her about Honey, how she came by this morning, dropping off the newspapers like she was Santa.

Aw, I need to call Honey. It's been a while.

Donovan comes into the living room from Kendra's bedroom. The three of us talk and drink wine and celebrate, celebrate.

to reconcile

We should talk. Kendra walks me outside. We stand
on the porch, shivering a bit because now that the sun
is gone, the temperature has dropped. *I never meant to
hurt you. I just—I really didn't know what to do, how to
handle the situation. But for the record, I didn't know they
had been together until after I took her on as a client. And
I just, I really thought that by not telling you I was being a
good friend. I'm sorry, Lena. I'm sorry and I love you and
I miss you.*

Kendra reaches out to hug me. I can't remember the
last time we've hugged. She is not the touchy-feely kind
of person.

I tell her I love her. *And I accept your apology.*

*Thanks again for coming by. Let's, um, let's connect
soon.*

risk

love is a risk, a trust in the uncertain,
a walk of faith, a calculated gamble. Love is not about
falling in, but growing in. It is a choice,
a confidence not in the person you love, not in yourself, but in the surety that even if your heart breaks,
it can heal.

rebuild

to build something again after it has been destroyed: to renovate, to restore, to make anew, to reconstruct, to reassemble, to revise, to re-vision, to readjust, to repair, to improve,

to give it another chance, to be patient, to try harder, to dream up a new possibility of what could be, to make good better, to let go of what's not working, to be intentional, to take a risk, to be uncomfortable, to not give up, to work, to work, to work.

change

A metamorphosis, a transformation, a new beginning. To make modifications, adjustments. A shift, a correction.

Me listening to my body when it tells me it's not hungry for food. Me listening to my body when it tells me it needs to go on a walk, when it needs rest, when it needs to be touched.

Me understanding that forgiving and letting go does not mean keeping the person, ignoring the hurt.

Change.

To switch it up, to develop, to do an about-face, to go another direction, to revise, remix, to be you but better.

To be familiar, as in new and improved.

first dates

Malcolm tells me over and over, *We can go slow. I'm not going anywhere.* We have settled back into each other. Seeing each other a few nights a week: Portland Art Museum, our favorite coffee shop, a happy hour at a new Cuban restaurant. This morning, we are at a hole-in-the-wall breakfast joint that has the biggest and best pancakes.

What's on your mind today? Malcolm asks.

Everything. I feel like I can't turn my brain off. I'm always thinking. Mostly about Aaliyah. I know it's not true, but I keep worrying that I've ruined her.

Malcolm swallows the bite of food he just stuffed in his mouth, says, *Do you want me to respond or just listen?*

You can respond, I say.

None of us survive childhood unscathed. When Aaliyah looks back on these days, yes, she might remember these painful moments, but I believe she'll remember all the days you showed up for her, that you kept loving her, that you kept on persevering for her—for yourself. The best way you knew how. If you believe you're passing down your short-comings and burdens to her, doesn't that mean she's inheriting the best parts of you too? She'll have to decide what to let go of, what to keep.

Thank you for saying that, I tell him. *I might need you to tell me that again and again.*

For the rest of breakfast, we talk about our to-do lists for the week—Malcolm has to go grocery shopping after this because he's hosting some of his mentees over to his

365

place for a game day this Saturday. I have to pack for an upcoming work trip.

We talk and talk and drink our coffee and eat so slow, our server is exchanging the breakfast menus for lunch. There are no getting-to-know-you-questions, no declarations of love, no deep commentary, not even any heavy flirting, there's just us. A regular date on a regular morning.

A Wednesday kind of love.

good times

The kitchen smells like peaches and cinnamon. It's the anniversary of Ms. Turner's passing, and me, Aspen, and Kendra are at Kendra's house reminiscing and comforting each other. Kendra says, *Thanks for coming. I know things have been... we haven't talked in a while, but I really appreciate you keeping our tradition.*

I hug her. *This is what we do. We show up for each other.*

The cobbler cools on the counter while we sit and talk. Kendra says, *I can't believe it's been twenty-two years. It doesn't seem like she's been gone that long. There are still moments when I want to call her and tell her something or ask a question.*

Kendra has Ms. Turner's eyes and smile. And definitely her style. Back in the day, I was obsessed with what the women at church wore, how they carried themselves. Honey, the classy one, Ms. Brown, the sophisticated one, Ms. Turner, the fly one. She didn't do church hats, and a lot of her clothes were black, the opposite of the sea of colorful dresses and suits moving about the sanctuary. Ms. Turner was the embodiment of the phrase Big and Beautiful. She was wide and warm, brown and bold. When Kendra starts talking about growing her business, about writing a plus-size style column for a high-fashion magazine, I see her mother, hear her. She is gone, gone but here still.

But what I remember most is her brilliant mind, how she knew random facts about the ocean, how she could name every bird and flower we came across. She could put a bookcase together without looking at the instructions, knew how to change her own tires, check her oil. She was a saved-sanctified-and-filled-with-the-Holy-Ghost Christian, but she also drank bourbon on occasion, and got tickets to see Luther and Anita Baker in concert.

I was always nervous around Ms. Turner. In the way you are nervous when you really want someone to like you, when you hope they enjoy being around you as much as you enjoy being around them.

Once, when Honey picked me up from Kendra's house, she came in and started apologizing profusely to Ms. Turner because she had dropped me off at the last minute—an emergency with one of the church members that needed her and Dad's attention. Ms. Turner put her arms around me, said, *This beautiful chocolate drop is welcome here anytime. Anytime.* She told me once, *I always wanted twins. Picked out names and everything. Didn't get my twins but God gave me Kendra...and you.* I never heard her mention an ex-husband or ex-boyfriend or ex-lover. There were no photos of Kendra's dad in the house. It wasn't until we were in high school that Kendra ever mentioned her father. She didn't come to school one day, so Aspen and I went over her house—unannounced—after school. She opened the door and broke down crying, telling us she hated that she never knew her father, hated that he didn't love her enough to get clean, hated that his body was found dead in the alley near Twenty-Ninth and Ainsworth.

That was the first and last time Kendra ever talked about her father to us. It was our junior year in high school. A year later, at the end of senior year, she was saying goodbye to her mother.

I often wonder how it is that Kendra was able to handle so much at only eighteen. How it is that she survived her early college years, her twenties, her thirties, without the woman who gave her life. I asked her, once, how she made it through. *I have your mom and Ms. Brown,* she told me. *Plus, I have my momma's wisdom too. She left me herself.*

And what will be said about me when I am no longer on this earth, just a memory, just a story passed down? What am I leaving behind for Aaliyah? When she is older and maybe a mother or someone's life partner, when she is navigating a career and friendships and she needs wisdom or inspiration or guidance, and she reaches back, will she find me healed, will she find me whole, will she find what she needs to survive?

I ask Kendra and Aspen, *Did you think our lives would turn out this way?*

Yes and no, Kendra says. *When I was younger, I didn't think I'd go through my twenties and thirties without my mom. I thought she'd live to be eighty or ninety, even. She died so young. I used to think being forty was old, but then she died at forty-three, and I realize now how young she was. How much life she had left to live.*

Aspen says, *I thought I'd be married with at least two children by now. I mean, at this age my mom had already had three children and was celebrating double-digit wedding anniversaries.*

Yeah, it's strange, huh? To be this old but to still have so much more to learn, to still be growing and changing, I say.

I look around the room, study my sisters. We've lived long enough where we can say to a teenager, *I remember when you were just a seed in your momma's womb.* This is the age when we joke about our Golden Girls Retirement

Plan. Kendra always says it: if we're single, divorced, or widowed in our golden years, we will be like Dorothy, Blanche, and Rose, living out the rest of our years splitting rent for a condo somewhere near water.

This is the age when death gets closer and closer. No longer a person at church we kind of knew, or an acquaintance we knew through a friend of a friend. Death is close: parents of your friends, former teachers, celebrities we felt like we knew because we grew up watching them on TV, because we lip-synced the lyrics to every song they sang. This is the age when we start taking account, enough time behind us to figure out what to do differently with the time ahead of us.

This is the age we have started half joking about creaking knees and having to squint to see small print. This is when yawning begins before the clock strikes midnight. This is the age where, if we let it, our best years can be ahead of us. If we decide to not waste any time on people or possibilities that don't align with our purpose.

This is what the old folks meant when they said, *Chile, I'm too grown for that*...a declaration that they have moved on, that they are never going back.

Kendra tells us to help ourselves: *Let's eat this while it's hot.* She dishes out Ms. Turner's signature dessert.

Aspen scoops ice cream into her bowl. *I was just thinking about your mom the other day when I drove past the exit we'd take to get to Jantzen Beach. Ms. Turner loved that shopping center.*

Girl. The hours I spent in Montgomery Ward, Kendra says.

Meanwhile, my momma had me up in Newberry's all day looking through bric-a-brac, buying stuff she didn't need.

We laugh. *Ms. Brown loves her some knickknacks, don't she?* Kendra says.

Talking about Ms. Turner being gone makes me think of Ms. Coleman, and those thoughts I keep having about losing Dad come again. I hate that while we are supporting Kendra and honoring her mom, I am thinking about who's next. I am thinking about how one day, all three of us will be gathering to say goodbye to Mr. Brown, Mrs. Brown, to Dad, to Honey.

There is a whisper in my spirit.

Prepare yourself.

Prepare yourself.

We finish eating our dessert and go into the living room. Kendra picks up the remote, says, *Ready for some dy-no-mite?* She spreads her arms out like JJ. We all burst into laughter.

Kendra presses play, and we do what we do every year to commemorate Ms. Turner's passing: we spend the day eating her favorite dessert and watching episodes of her favorite show, *Good Times.*

peach cobbler

Ingredients

Filling

5 cups (750–800 g or 2–2.5 lbs.) chopped peaches
   (peeled or unpeeled)
¼ cup (31 g) all-purpose flour
½ cup (100 g) raw cane or turbinado sugar (go up to
   ²/₃ cup if you like it really sweet)
a pinch of salt
1 tablespoon (15 ml) fresh lemon juice
½ teaspoon caramel extract (pure vanilla extract also
   works)

Topping

½ cup (100 g) packed dark-brown sugar
²/₃ cup (84 g) all-purpose flour
1 teaspoon ground cinnamon spice blend (cinnamon
   + nutmeg, with tiny dashes of ginger and allspice)
a pinch of salt
½ cup (113 g) salted butter, very cold, cubed
²/₃ cup (57 g) old-fashioned whole rolled oats
optional: ²/₃ cup (95 g) crushed unsalted pecans

Instructions

Preheat the oven to 350°F (177°C). Lightly grease any
2–2.5-quart baking dish; a 9 x 9 pan or 10-inch cast-iron
skillet also works. Set aside.

Gently mix all of the filling ingredients together in a large bowl, then spread into the baking dish.

Make the topping: Whisk the brown sugar, flour, cinnamon, and salt together in a medium bowl. Cut in the butter using a pastry cutter or fork until the mixture is crumbly. Fold in the oats and crushed pecans. Sprinkle evenly over filling.

Bake for 40 to 50 minutes—it really depends on your oven, so I'd take a peek after 30. Look for a golden-brown topping and fruit juices bubbling around the edges. Remove from the oven and allow to cool for a few minutes before serving warm.

mile high club

A library in Arizona heard about what we are doing here in Portland, and I've been invited to speak at a conference about preserving local history and honoring Black communities.

Malcolm gives me a pep talk when he drops me off at the airport. *You got this. You're going to blow them away and get a standing ovation.* He sends me off with a soft kiss. It is comforting, but it doesn't ease the anxiousness I feel about going into the airport. I am actually more nervous about this flight than I am about speaking in front of hundreds of people.

I hate airports. I hate airplanes.

I hate the long walk from the check-in counter to the gate. I hate the way people bump into me, without saying excuse me or acknowledging my presence. I hate how when I get to the gate, I notice people sticking out their legs, putting their bags on the chair next to them—anything to send the message that they do not want me sitting next to them. I hate how when I get in line for preboarding, the attendant always says, *This is for people with disabilities or people who need more time.* I hate how when I say, *I need more time,* I either get a blank stare, a look of confusion, or a look of disgust. I hate how I get on first, rush to put my carry-on in the overhead bin, then discreetly take out my seat belt extender, clicking it in place.

All this I try to do before anyone else boards the plane. Me, against the window, buckled in and tucked away so that I am not in the way. Me, against the window and buckled in, knowing that if I have to go to the restroom, I will hold it. I will not get up from this seat, will not get in the way, will not draw attention to myself. My big self, who will ask if the armrest can be left up, knowing the answer will most likely be a hard no. Knowing that the person next to me will do everything possible not to brush up against my fat arm.

And then it happens. The best surprise. The cabin doors are closing, and no one—no one—is seated in my row. I have the whole row to myself. I lift the armrest, spread my legs out a bit, exhale.

The flight attendants do their routine announcements and walk down the aisle, checking to make sure all seats are upright, all seat belts are fastened. The attendant stops at my row, says, *You are in an exit row. In case of emergency, you may be called on to assist in an evacuation. If you wish to move seats, I can move you.*

I'm fine, thank you.

She walks away, to the front of the plane.

And then.

Another attendant walks over to me. He doesn't say anything. Just looks me over and walks away.

And then.

There is whispering and more looking over at me and more whispering.

And then, one of the flight attendants from the back is standing at my row with a passenger from the back of the plane.

Excuse me, you're going to have to switch seats. You can't sit here if you're not able to assist in case of an emergency.

But I—I said I didn't mind assisting—

You can't assist. You have a seat belt extender. You

can't... Ma'am, please don't make a scene. You're holding us up. We need to take off. I need you to move.

I'm not making a scene. I undo my seat belt, get my bag. I don't ask questions, don't try to explain that just moments ago, the other flight attendant saw me sitting here, looked at my seat belt extender, said nothing. I just do what I'm told as quick as I can. I don't want to prolong this. I feel like the entire plane is looking at me, waiting on me.

I do the walk of shame. Squeezing my big, Black self down an aisle made for bodies that don't need to twist and turn and shimmy. I am sweating now, and I feel like I might drop my headphones or that the book I was about to crack open might slip from under my armpit. And God knows I don't want to have to bend over in the middle of this aisle.

On my way to the back of the plane, I pass a woman who looks at me with eyes full not of pity but of understanding. She is a pale woman, and as big as me. Her arm hangs off the armrest, her hips spill out of the seat. She gives half a smile, soft like the petal of a flower. She is the first person since I got to the airport and boarded this plane who has looked me in the eye.

I make it to my seat. A man is sitting in the aisle seat, and a woman is sitting at the window. Both of them look so annoyed. The man gets up, lets me in.

People are huffing and puffing and murmuring about being late, about me holding everything up. In this moment, to keep from crying, I think about Kendra. She would probably cuss the flight attendant out, put her headphones on and ignore them all. I don't cuss anyone out, I don't say a word. I just get in my seat, attach the seat belt extender, and settle in, immediately putting my headphones back in and turning up the volume.

skin & bones

Squeezed in.

This physical feeling, as uncomfortable as it is, is not as difficult as all the other times I have had to navigate spaces not made for me, push down my emotions, dim my light, act less brilliant.

My entire life, I have had to learn how to adapt, adjust, shrink. I wonder sometimes what it would be like for me to expand, to take up space, to exist in all my fullness without apology.

I exhale, let my shoulders relax, and say to both of my new seatmates, *Do you mind if I put the armrest up?* I don't wait for an answer, I just do it. I straighten my legs out front of me, stop holding in my belly. *Relax, Lena,* I tell myself. *Just sit here and let your body be.*

When the snacks come down the aisle and the flight attendant doesn't ask me if I want anything, I reach over the man sitting in my row, who is manspreading all over the place and feasting on cookies. I say to the flight attendant, *You didn't ask me what I wanted.* I take a bag of chips and eat them one by one.

landing

When we get off the plane, I head straight to the restroom. I've had to go for the last hour, but there was no way I was going to ask that man to let me out of the row. As I'm washing my hands at the sink, a woman comes over to me, whispers, *I'm really sorry you were treated that way on the plane. You should make a complaint. That was unacceptable.*

I can't thank her. Not for coming up to me now, after the fact. Why didn't she stick up for me on the plane? I can't appease her or make her feel better about how bad I feel. I just keep washing my hands.

Excuse me, miss? Did you hear me? I just wanted to say how sorry I am that you were treated so badly . . . hello?

I put my hands under the dryer. The whirlwind noise fills the restroom, drowns out her voice. She huffs and walks away, mumbling something I can't quite make out. . . . *bad attitude* . . . is all I hear.

And then I see the woman from the plane, the woman who smiled so gently, so knowingly, standing in line waiting to enter a stall. When one becomes open, she lets the woman behind her go. *I'm waiting for that one,* she says, pointing to the handicapped stall. When I walk past her, she says, *it's quite the club to be in, isn't it?*

vip

The conference is at a local high school. The auditorium will hold all the main-stage speakers and panels, and smaller breakout sessions will happen in the classrooms. I can't help but think about the last conference I went to. How the signs were both welcoming and offputting, how so many bodies looked like mine. How so many hellos and smiles were exchanged between strangers.

I am hoping today is like that, especially since last night's dinner was so wonderful, and the host was smart enough to invite women of color to join us. We didn't talk about equity or activism or social justice at all. We talked about our favorite reality shows and lamented the state of R&B music.

I am expecting good vibes today, but when I arrive at the backstage door, the volunteer looks me over, says, *This entrance is for speakers and staff only.*

I'm a speaker, I tell him. *Actually, I'm giving the keynote.*

He looks perplexed and shocked, his face scrunched up in disbelief. He looks me over again. *This entrance is for speakers and staff only.*

Sir, I am a speaker. I'm giving the keynote. How do you think I even know about this private entrance?

Your name?

Lena Baker.

He checks the list that's attached to his clipboard.

Wait, so you have a list, and you didn't even check first before telling me this entrance isn't for me?

He skims the list, and I look over his shoulder, see my name right away, and point to it. *That's me. Lena Baker.*

Give me a moment, he says. And he walks into the building. A line begins to form as I wait. A woman walks up to me, her pale cheeks decorated in freckles. *Are you Lena Baker? Oh my goodness, I'm so looking forward to hearing you today.*

Thank you.

The volunteer is back with reinforcement. A wide, short man is with him. Kindness exudes from his eyes. The volunteer points toward me. *She says she's Lena Baker.*

Lena! Welcome. We are thrilled to have you. Come, come with me.

I walk with the pudgy man, a trail of speakers behind me. We follow him to the green room.

When I walk onto the stage for sound check, I realize how massive this place is. The auditorium has been remodeled and is better than some prominent theaters I've been to. I scan the stage. The podium is on the left, and two chairs are in the middle.

Two director's chairs.

Um—those chairs, I say.

For the conversation after your keynote.

I tell myself, *Ask for what you need, Lena. You deserve to be comfortable.*

I tell the man, *Those—those don't look comfortable. At least, not for me. Is there another chair we can use? Those are very high and don't look stable at all.*

Um…yes, let me…I'll be right back. The man disappears into the darkness of the theater.

I do my sound check, the whole time panicking about having to lift my big self into that joke of a chair. What if it breaks when I sit on it? What if my hips spill out of the sides of the chair?

When I'm finished testing the mics, the moderator who I'll be in conversation with comes out to check the lapel mics we'll use for the conversation. She is thin, not a twig, but not round or plump in any way. When she sees the chairs, she says, *We're sitting there?* And the way she says *there*, it sounds like she is terrified. *I have on a skirt*, she says. *I am not trying to give the audience a peep show.* She laughs, but there is terror in her voice. *And I'm short. My feet are going to dangle through the whole conversation like I'm a child on a swing.*

I laugh. *Oh, thank God it's not just me. I asked the host to find something else.* We wait for a different set of chairs to come. The host seems happy to have made the change, but I hear two people from backstage talking.

She should have put in her rider that she needed handicap-accessible considerations.

Oh, I don't think—um, she's not handicapped. She's just too big to fit in the chair.

It's not our fault she can't fit in the chair.

Well, these days, everything is about inclusion, so you know, that means fat people get to make the rest of us feel bad because they can't do what normal people can do. It's fine, I guess. Just sucks that the photos will have those plain chairs in them. Messed up the whole aesthetic.

I swear, if it's not people like her crying about racism, it's people like her ranting about their diabetic, asthmatic, out-of-shape bodies. Always blaming everyone but themselves.

The moderator hears the staff talking too. I can tell by the shift in her body, the way her eyes look at me, then away. How she starts talking about the weather, the

Pacific Northwest, the difference between there and here. Anything but the conversation that is happening backstage. We check the lapel mics, go to the green room, where there are plenty of comfortable seats and a table full of charcuterie boards and lemon water and tiny mints and chocolates and nuts. I don't sit at first. I just stand at the door, take it all in. I belong here. My big, Black body belongs here, and everywhere I choose to go.

keynote

Good evening,

I want you all to take a good look at me. It's okay, I am
giving you permission to stare and notice and look me
up and down. See me. All of me. Notice the shade of this
brown, look at the crinkle of this hair—no really, this is a
good twist-out, so I really do want you to take that in.

Notice that my nails are a neutral color, enough to be
noticed but not enough to overwhelm. See how my hips are
more ocean than creek. See the scar over my left eyebrow
that is fading, fading but still there, been there since a fight
in the sixth grade when I stood up for the new girl who
was being bullied because she brought pancit to school for
lunch, and we Black kids did not know anything about Fil-
ipino food, so she was teased and ostracized, and I took on
the loudest mouth. I won that fight, but you wouldn't know
it by this scar—she got a few good punches in, and her ring
scraped my face and tore my skin apart, just enough to
need stitches.

Now, I have to say that was my first and last physical
fight—my parents weren't having that. But I am still fighting. I learned how to fight for people who are being pushed
to the side, ignored, erased. I became passionate about
learning people's stories, digging past my own assumptions, a stereotype, or a simple summary of their experience. I learned how to ask questions, how to listen, how to
amplify voices that are quieter or, in some cases, silenced.
I became determined to showcase and highlight what the
dominant culture wanted to hide. This is the work I am

doing in partnership with Starshine & Clay. Portland: Black is about reclaiming our stories, centering our experiences. It is about taking up space.

I know I am here to motivate and inspire you to find your way into this work. But first, I need to say if you are going to be in the fight for standing up for yourself, for the marginalized, you have to expect scars. You can see this scar above my eyebrow, still here after a sixth-grade tussle. But you can't see the emotional scars that microaggressions leave, the tearing apart that happens to my Black soul every time a White person who sees themself as a friend, as an I'm-not-one-of-those-kind-of-White-people person, says something racist. The bleeding from an onslaught of passive-aggressive comments about my body, my weight. Where there's a fight, there are scars...

And then, even though I didn't plan it, I say the thing that needs to be said. I almost bite my tongue, hold it in. But no. Not at a conference about making the invisible visible. Not when I have a Black daughter who needs to know her momma can and will speak up, can and will show her how.

I am leaving here today with wounds that I am sure will become scars soon. Disappointed by some of the staff and volunteers you have here, who clearly chose to volunteer and work for this cause, but have not done the work to inventory their own biases. Working here does not mean you are actually doing the work. The real work is in your own personal heart. If you don't care for real, if you don't put into practice everything you all have been meeting about and hearing about on these panels, I promise you your disregard, assumptions, and judgments will seep through your practices and show up even in how you greet new folks to the space, how you set up the space, how you make excuses when you mess up.

Yes, I will heal. I am accepting more and more that to be a fat Black woman is to be in a constant state of hurting and healing.

I speak this out loud so that my humanity is centered more than my accomplishments. I say this out loud so that I remind myself that I belong here, and I deserve to be believed when I show up and say I am the keynote speaker. Yes, me, a person who looks like me. I deserve to have a comfortable seat to sit in for a forty-five-minute conversation in front of hundreds of people. Yes, me, a person who looks like me. I deserve to be heard when I speak up for what I need. And not just me—you deserve it, and so do the members of the community you serve.

This is what I learned. My takeaway from Portland: Black is that not only do the stories of my ancestors matter, but my story matters too. They were here, and I am here. And I will make good use of this breath.

purpose

I am starting to be
who I always thought I was.

black, powerful

Janice keeps telling me, *Don't look at it like your daughter needs fixing. She needs healing. Healing takes time.*

So, once a month, I make sure I am intentional about spending time with Aaliyah. I call them Sunday fun days. Aaliyah and I skip church and spend the day doing something she wants to do. Oregon Museum of Science and Industry, brunch, manicures. Today we are having afternoon tea at a downtown restaurant. It's the fanciest place she's been in, and she is in awe of all the lavish, dainty decorations. She loves trying all the flavors of tea, and has decided that vanilla crème is her favorite. I am surprised that she likes the fig and goat cheese scones. We both devour the cherry-almond ones. My little girl's tastebuds are expanding, so much of her growing, changing.

After we leave the restaurant, I take Aaliyah to Starshine & Clay. It's closed on Sundays, but Aspen has arranged for me to give Aaliyah a private tour of the exhibit. The space feels solemn today, with no people, no music, no food. Just the oversize portraits hovering around us.

Aaliyah walks through the space with reverence, like she knows this is something to behold, something to cherish. I take her to each and every piece. She reads the bios out loud, and I help her on the words she gets stuck on, answer all her questions.

We make it to the end of the exhibit. It's my favorite part of the experience. A local Black artist made an installation of a map of Portland, using black-tinted mirrors. It's not obvious that the glass is a mirror. At first glance, it looks like a glass rendering of a map in the shape of Portland. The landmarks of Black Portland history are identified in small gray letters. Aaliyah says, *This is so cool. I've never seen black glass.*

I touch her shoulders, position her in just the right spot. *Look,* I whisper, standing behind her with my hands still resting on her shoulders. *Depending on where we stand, we see our reflection in the map.* Our reflections come and go, faint, like a ghost, a spirit. We stand for a while staring at our ghostly selves, see our Black selves embedded in the city.

Aaliyah, do you know how powerful we are, how powerful you are?

She smiles and shrugs. Like she knows, but also like she wants me—needs me—to tell her, like she's been taught to be humble, not to brag, not to think too highly of herself.

But, oh, she knows. She knows.

daddy, daughter

It's becoming the norm now. Bryan spending time with Aaliyah. Picking her up for planned outings and just-because. I didn't see it happening, but here he is—growing into the father I've always wanted him to be. Change is quiet sometimes, still like water, but movement is happening. Things are shifting, shifting.

harvest

Tulips have arrived, and the trees are a revival of blossoms. The church is packed, folks stuffed all the way up in the balcony.

Dad is not here.

This morning, he woke up not feeling well, Honey tells me. *He called Malcolm, asked him to preach.*

And you left him home by himself? Is he—is he okay to be alone? I instinctively grab my keys, ready to drive over to the house, sit with him.

He's fine, Lena. Just tired. Just needs to rest today.

Prepare yourself, my heart whispers. *Prepare yourself.*

I find a seat next to Honey, which I haven't done since I was a child. But today, I want to be close to her. The choir sings, offering is taken, announcements are made, another song, and then Malcolm walks up to the pulpit.

Malcolm begins by saying, *In full disclosure, I wasn't prepared to speak today. Pastor Baker isn't feeling well and asked me to preach. I asked him what he had planned to talk about. He told me he was going to kick off a new series on legacy. That seems fitting, being that he is my mentor. Many of you know my story, that I spent most of my childhood in and out of foster homes. When a word like* legacy *comes up, it is daunting. If I have inherited what my parents left for me, does that mean drug addiction and reckless living? What does it mean for one generation to give something to the next? What if we don't want what's being passed down?*

Malcolm takes a sip of water. *I wrestle with these questions daily. And in that grappling, that searching for an understanding, I've come to realize that it's not just about the legacy we've been given.*

Today, church, I want to talk about the legacy we leave. The footprints we make. Because the truth is, we can't do much about what's been given to us. We can learn from it, hopefully find encouragement from it, and in some cases we need to vow never to repeat it, not to continue it.

But more important than all of that is thinking about the actual impact we are making. Right here, right now. In real time.

There are amens and heads nodding. Malcolm isn't the nervous orator I had to pray for years ago. Today he is standing at the pulpit so sure, so relaxed. What I love most is that he is simply talking with us. There is no preacher voice he puts on to sound super spiritual.

I'd like us to think about being a living legacy, the same way we talk of living legends—people who haven't even reached the pinnacle of what they will do, and already we know we are witnessing greatness. Folks who accomplished so much that even before they are gone from this earth, we talk about how they changed it.

He pauses, wipes his brow, then continues. *The conversation about legacy can't just be reserved for the old, or the rich, or the famous. All of us should be taking account of how we are living. What would life be like for you if you saw every single moment, every word, every deed, as a seed? What would your harvest be?*

Now that's a good question, the man behind me says.

And I'm talking about a harvest to enjoy now. The Bible speaks to this in Matthew 7:16—we know a tree by the fruit it bears. Church, what fruit are we bearing? What is our living legacy?

Malcolm's sermon gives us all inspiration and rebuke too. He challenges those of us with rotten fruit or no fruit.

He admonishes us to do the hard work of plowing and pruning.

Honey leans over to me whispers, *I think the torch is being passed today. No pomp and circumstance. It's happening, he's ready.*

rare

The forecast promised a dry day, but the sky is gray and misty. May is moody like that. She is unpredictable and changes her mind without care for what the day's plans are. But May is also gracious; at least she is giving a comforting rain, not a downpour. I decide to go on my morning walk as planned. A younger me with pressed hair would've never walked in the rain. Not without a hood or umbrella. I laugh at the girl I was back then, so afraid of getting my hair wet because of Grandma's warnings that she wasn't going to do any touch-ups if the press didn't last, so I better take good care of it, which meant wearing a bonnet at night, and not getting my hair wet.

I walk through the neighborhood, replaying Malcolm's sermon. On my way back home, I see that the new ice cream shop has finished construction. There's no sign about when it will open, but seeing all the scaffolding gone means it'll be soon. I'll have to bring Aaliyah here on a mommy-daughter date for a spring treat.

I walk home and get ready to meet Malcolm. He made a ten o'clock appointment for the Rare Books Room at Powell's.

We are early, so we meander through the gifts and greeting cards for a bit. As soon as we go to the Rare Books Room, I am immediately transported away from the store's industrial vibe, with its bright lights, and into an elegant, dimly lit space. The one-of-a-kind books are shelved on dark wood bookcases. *I can't believe I've lived here my whole life,* I say, *and have come to Powell's a million times, but never been in this room.*

Malcolm teases, *And to think you were once a librarian!*

We walk around the room, take in all the ancient treasure. The space houses literature from the 1600s and 1700s, all the way up to signed books by Tennessee Williams and Shel Silverstein.

Malcolm is walking behind me as I lead the way, oohing and ahhing, pointing to books. *Do you see that one? Look at this!*

And then Malcolm says, *Did you see this one?*

When I turn around to face him, Malcolm is on one knee, holding up a ring. *Lena, you are exquisite and one of a kind, and like these books, what we have is rare. We are in this room full of words and ideas and stories that were outlined, drafted, revised. Chapter by chapter these stories became complete. Ours is a love story still being written. A tattered love knitted together by grace.* Malcolm takes a deep breath, says, *Thank you for loving me. I would be honored if you would allow me to love you and Aaliyah for the rest of our lives. Will you keep writing our story? Will you marry me?*

Yes, Malcolm. I will marry you. Yes, yes!

port

As in haven, as in harbor. As in hold me close, keep me safe, bring me what I need to survive, keep me from anything that means to harm. Take me to faraway places, but never let me forget the beginning, never let me forget home.

age 41

I celebrate turning forty-one on an airplane heading to Hawaii. I've been holding on to this honeymoon ticket, not sure when or if I'd use it. Honey kept asking, *You sure you want to go all by yourself?* Yes. A week to rest and reflect all by myself is what I need, what I want. Malcolm and I have decided we'll honeymoon someplace else. Jamaica maybe, or Mexico.

Being in the sky, hanging out with the clouds, makes me feel closer to God and all the people I love who've gone on. I don't think they are looking down on me—I hope not, anyway. I hope heaven is a place so good that once you're there you never want to look back, go back to what was. That's the kind of afterlife Grandma and Bryan's mom, and Kendra's mom, and Dr. Unthank, and Beatrice Morrow Cannady, and Marcus Lopez deserve.

They are gone, but here. Their strength, their wisdom, their shortcomings all here for me. How they've taught me to love a country, a city, a community, a neighbor, a friend, with a fierce love, a love fierce enough to demand it to live up to what it could be, should be. How to love my body, my hair, my skin, my culture, with that same relentless love.

sunday sermon

Dad preaches, *Genesis 3:19 tells us, "By the sweat of your brow you will eat your food until you return to the ground, since from it you were taken; for dust you are and to dust you will return."*

Church, all of us, all we are is dirt.

This body is just a shell, a container.

Skin and bones, ashes to ashes...

All that matters is your soul.

acknowledgments

It begins with my mother, Carrie Elizabeth Watson, who died just as I finished the first draft of this novel. Oh, how I miss you every day. Oh, how I felt your presence, your wisdom, your encouragement, as I worked on the revisions for *skin & bones*. Oh, how I carry you with me, always. I am so thankful to have been your daughter, to have known what is means to be anchored by your love.

Thank you to my brother, Roy, and my sisters, Cheryl, Trisa, and Dyan for being my first friends, for celebrating all the wins with me, for tending to the bruises life has given me, for modeling perseverance so that I could see how to survive. Thank you especially in this moment for believing I could write this book, that I should write this book.

Thank you to the women who hold me down and lift me up: Chanesa Hart, Jonena Lindsay, Kendolyn Walker, Ellice Lee, Ellen Hagan, Lisa Green, Rajeeyah Finney-Myers, Tokumbo Bodunde, Nanya-Akuki Goodrich, Olugbemi-sola Rhuday-Perkovich, Jennifer Baker, Robin Patterson, Catrina Ganey, Shalanda Sims, Velynn Brown, DéLana R. A. Dameron, and Caroline Loftin. My prayer, always, is that everything you have poured into me comes back to you. This book would not exist without our conversations—and sometimes debates—about dating, motherhood, friendship, faith, beauty standards, and self-love. Thank you for sharing your experiences and insights, your fears and regrets, with me. Thank you for doing life with me. You've walked

acknowledgments

alongside me, witnessing the miracles and the mundane. I love you deep, I love you always.

Thank you, Linda Christensen, for taking me out for breakfast on that rainy, gray Portland morning to talk with me about these characters and the themes of the book. Thank you for reading and rereading drafts, for all the text messages encouraging me to keep going, for the guidance you offer. I was honored to have you as my high school English teacher those many years ago, and now to call you friend is a great privilege that I don't take for granted. I will never tire of saying how much you mean to me.

Thank you, Kori Johnson and Dana Brewington. You are an answer to prayer. Thank you for reminding me to rest, for encouraging me to trust my instinct, for dreaming big, wild dreams with me.

Thank you to my editor, Tracy Sherrod. Tracy, you are such a force, such a gift to the literary community. Thank you for your guidance, for the hour-long phone calls when we'd talk about Lena, Aspen, and Kendra like they were real people.

Thank you to my agent, Rosemary Stimola, for being intentional and for handling not only my career but me with such care.

And to the Black pioneers of Oregon. Thank you for your sacrifice. It was not in vain. Your legacy lives on and on.

about the author

Renée Watson is a #1 *New York Times* bestselling author. Over the past decade she has authored eighteen books for children and teens. She received a Coretta Scott King Book Award and a Newbery Honor for *Piecing Me Together* and high praise for *The 1619 Project: Born on the Water*, coauthored with Nikole Hannah-Jones. Watson is on the Writers Council for the National Writing Project and is a member of the Academy of American Poets' Education Advisory Council. She splits her time between New York City and Portland, Oregon.